May ~
Keep your light
& Spirit bright
Be brave
Best Wishes ~
Sousanna

Sousanna

Sousanna

the lost daughter

by

Sousanna Stratmann

Tranquility Press
2018

For information:
Tranquility Press
723 W University Ave #300-234
Georgetown TX 78626
www.TranquilityPress.NET

Though inspired by true events and deeply rooted in years of research and family histories, this is a work of fiction. Names and some characteristics have been changed to protect the privacy of individuals involved, and some scenes have been fictionalized or entirely imagined. Nonetheless, every eff ort has been made to capture the essence of truth, if not always the precise facts.

Afterword by Teresa Lynn
Cover design by Rob Williams

Publisher's Cataloging-in-Publication data

Names: Stratmann, Sousanna, author.
Title: Sousanna : the lost daughter / Sousanna Stratmann.
Description: Includes bibliographical references. | Georgetown, TX: Tranquility Press, 2018.
Identifiers: ISBN 978-0-9904977-3-8 (Hardcover - Lam) | 978-0-9904977-5-2 (Hardcover w/jacket) | 978-0-9904977-8-3 (Trade paperback) |978-0-9904977-4-5 (ebook)
LCCN 2018907817
Subjects: LCSH Intercountry adoption--Greece--Fiction. | Family--Fiction. | Child traffi cking--Greece--Fiction. | World War, 1939-1945--Influence--Fiction.|BISACFICTION/ Biographical
Classificati on: LCC PS3619.T742555 S68 2018 | DDC 813.6--dc23

This book is dedicated to
Emilia and Panayiotis

Acknowledgements

I would like to express my gratitude and appreciation to the following people who supported me in the writing of this book.

Many thanks to my husband Bob, who tirelessly listened, read, reread, contributed, laughed, cried, and remembered with me; my children, Nikki and Ben, and their spouses, Matt and Mary, for enduring my countless stories; and to my grandchildren, Hudson, Emma, and Easton, for the sheer joy they bring to my life.

I also want to thank my editor, and now my friend, Teresa Lynn, whose expertise finessed my words into this beautifully interesting and timely story, and Linda Jones, for re-teaching me high school grammar at her dining room table.

I'm grateful for all the dear friends who faithfully encouraged me while walking and praying beside me through this journey.

And, as a woman of faith, I thank God for all things, and all experiences. I am a woman blessed beyond measure and so grateful for the love poured, by so many, into this story.

Author's Note

I have always wondered about and, quite honestly, accusingly questioned the narcissism of those who choose to write about their lives. Why would they record their most intimate details, private experiences, and raw emotions, then send them out into the public forum of strangers?

But here I am, not without soul searching, compelled and strangely obligated to write my story, to join all those whose motives I never understood before. I now chastise myself for having called this narcissism, when it is really courage.

I grappled with telling my story for ten years. It's interesting, but is that enough of a reason to tell it? The compulsion I felt had to have a deeper reason, a meaningful purpose.

Then, pressing through, the story slowly started to give way its intention, and I realized this is not just my story, but the story of many people whose lives, culture, and destiny were changed, and are still being changed, by the generational effects of war. In my necessary research, I learned of thousands of other people with similar stories, many of whom are still searching and hoping to find answers.

Reaching back into my own life, reviewing old pictures, letters, and family stories, and allowing memories to flood my thoughts, a wound I had long ago sealed opened again. I had to confront the horror and desperation that forced so many people to make unimaginable decisions just to survive. I wanted—no, I needed—to record this history for them. For us.

As my days of writing turned into months, I rode emotions from sadness, to anger, to uncertainty, and finally to peace. I came to understand that people must often make desperate decisions in desperate times; that we cannot scorn someone without understanding what brought that person to that place; that good people sometimes make bad decisions; that words spoken over children have lasting effects on their destiny; and most of all, that war, love, greed, desperation, and determination each have effects that last for generations.

This book is part of my true story, with parts of others' true stories, written in novel form so that it's *our* story. I hope it will show the strength of the people who endured a time in history that few even know took place.

Sousanna

I am not saying this because I am in need, for I have learned to be content whatever the circumstances. I know what it is to be in need, and I know what it is to have plenty. I have learned the secret of being content in any and every situation, whether well fed or hungry, whether living in plenty or in want. ~ Apostle Paul

Chapter 1

Sousanna

October 1958; Pirgos, Greece

Papa is ready to go to work, but he does not go. He's watching Mama.

My brother Ilias is ready to go, too, but he's also watching Mama. Ilias is only eight years old, but he thinks he's grown up because he goes to work with Papa. He even dresses the same as Papa, in a buttoned-up shirt tucked into brown pants held up by a braided belt. Mama and Papa say people should always be neat and clean, even if they're only going to the fields to plant seeds or gather vegetables. That's why Mama always mends the knees of their pants when they get the tiniest hole, and Papa ties together their shoelaces when they break so they won't flop around loose. They are neat and handsome. Especially Papa, with his thick, blond hair combed away from his face.

Usually when Ilias is ready early, he makes sure Mama and Papa aren't watching then teases me by sticking his tongue out at me. I wrinkle my nose to make a mean face and do the same back to him. It makes us giggle. But this morning he just stares at Mama with his eyebrows pulled together and his mouth turned down.

If Marios were here, he'd play with me. Marios is my oldest brother, eleven years old. He left many days ago, and I don't know where he is. Every day I think, *Maybe Marios will come home today.*

Mama should be helping me get dressed in my soft, white—well, almost white—shirt and my green play skirt with the tight elastic that hurts my tummy. I don't tell Mama about it pinching my tummy because I don't want to make her sad.

Sousanna

Since she hasn't put my clothes on me yet I'm shivering in only my baggy white—well, almost white—underwear. I jump up and down to get her attention.

"Mama, I'm cold. Help me get dressed."

No one seems to hear me. They keep watching Mama, busy over a pot hanging in the fireplace at the end of our one-room house. I'm too little to see what she's doing. All I see is the gray fabric of her dress pulling across her shoulders as her arms move, her darned white stockings, and her pinned-up braid.

My sister Anastasia stands near her. She helps Mama with just about everything. That's because she's almost grown up, already thirteen years old. This morning Anastasia stands by the concrete wall and watches Mama, swaying a little so her blue skirt swishes back and forth. Her mouth is turned down, too, and her eyes are extra shiny. She keeps sniffing.

I pull on the back of her swishing skirt to get her attention.

"What's Mama doing?" I ask. I want to know why everybody is watching her, and nobody's doing what they usually do.

Looking down at me, my sister whispers, "It's a surprise."

It can't be a good surprise because her voice is sad. Surprises should be happy and exciting.

"Is it for me? What is it?"

"You'll find out soon enough."

"I want to know now. Pick me up so I can see."

"Don't worry; you'll get it in a minute," Ilias says. His voice is nice, not cross or teasing like it usually is when he talks to me.

Mama turns and hands something to Papa. He steps toward me and holds out a boiled egg that has been peeled and is ready to eat. So that's what Mama was doing. I love eggs. When Aunt Georgia brings us some, I can hardly wait for Mama to find a sewing needle and poke a hole in the end of one so I can suck the raw egg from its shell. A boiled egg is a special treat.

"Sousanna, this egg is for you, who will go to the foreign country." Papa's words are slow and his voice is quiet. He looks at the floor for a moment before lifting his head to speak again. "It will keep you strong until we are all together again."

I don't know what a foreign country is, but he must mean YiaYia's house. That's the only place I go that's far away, where I have to eat before I leave because it takes a long time to get there.

I giggle at Papa's funny words and reach for the egg. I use a low, funny voice to say, "Let me eat it all, since I am going away."

The egg slips from Papa's fingers to mine. I'm close enough to see the crease between his heavy eyebrows pressed deep into his skin.

As I gobble up the delicious egg, Mama and Ilias and Anastasia stand close behind Papa. They all stand still, with strange looks on their faces. I don't know this look, or why they're staring at me. Something in my tummy feels wobbly. Maybe it's the egg.

Papa's chest lifts as he takes in a deep breath. This time he speaks clearly, using his strong, familiar voice. "This is Sousanna, the best of my children, who will go to live like a queen."

I giggle again. "Are we playing a new game?"

Papa loves to play games with us. My favorite is when he lifts me onto his shoulders and walks me around our town, telling his friends, "This is my Sousanna. Look how tall she has grown."

It always makes me laugh, and I ask, "Do the people really think I'm this tall?"

Papa doesn't say if we're playing a game. He bends down, one knee on the hard dirt floor, so that his blue eyes are even with mine. He holds my small shoulders in his heavy hands. I stop giggling because I can see worry on his face and tears in his eyes. It must not be a game after all.

Looking into my eyes, Papa says, "Sousanna, be brave. Do not cry when you are away from us. Be brave."

Then he kisses me on both cheeks and pulls me into his arms. I lay my head on his shoulder and wrap my tiny arms as far as I can around him. He holds me for a long time. When he releases me, almost pushing me away, I don't want to let go. I'm not ready to leave his arms, and I'm not done holding him in mine.

As he stands I tilt my head way back so I can see his face, far up because he's so tall, and smile. I love him so much—my handsome, giant father who will always take care of me and keep me safe.

He turns and waves his hand to bring Ilias to him. "Come, Ilias. It's time for us to go to work." Papa puts his hand on Ilias's shoulder and they walk out the door, their striding legs in drooping yellow socks taking them away from me.

What is a foreign country? What if I don't like how a queen lives? I'm too little to go away. Why did Papa say not to cry?

Chapter 2

Peter

Three weeks earlier; Tulsa, Oklahoma

Peter hung up the phone and picked up his scotch. "That was the guy Father Andreas told me about who wants a kid," he told his wife after taking a drink. "Sounds like a nice guy. He's going to bring payment to the office tomorrow. With Alice's and the rest, that makes seven kids. Guess it's time to go get them."

Hazel lowered her book and peered at him over her cat's-eye glasses. "You make it sound like the children are groceries."

"You know what I mean."

"Still. It's not like they're buying a child off the shelf at the store."

If she only knew. It was exactly that way. American couples wanted a child; Peter wanted to make money. What could be simpler than using his position as an attorney to arrange adoptions?

"I ever tell you about the first time I went to pick up some kids?" he asked, even though he knew he had. They talked about it every time he went to get a group of children.

"When you met the man from that adoption agency that was taking all the sick babies?"

"Yeah." He pinched the bridge of his nose under his wire glasses then took another drink. "Those kids were practically dead. All their hair and teeth had fallen out. Some of them could barely move."

"That must have been terrible to see."

It was. And he never told her the worst part, about the ones who'd already died but still lay in the orphanage beds. It still haunted his dreams sometimes. He never went to an orphanage to get kids again. There, even the children still relatively healthy were listless and—what was the word? Hollow. There was no spirit inside the scrawny bodies. He couldn't use them; no one would pay good money for kids like that. He had to have children with some life in them, so now he always took kids from families. Of course, Hazel didn't know that. She thought he still brought orphans.

"Well, I remember something else about your first trip," Hazel said. "I remember you reading me that Greek newspaper article about how many orphans were left after the wars, and how you wanted to help them. To bring them here to America where they would have hope of a better life. How proud I was of you."

He didn't remind her that she was the one who'd wanted to help the babies. It was that comment she made—"They have so little in Greece, and we have so much here. I wish there was a way we could share it with them."—that got him thinking about ways to take advantage of the situation in his home country.

When he overheard one of his neighbors mention adopting a child, it all came together. Peter wrote an article in the community paper about the tragedy happening to the children of Greece. How the wars had left countless widows and orphans with no way to provide for themselves. How desperate mothers abandoned their children rather than watch them slowly starve. How the orphanages overflowed, and even they could not properly care for all the children. He could almost hear the yearning hearts of those wanting to help the children as he wrote.

It worked. Couples came to him anxious to adopt those poor, Greek children. He knew some of the parents-to-be had been denied by adoption agencies. They didn't qualify as suitable parents. That was none of his concern. If they paid his fee, he'd bring them a kid.

"Anyway, this time will be special." Hazel was still talking. "I'm glad Alice is finally getting a son. I'm ready for a grandchild to share our blessings with. You'll find the perfect little boy for her, won't you, Peter?"

Peter didn't care about being a grandfather, but his daughter wanted a son. When she asked him to bring her a little boy, what could he do but agree?

Chapter 3

Sousanna

Confused, I squeeze my eyes shut and fold my arms against my bare chest, letting out a noisy sigh. I want to run after Papa and ask him all my questions, but I know he won't answer. He'll just say, "Sousanna, go back in the house. Ilias and I can't be late to the fields."

I'm certain that when he gets home from work he will, as always, answer my questions. He'll sit in his broken-down chair outside our house and spread his feet wide on the ground to keep the chair balanced beneath him. He'll call out to Mama, "Katerina, I'm here."

Then he'll reach into his coat pocket and take out his strand of amber worry beads, and he'll flip it over and around the top of his hand and then back to grab it tightly inside his fist. He'll repeat this motion over and over, quickly at first so the beads will clash loudly together when he catches them. After a long while, the beads will move more slowly, with an even rhythm that is soothing to my ears. That's when I know it's time for me to say, "Papa, I have so many questions for you."

Laughing, he'll lift me onto his lap and wrap his strong arms around me as I snuggle close to his body where I'm safe and warm. Then we'll talk.

As I stand dreaming of the evening when I can ask Papa my questions, Anastasia wraps her arms around me and pulls me so tightly against her body I can't breathe. I hear her crying, and with each sob her chest moves up and down. She says, "My little doll, I love you. God protect you."

Protect me from what? I want to ask, but I don't because she's crying.

When she releases me I take a big breath. Anastasia takes my face in her hands and looks at me with the same strange look that was in Papa's eyes. Quickly she kisses my cheeks, then turns to hurry out the door. Watching her leave, still sobbing, makes me want to cry too. Maybe when she's home from work we can play with bubbles in the dishpan. That will make her happy again.

Now only Mama and I remain in the room that is our house. She stands for a long time, not moving, looking down at the dirt, packed hard as the concrete walls. I've never seen her so still; usually she's moving all the time, busy with some work. Why doesn't she move? Does it have anything to do with the strange words Papa said? Or Anastasia crying? I don't like it when so many things happen that I don't understand. I start to cry.

Quickly Mama gathers me into her arms and rocks me. Stroking my hair and kissing my cheeks, she says, over and over, "I love you, my child. I love you, my child," until I stop crying.

One more time she kisses my forehead. Holding me back so I can see her face, she asks, "Who will wipe your tears away when I am not there with you? Who?"

I don't know who, so I don't say anything.

She shakes her head. "What have we done?"

Why is she asking that? We haven't done anything.

She sighs and says, "We must get you dressed."

Mama lifts my dress from the cord that stretches across one corner of our house, holding all of our clothes. The cord is not very long because we don't have many clothes, unlike my cousin Nefeli. Her family has so many clothes their cord stretches over two corners. Nefeli gave me the dress now draped over Mama's arm. It's my only dress.

My dress is very pretty because it has puffy sleeves and long pieces of fabric attached to the back that Mama can tie into a big, beautiful bow. The collar still has bits of lace here and there. I don't care that the flowers have faded on the fabric; I love my dress.

Mama also takes my red sweater from the cord. This is my sweater. Mama knit it just for me and it's the only thing I have that is really, truly, only mine.

I remember when Mama made the sweater. From under the bed she pulled out the wicker basket that held the red yarn and her silver knitting needles, the ones that had belonged to her mother. She held the wicker basket under one arm and with the other hand pulled a chair from the small table across the room, close to the giant fireplace. There she gathered the needles and yarn from the basket and began to knit.

I sat by her feet and listened to the music of her clicking needles, watching her hands dance as she guided the thread around and through, around and through, until my red sweater began to take shape. Excited and impatient for it to be finished, I continually asked, "Is it ready yet? Can I try it on? When will it be done?"

Laughing, Mama said, "You must be patient, Sousanna. It will be ready soon." Finally, one day she asked, "Are you ready to try on your sweater?"

I clapped my hands and jumped up and down, squealing, "Yes, yes!" My beautiful, red sweater. It was soft and warm against my skin, and it was mine.

Now, Mama drapes the sweater over the dress on her arm. Then she slowly bends over and picks up my shoes, with socks tucked deep inside. These shoes had also once belonged to my cousin Nefeli. Nefeli likes to show off and she said to me, "When my mother bought those black shoes for me, they were shiny and the buckle worked. Now they are ugly and dirty." Nefeli likes to be mean to me, as her mother is to my mother. I don't care; I'm happy to have shoes that I can wear to church, even if they did once belong to Nefeli.

Mama lays everything on the table and turns to me. "Lift your arms high in the sky, Sousanna. It's time to get you dressed."

I grin, because lifting my arms means we'll play the tickle game. When I reach into the air, she'll tickle under my arms until I pull them close to my chest, making us both giggle.

She does not play our game this morning. She quietly slips the faded dress over my head and down my body, giving it a tug to settle it in place. She turns me around and I feel her close the four buttons on the back of my dress and tie the bow. Why does everyone seem so sad this morning?

Often Mama tells me the story of the dress as she ties the bow. "Sousanna, once this dress was bright yellow with thousands of tiny pink flowers on the fabric. After many years the color of the dress began to change. It changed just for you, Sousanna. Now it is the color of soft butterfly wings, and many of the tiny pink flowers have stayed on the dress because all little girls should have at least some flowers on their dress."

There is no story today.

Chapter 4

Peter

October 1958; Greece

At the Athens airport, Peter looked for a car to rent. Something that would show people he was rich and important. They had to respect him, believe he was better than they were, for his plan to work.

"This one," he told the attendant escorting him around the parking lot when he spotted a green and white Chevrolet convertible. A couple years old, but in mint condition. "It's perfect. I'll take it."

"Yes, sir. Good choice."

The attendant led Peter back inside to the rental desk, where they completed the transaction. Then Peter took the keys and unlocked the car. He unlatched the top hold-downs, slid behind the wheel, and switched the lever under the dash. The top eased back with a smooth hydraulic hum. Nice.

His first stop was Town Hall, to make sure the judge would still sign any necessary papers. Five hundred American dollars for one stroke of a pen? Of course the judge agreed.

Next he found a store that sold toys. Picking up the kids went so much easier if he had something that would lure them into the car. A shiny, black and red train and a tall, blond doll—those should do the trick.

Finally Peter headed to the Peloponnese region. This time he couldn't get kids in Athens. The city had enough industry and international trade that it was beginning to recover from the wars, and people weren't so desperate. The Peloponnese was still struggling with widespread poverty; he had a better chance there. Besides, it was one of the most beautiful areas.

Sousanna

As he drove commercial buildings gave way to homes, then countryside. Large swaths of uncultivated land were broken up by villages surrounded by olive orchards, vineyards, and fields of vegetables. Thin, weathered men and women in tattered clothing bent over in the fields, gathering the last of the fall harvest.

All that work, for just a sack of potatoes or onions. Why do they stay here? At least the kids I take will have hope for a better life.

He'd found what he was looking for: desperate, hungry people. It was time to stop and look for the first kid.

He eased into the next village. Some of the little concrete houses didn't even have doors, just a cloth draped over the opening. Old yiayias gathered in bunches, gossiping as they watched their grandchildren while the parents worked. This time of day, while people worked in the orchards and fields, the square was mostly empty. No point going to the usual gathering places right now.

A figure in a black cassock and skufia outside an Orthodox church caught Peter's attention. Ah, the local priest. He might help. Peter parked quickly and caught up with the man, approaching with cupped hands.

"Father, may I have a blessing?" Peter asked, using the traditional ritualistic greeting. Surely the priest would appreciate that.

The priest placed his hand on Peter's and recited the blessing. When he was finished, Peter kissed his ring.

Then he was able to get to business. "I'm Peter Bakas. Do you have a moment?"

"Yes. I am Father Mitropoulos. How may I help you?"

"I am a Greek, living in America. My poor daughter lost her husband before they had children." No need to tell the priest it was a loss due to divorce; let him think what he wanted. "Father Andreas, our priest in America"—*surely he won't turn down another priest's advice*—"feels that she could cope with her grief better if she had someone else to give her attention to. I know there are many children here who need help since the wars. My daughter —"

"I believe I know what you seek," Father Mitropoulos broke in. "Come into the church; let us talk this over."

Peter left the village a few hours later, with a little boy in the back seat.

It never failed to astonish him how easy it was to get kids. He sometimes forgot, between visits, how naïve the Greek people were.

They knew nothing about the outside world. Most of them couldn't read, and they were too poor to travel. With their immediate and implicit trust in him, he found his first six children within a couple of weeks. They were too thin but otherwise decent looking, with the spark of life from being loved that made them marketable. He left them with a hired caretaker while he looked for the last kid to complete his search. All he needed was one little blond girl.

Chapter 5

Sousanna

Mama lifts me up and stands me on one of the two chairs at the table. She kneels onto the floor to put on my socks and shoes. I don't like to wear shoes. Usually I go barefoot, but I wear my shoes to look pretty at church for God.

"Why are you getting my shoes?" I ask. "It's not church day."

Mama says, "You must look nice today."

I still don't know why.

I don't like it when she pulls the first sock over my bare foot. "Mama, it hurts. My socks are lumpy and they itch my feet. And I don't like to wear shoes if it's not church. I want to feel the cool dirt under my toes." She pushes the un-shiny black shoe over the thick, itchy sock anyway. Even when it pinches and I say, "Ouch!" she continues pushing until my foot is deep inside the shoe, then pulls the worn strap over the top and through the buckle on the other side. I lift my other foot, leaning onto Mama's shoulders to keep from falling off the chair. Repeating the same motions, she pushes the other shoe into place. As she struggles with the broken buckle of the second shoe, I see the knife on the table. Remembering, I look away quickly, but it still makes me cry again.

Mama takes my chin into her hand and looks in my eyes. "Sousanna, you must not cry." Her voice is soft.

Between sobs I tell her, "I miss Marios. Where is he?"

"He has gone to the big city, Athens, where he can find work. We must all work right now. You know how clever Marios is, and we are all proud of him. Soon, Sousanna, he will be home."

I try to stop crying. With the back of my hand I wipe the wet drips from my nose and reach my tongue to lick up all the salty drops on my cheeks before they fall onto Mama. With one last sniff, I smile so she'll see I'm glad about Marios.

Sousanna

Sitting back onto her knees, Mama tries to finish buckling the shoe with the broken buckle. When it's as secure as it's going to be, she pushes herself up from the floor and lifts me from the chair to stand beside her. She holds my red sweater open for me to push my arms through the holes until my hands appear at the end of the sleeves.

Now fully dressed, I wrap my arms around her legs. "I love you so much, Mama."

She takes hold of the collar of my sweater with both hands and pulls it snuggly around my neck. Her face is so close to mine I can see water filling the bottom of her beautiful eyes. Her eyes are not green or brown but a color somewhere between, and they are gentle and kind. Her eyes explore my face, moving from one side to the other, then from top to bottom, then looking straight into my eyes with the same look I saw earlier in Papa and Anastasia's eyes. We stay this way a long time, until she walks to the small, round table next to her and Papa's bed, the only bed in our house.

I love my parents' warm, soft bed. I love to wake up nestled between Mama and Papa. My brothers and sister don't seem to mind that I'm allowed to sleep in the bed with my parents, because I'm the youngest and the smallest. At night we all laugh when Papa calls to me, "Come, Sousanna. Jump!"

Running to the bed, I jump as high as I can and land deep in the middle of the soft mattress. I sink deeply into it. When Marios was there, he'd say, "Look! The bed has eaten Sousanna!"

But when it's cold, I don't like to sleep in their bed. I want to be on the dirt floor close to the warm fire with my brothers and sister. Anastasia and I share her bedroll, cuddled close together watching the fire dance on the walls of our house, lighting our faces in the dark of the night until we fall asleep.

I'm distracted from these happy thoughts when Mama picks up the yellow comb and the new, shiny, blue ribbon from the small stand beside the bed.

Papa brought the ribbon home yesterday. Anastasia, Ilias, and I all asked Papa if we could feel it. He held the blue fabric out so each of us could rub it between our fingers. Ilias said what we all felt. "It's so slippery."

Taking the ribbon from Papa, Anastasia twirled it high over her head, skipping and dancing around the room. She pulled it across our necks, first Ilias's, then mine, causing us to laugh with delight as it tickled our skin. Anastasia sang out, "A ribbon the color of the ocean. Oh, Papa, who is this ribbon for? It's the most beautiful ribbon I've ever seen. Is it for me?"

Papa's head dropped. "Anastasia, my dear daughter, one day I will buy you ribbons the color of the rainbow; but this ribbon is only for Sousanna." His voice sounded like Marios's does when he gets in trouble and says he's sorry.

Anastasia stopped dancing and handed the ribbon back to Papa. "I know you will, Papa." It sounded like tears in her words. "This is for Sousanna. I understand."

Ilias turned away with a scowl, folding his arms over his chest as he kicked the dirt.

The ribbon should be for Anastasia. Her long hair falls to her waist, and the blue would be so pretty at the end of her dark braid. I don't need the ribbon—my hair is short, and it's always tangled and straggly from my playing.

"Papa, I don't want the ribbon. I want Anastasia to have it. She's the oldest and has the longest hair."

"The next ribbon will be for Anastasia. This one is for your hair, Sousanna; I bought this one just for you."

Mama lays the beautiful blue ribbon across the bed. She calls me to her and combs my short, blond hair. I feel her pull the comb across the back of my head and down the side. She ties the blue ribbon around a bundle of hair beside my face.

She turns me to face her once again, pushes my hair behind my ears, and kisses my cheeks. Her head drops so all I can see is the part in the center of her dark hair. She covers her face with her hands. I pull her hands down. Her eyes are pressed shut but tears squeeze out onto her long, black lashes. In a moment she blinks her eyes open, takes in a deep breath, and wipes away the tears. Her mouth wobbles until a smile comes. It's faint, but it's her sweet smile that lets me know how much she loves me.

"My lovely Sousanna, you are ready to go. My beautiful child, every day I will think of you in my arms, of kissing your cheeks. Don't forget me while you are away. I am always here, and I am your mother."

Of course Mama will always be here; this is where we live. I still don't understand. So many strange things have been said, so many tears have fallen this morning. And now I'm wearing a new, slippery, blue ribbon in my hair with my faded yellow dress, itchy socks, scuffed black shoes, and beautiful red sweater, when it's not even church day. I never had to get dressed up like this to go to YiaYia's before.

Mama pulls me tightly to her again. I barely hear her words in my ear. "I don't want to let you go. I want you to stay here with me so I can care for you."

"Mama, do you want me to stay here and get the hoe and come with you to the fields?" I don't like to see Mama sad. Maybe if I show her I'm big enough to work I can stay here with her and not go to YiaYia's house.

She doesn't answer. She reaches for her only pair of shoes. Holding onto the cold concrete wall for balance, she puts one stockinged foot into a black, lumpy shoe, then the other. She bends down to pull the laces tight across her foot, finishing with a perfectly-tied bow. Her shoes aren't very pretty, but her bows are beautiful. She walks to the small table and falls softly into one of the two chairs.

She looks tired, like the days after she has worked in the fields, or when she's worried that we don't have enough food to eat. Again she is looking at me in that strange way. I don't know what to do, so I don't move.

Then I say, "Look, Mama," and make funny faces, rolling my eyes round and round in circles to make Mama laugh; but she doesn't laugh and I'm getting dizzy, so I stop. When the room stops spinning I notice something on the table under Mama's hand.

It's a white envelope. Mama stands and puts it in the pocket of her dress, running her hands down her skirt to smooth it into place. She comes to me, takes my hand in hers, and we walk out the door into the yard together, only Mama and me.

I look up and down the street to see if my friends are outside playing, but there is no one. No one anywhere.

Where are all my friends? I love my friends, especially my best friend Emilia. We all play together every day. Sometimes we play my favorite game, The American.

Our parents tell us the Americans helped us during the war. "They are good and brave people," our parents say. Some of them say they'll go there someday, because "In America no one is poor." They love the Americans, so we do too. Hearing so much about Americans, my friends and I made it a game and now it's our favorite. Of course, we all want to be The American.

I especially want to be The American every time, and if my friends won't let me, I bite them. One day I had to bite Christos really hard so he'd let me play the part. He went home crying and I got in trouble for being mean to my friends. But they don't try to be The American anymore.

When Marios was home I didn't have to bite anyone. He'd say to them, "Please let Sousanna be The American. Some of you can be brave Greek soldiers. And look, I have rings for everyone, rings for the girls and rings for the boys to give the girls, hey, hey."

Everyone loves Marios and wants to be his friend so they'd give in. Then Marios would pass out cigar rings he gathered from the cigar stand near the square. When Marios found a very beautiful ring, he saved it just for me. Putting it on my finger he'd say, "Look at you, Sousanna—you're married."

None of my friends are outside. Not even the old yiayias who are always walking up and down the road peering into everyone's yard looking for something to gossip about are out. There's just Mama and me.

I shiver as the wind blows my dress around my knees. Mama stares past our tiny dirt yard to the street.

What is she looking at? There's nothing to see.

I want to go back into our house.

Chapter 6

Peter

It was quiet when Peter arrived in Pirgos. After driving all day, he could use a drink. A taverna, that's what he needed. Not only could he quench his thirst, but it was the best place to meet the locals. There was always someone willing to point him to a desperate family for a drachma or two. And what luck—there was a pub just down the street.

Stepping through the door, Peter choked on the foul smell. Stale beer? Rotten food? The sweaty men draped over the small tables in animated conversation? Probably all of them. *Good thing I won't be here long.*

The room fell silent when the men inside noticed him standing at the door. Peter stood tall and held his head high.

Someone shouted, "Who is this fancy man at the door? He must work for the government, dressed so fancy in his white suit and hat. Have you come to take us all away for not paying our taxes that you and your families use to fill your fat belly? My name is Spiro. You can take me if I can wear your fancy white hat."

The entire room roared with laughter. Peter joined in. It was all part of the game, winning their trust as someone who understood them and would play along. "No, I am not with the government. My name is Peter Bakas. I am traveling through and need something to eat and drink."

He walked across the small, dark room to the table where the squat little man who'd taunted him sat. Peter hid his disgust at the hairy rolls of fat oozing from the man's open shirt and over his belt. The excess flesh showed this man had purchased food on the black market. Just the kind of person Peter needed.

"May I sit with you, Spiro?" he asked in his most affable voice.

Spiro looked Peter up and down. He put his hands on his hips and moved his shoulders back and forth, speaking in a high-pitched voice like a woman. "Why, yes, you may."

The room roared at the mockery.

Peter wasn't going to be made a fool by this half-wit. He called to the man behind the counter. "Bartender, I want to buy this woman a drink. In fact, I'll buy everyone a drink."

Men slapped their legs and threw back their heads with howls of amusement.

"What do you want here?" Spiro demanded. "Sit down and tell us your business, funny man."

Peter tipped his hat to Spiro, then removed it and placed it on the table as he sat down. Spiro was obviously the town blusterer. With little effort Peter would be able to get the information he needed.

Everyone was still watching him. Peter understood small villages. They all wanted in on the action, to find out who the stranger was and what he was doing there, so they could swap stories about him later. Peter addressed the room.

"I've never been to Pirgos. This is a fine town you have. You must be proud of your crops; I've seen many prosperous fields."

"Our fields?" a man in the corner said. "They're not our fields. We work our hands to the bone for the people who own those fields, just so they can buy more fields. We have nothing and they have everything. Our fields, bah."

"It sounds like these are hard times for you. I am sorry. But that's why I've returned here from America. This is my homeland; I grew up not far from here. As a Greek like you, I understand your problems. Many of you are suffering misfortune. Now I am a successful lawyer in America—"

Another man jeered, "Oh-ho, a successful American lawyer. You had to go all the way to America to be successful? You are a Greek and should live here in your own country. Just think, you could be a successful Greek field worker like all of us."

Someone else said, "Go away. You're too fancy for our town. We're all hungry and poor here, trying to feed and care for our families. Or maybe you'll tell us how to become successful lawyers like you?" Men chortled with glee.

Idiots. Peter raised his voice over the laughter. "I want to help you. That's why I'm here—to offer hope where there is no hope. Maybe you know of a family that is in need of help. As I said, I am a Greek, like all of you, and I love my native country." He said it so smoothly he almost convinced himself. "My heart is broken to see so much poverty. I can help one family by taking their young child back to America with me until things get better."

Now the room was quiet. Some of the men seemed to be considering his words, especially Spiro.

He's my man, I know it.

A man at the next table stood up. He spoke with authority. "Get out. Go back to America. Take your fancy clothes and drive away." He turned to the other men, waving his hand toward Peter. "He's a fool. Don't listen to him. Drink your beer and mind your own business."

Peter ignored the man, focusing on Spiro. He could almost see the wheels turning in the man's head. Peter waited, taking his time to drink the ouzo before him.

Spiro kept watching him as the tavern again became loud with the voices of the men. Finally, he leaned toward Peter, cautiously looking around as he spoke in a hushed voice, obviously not wanting the other men to hear him. "Is there money for what I tell you?"

Like reeling in a fish. Peter leaned away from the stench of Spiro's breath. He was everything Peter despised, a useless man who would do anything for a drachma.

"Of course, if what you tell me is useful."

Leaning deeper into the table, Spiro whispered, "I know someone who cannot feed or take care of his family. Nikolas— we call him Niko. He'd never admit it, but we all know he can't feed his family. Often his wife has to take the bones from other people's leftovers and boil them for their children to suck the marrow from. He has a little girl named Sousanna. She's clever, but here in our village she'll never have a chance. He lives down this road. Count eight houses, and his will be on the left side of the road, the one with the red door." He sat back with an air of smug satisfaction, his voice no longer a whisper. "Go there and take Sousanna to America with you."

One of the men sitting nearby shot out of his seat at Sousanna's name, his chair falling to the floor behind him. He shook his fist in

Spiro's face. "You son of a bitch. Niko is your cousin. What kind of man are you? No one here..."

Peter got up, threw two drachmas on the table, and walked out, not waiting to see the commotion.

It took only a couple of minutes to find the house with the red door. Peter stood outside the gate and brushed off his trousers and straightened his hat with anticipation. His next five thousand dollars might be on the other side of this gate.

A man sat on a chair beside the door in front of the house, tossing worry beads. He appeared lost in thought and didn't seem to notice Peter. He was a handsome man, slender but tall and strong looking. Best of all, he had blond hair—a rarity for Greek men. Peter felt the swell of success in his chest even before he saw the child.

On the other side of the door, a pretty little girl played in the dirt. Evidently the man's daughter, she also had fair hair, and looked about five years old.

Perfect. This child was exactly what Peter needed to complete his quest and leave this destitute country.

Chapter 7

Nikolas

Nikolas sat in his favorite chair outside the house, resting from the day's work. Sousanna crouched on the ground a few feet away, using a stick to make pictures in the dirt. He was so lost in his own thoughts, tossing his worry beads to and fro, that he didn't notice the man until he heard someone call his name. "Hello, Niko. How are you today?"

The voice was not familiar, and when he looked up he didn't recognize the man who called him by the name only his friends used.

The stranger walking up the path toward him looked out of place. He wore expensive clothes—a well-fitting white suit with a white shirt and white tie, a white fedora that he was waving in the air, and even white shoes. Only his glasses were not white. They were silver wire.

"I am good; how are you?"

The man didn't answer the question but said, "I would like to introduce myself. My name is Peter Bakas. I am from America, although I was born in Greece and am a Greek like you. I have been in the taverna with your friends. Your cousin told me that you are having a hard time caring for your family, to have enough food for them."

What could Niko say to that? It was true times were hard, but it was none of this stranger's business. Besides, the man wasn't even looking at him as he talked to him; his gaze was focused on Sousanna. He looked at her the way a hungry wolf looks at a rabbit.

"Come, Sousanna." Niko stuffed his strand of worry beads in his pocket to free his hands and lifted his young daughter protectively into his lap. She leaned over his arm, admiring her picture in the dirt, not paying attention to the grown-ups. Good. It would be best if she gave the wolf no notice.

Finally Nikolas answered the stranger. "I can take care of my family; this does not concern you. I don't even know who you are. By the way, which of my cousins told you this?"

"Spiro told me of your struggles, and you should thank him. You see, Niko, I am here to offer you help. I have come from America to help families that are suffering from the war. I can help you with your little daughter. I can give her hope where there is no hope. Let me take her with me to America where I—"

Nikolas stood from his chair so fast he dropped Sousanna, his chair falling beside her. He stabbed his finger toward the gate. "Get out of my yard. Now! Get out, and never come back."

The man replaced his white hat and quickly walked out the gate and up the street until he disappeared.

Nikolas set the chair back on its feet. "Get up, Sousanna. Get out of the dirt." His anger at the stranger and at Spiro made his voice sharper than he intended.

He felt in his pocket for the amber beads and twirled them fiercely as he strode into the house for his tattered cap, then headed to the taverna. Each step reached for as much of the road as possible. He'd teach Spiro a lesson he'd not soon forget.

"Spiro, stand up," Nikolas roared as he entered.

Spiro startled and looked up, then away, not meeting Niko's eyes as he said, "What do you want with me, Niko? I'm relaxing, having a drink. Let me be."

"Let you be? Let you be? After you sent a man to my home to take my daughter from me?"

Nikolas crossed the room to Spiro in three steps. He grabbed the fat man by the ear, jerked him up, and spit in his face. "Never come near my home again. You are not my family anymore. You, your wife, and your spoiled children, all of you, stay away from my home and my family."

He pushed Spiro back into his chair, making the man's legs sprawl wide and his arms hang limply by his side. There was not a sound as Niko turned and walked out of the taverna.

As he strode home his thoughts went crazy in his head. *What the man in white said was true. I can't feed my family. What will happen to my children? To Sousanna?*

34

Nikolas

He lifted his head to the sky and shook his fist toward it. "Damn you, God! Why all this? Why us?"

Only a moment later, he dropped to his knees and buried his fingers in his thick blond hair. He felt the sting of tears in his eyes as he bowed his head. "No, God. Forgive me. I have my family. You have kept us safe. Thank you. I have some work, and with your help we will find our way. Forgive me; I am afraid."

Chapter 8

Peter

That evening and deep into the night, Peter thought about the small girl drawing in the dirt. It was rare to find such fair skin and light hair in this country. The child reminded him of his own daughter—Alice was fair complected, too, and many were the days he'd sat and read the paper on the porch while she played in the yard, just as Sousanna did while Niko sat nearby.

Images of Niko's crystal blue eyes full of pain broke into his thoughts, but he pushed them aside. This was no time to get sentimental. One way or another, he'd get the little flaxen-haired girl. Her fair complexion would surely please the American couple; she'd look more like them. Maybe he could even raise the price a little for this one.

What could he say to Niko? This father wouldn't let his child go easily. Peter would have to tell him more than was true. Words Niko wanted, needed, to hear. The right words would get him the girl. He just had to make Niko think of the future—Sousanna's future.

The next morning Niko sat in the same chair, but Sousanna was not with him. Peter opened the gate and approached cautiously, trying to speak as a trusted friend would. "Niko, listen to me, my friend." He spoke quickly, before Niko could stop him. "Children in America are not poor. They have plenty to eat, and they all go to school." He walked deeper into the yard. "Let me give this life to Sousanna until you can. Let me take her to America, where she will have a good life. When things are better she will come home to you again. You are a wise man, Niko. This life is not your fault, but keeping Sousanna here to suffer will be."

When Niko stood, Peter couldn't help it; he flinched. Niko grabbed him by the arm and shoved him toward the gate, shouting, "Get out! I told you never to come back here."

Peter jerked his arm from Niko's grip and turned to look at him. "You have nothing to offer her. Look at this house, this street...only poor people who can barely eat. What kind of father would let his daughter live like this?"

Something in Niko's eyes changed. Defiance became despair. He lowered his head. "Please, just leave us alone. She's my daughter; I will care for her. Please leave us alone."

The girl's father would not be able to forget what he said. *Just give him some time to think about it, and I'll have her.* Satisfied, he placed his hand on Niko's shoulder.

"I'll go now, but I'll be back. Think about what I have said, Niko. It is hope I am offering Sousanna. Surely you would not take this opportunity from her. I know you, as her father, want her to have a life of possibilities."

As he turned to leave, Peter saw a small boy peering around the corner of the house. "Who's there?" he called, but the child disappeared.

§

The café's fountain gushed water into the air, where the drops sparkled in the evening sun before splashing back into the pool beneath. Peter stared at the fountain as he waited for his ouzo and fish. He couldn't forget Niko's face, or the humility in his final plea, "Please, just leave us alone." The change he'd seen in Niko's eyes haunted him. The despair—had he caused that? These poor parents wanted hope for their children, didn't they?

*They're desperate...*But Niko's eyes convicted him. Peter's stomach soured and he left before his food arrived.

§

Sousanna. I want Sousanna. Peter woke up thinking about her. Before his eyes opened, he remembered her face puckered in concentration, as it had been when he first saw her playing in the dirt.

It's not my fault her father is a poor fool who can't feed his family or take care of his own daughter. I'll convince him to let me have her.

On his third walk to Niko's house, Peter passed a group of children outside playing in the street. One of them was Sousanna.

Sousanna

Ah, a chance to see what she's really like. He stood behind a lemon tree in an open yard and watched. The children held hands and ran around in a circle until they got dizzy and fell to the ground with laughter.

Sousanna held her hand into the sunlight, looking at something on her finger. It looked like the ring off a cigar. "Look at my beautiful ring, everyone," she said. "I'm married."

This child was happy and loved, and he was going to steal her away from that. The sourness returned to his stomach.

No; I'm taking her where she will have more, where she'll have a chance to be even happier. I'm giving her hope where there is no hope. He left before the kids noticed him.

Nikolas was sitting in his usual chair. In a sudden burst of inspiration, Peter thought of the perfect words. This time there was no hesitation as he walked into the yard and stood close to Niko's chair. "Niko, I am here again to ask you, do you want your little Sousanna to become a whore in the streets because you cannot care for her?"

Tears filled Niko's eyes as he slowly slid the familiar cap from his head and looked down at the dirt beneath his feet. "I know she has no life here." His voice was resigned. "I want the best for her, but I have nothing to give her. I need time to earn money and make a better life. If I let you take her, you'll bring her home again, when I can care for her properly?"

"Yes, of course; this is only temporary." It was a necessary lie. Another burst of inspiration hit. "I'll even send you photos of Sousanna in America, and letters, so you can see for yourself how well and happy she is."

"Then, I will let you take her. Just for a little while."

The fool didn't even ask for any money. I got this girl for free, and she's one of the best ones. He should reassure Nikolas before the man changed his mind. He stepped even closer to Niko and patted his shoulder in reassurance.

"You've made a good choice, Niko, a good choice. It is best for Sousanna. I'll meet you and your wife in the square in two days. That will give me time to get a translator so you and your wife can write a letter to the new mother and—"

Niko hit his hand away and his eyes narrowed. "What? The new mother? Katerina is her mother. What do you mean, new mother?"

38

"Niko, calm down. Don't worry that I said 'the new mother.' That's what they say in America about any woman who is looking after children. It means she'll care for them as if they were her own. That's what you want for Sousanna, isn't it?"

"But you said you would care for her. Who is this woman you call the new mother?"

"I'm helping many children, Niko; I can't care for all of them myself. I promise you, Sousanna will be in a good home. I have met these people. They are good Christians—Orthodox Greek, like we are." Well, they were Christians, even if they weren't Orthodox. Niko would never know the difference, anyway.

Peter continued, "They'll take Sousanna to church and to school until she returns to you. Just think, Niko—while you are improving your situation, Sousanna will be getting an education."

Nikolas was silent for such a long time Peter thought he'd changed his mind. Finally Niko said, "Okay, I'll bring Katerina to the square, but you must keep your promise. When things get better here, you'll bring Sousanna home. And she will always know that Katerina is her only mother."

He had to momentarily look away from Niko's glaring eyes. "Of course, of course. Now, as I was saying, I'll bring a translator. He'll write your wife's words into English for the woman in America." Peter made sure not to use the word *mother* again. "I'll pick up Sousanna the next morning and take her to Patras. She'll stay in a big house with other children for a couple of days while we buy them nice clothes for America. Then we'll go to Athens, where we'll get on the plane to America."

Chapter 9

Katerina

"No, Niko. No! We can't." Katerina couldn't imagine such a thing as her husband was saying. Send little Sousanna away? To America? Yes, it was a struggle to feed the children. Yes, they were thin. But not emaciated like she'd seen so often during the war. Their children weren't starving, even if they often had to settle for broth made from discarded bones. They were getting by. "You can't agree. Tell him no. Please, Niko, tell him no!"

"Everything has already been arranged. We are to meet Peter Bakas in the square in two days, and you will write a letter to the new mother in America."

"I don't know how to write."

"I know you can't write, Katerina. Mr. Bakas will bring a translator. You tell your letter to him, and he'll write your words in English."

What does he mean? Why did he agree to this? It makes no sense to tell a letter to a new mother; I am Sousanna's mother. I will always be her mother. She can't have two mothers. Only one—only me. She's too young to be away from me.

Katerina continued her protests to herself but said nothing aloud. She would do what was expected, as she always did. As she had to. Follow her husband's direction, even when she didn't agree. It's what a good wife must do.

How would she tell the children? Well, not Sousanna—the child was too young to understand, it would only frighten her. No need to let her last days at home be filled with dread; better to let her have happy memories. Ilias was probably too young to tell, too. But Anastasia would know something was going on, and she was old enough to understand. She'd have to find a way to prepare Anastasia.

The words never came. Katerina couldn't speak of it. For two days she convinced herself the horrible thing her husband had arranged wouldn't really happen. It was just a bad dream. Or a misunderstanding. Nikolas hadn't really agreed to send Sousanna away. Surely, he couldn't. Even as she got ready to go meet the men who would take her daughter, it didn't seem real.

"Why are you putting on your mother's lace collar?" Anastasia's words broke into Katerina's thoughts. "You only wear it for special occasions or church."

Katerina swallowed. She wasn't ready to answer these questions. "I'm going to the square with your father today. I want to look nice." She made her voice normal, like nothing was wrong.

Anastasia knew better. "To the square? You and Papa never go to the square. You can't afford to eat at the cafés or buy anything in the shops."

Katerina finished tying the bow at her neck to secure the collar before turning to her daughter. It was time to tell Anastasia. If she spoke quickly, maybe she could get through without breaking down. At least the younger children were outside and wouldn't hear.

"We're going to meet a man who will write a letter to a woman in America that will be a new mother to Sousan—"

"What? A letter to a new mother? Are you playing a joke on me?"

"No, Anastasia. Come sit at the table with me. I have something very difficult to tell you." Katerina explained everything she knew about what her husband had arranged for Sousanna. Niko came in as she finished talking. Anastasia jumped up and ran to him.

"Please, let me go," she pleaded. "Don't make Sousanna go— she's too little. She won't know what's happening, and it'll frighten her. Please, father, send me instead."

"No, you're too old. The man can only help Sousanna because she is still a little girl." He turned to Katerina. "Come, Katerina. We must go now."

Outside, the mid-morning sun shone warmly but a slight breeze nipped at her ankles. The day's brightness could not lift the darkness in Katerina's soul. She felt numb, as if she were walking in a trance. Niko, also, seemed to move slower and more stiffly than usual. They didn't speak. What was there left to say?

When they got to the square they paused and looked around the familiar scene. Children running and playing around the central fountain, their shouts of laughter at times drowning out the splash of the falling water. Adults visiting and gossiping over coffee. Gypsies in bright clothing jingling trinkets for sale. Businessmen making deals over papers on small tables outside the cafés. The familiarity brought no comfort. Katerina felt as cold and dead inside as the marble tabletops.

Niko pointed to two men sitting at a small outdoor café drinking coffee. "Over there, that's them. That's Mr. Bakas in the white suit."

They approached the table silently. The two men did not stand to greet Katerina and her husband, as was customary. Mr. Bakas didn't even look at them as he gestured for them to sit in the two empty chairs.

Sitting across the table from these strangers, Katerina's anxious hands fidgeted with her dress. She clasped them together in her lap to still them. Niko was uncommonly silent. He'd removed his cap and was twisting it this way and that between his knees, staring at the table.

Mr. Bakas broke the silence when he addressed her. "Katerina." His voice was not kind. This stranger reminded her of the German soldiers that had come to Pirgos during the war and treated her family and neighbors as though they were nothing.

Why do bad people take so much from us? Why do we think we have to give them what they want? Why all this to my country, and to my family?

Mr. Bakas nodded to the translator but didn't introduce him. "Let's get this over with," he said.

The translator looked at her. "Tell me what you want to say, and I'll write your words in English," he said. "Please speak clearly and slowly."

What should she say? She began, "Dearest Mrs.—I'm sorry, I don't know her name."

"Brown. It's Brown." Mr. Bakas's voice was impatient.

How could she know what to say to a strange woman? One taking her child from her? Unable to choke back the sobs, she could barely speak.

No one comforted her. Not Mr. Bakas, who took deep puffs from his cigarette and blew the smoke up into the sky he was now admiring. Not the translator, focused on the paper in front of him. Not even Nikolas, who was still looking at the table and twisting his cap.

Katerina began again. Unable to swallow her sorrow or her tears, she spoke through them. The translator scribbled her clumsy words onto the paper.

Dearest Mrs. Brown,

Please take good care of my Sousanna. Please be patient with her if she is scared. She is a good girl, and a smart girl. I know she will have a better life in America. Kiss her often as she leaves my loving arms to yours. We will wait with agony for letters and pictures, and one day for her to return to her home.

Her mother,

Katerina Nikolas Demetriou

Chapter 10

Nikolas

Nikolas lay in the small bed staring into the darkness. Morning would be here too soon. He didn't want to think about what it would bring.

What have I done?

He turned, pressing himself against the wall to make more room for Sousanna, nestled between him and Katerina. In the darkness he could faintly make out his wife's body on the other side of the bed, lying with her back to him. Though her face was buried in her pillow, he could hear her sobs. There was nothing he could do to comfort her.

Their youngest daughter slept peacefully, unaware of the heartbreak tomorrow would bring. One arm stretched over her head; the other hand rested on her cheek. Niko brushed soft wisps of tangled blond hair off her face. In the stillness he could hear her soft breathing as he watched her bare chest lift, then sink deep into her belly, revealing the outline of every rib.

Putting his cheek close to her face to feel the warmth of her breath, he whispered, "God, she is so innocent. I want to give her the best of everything, but how? We have nothing. There is nothing here for her. What else can I do?"

He rolled onto his back again. His own tears flowed, matching those of his wife. His throat tightened and he could not find enough air to fill his lungs. He turned to face the wall, hoping to silence his sobs.

From the day she was born, when he first held her in his arms, Nikolas had loved Sousanna differently from his other children. It was not something he understood or could explain. At times, with her eyes that seemed a mystery of joy and sadness, he believed she could see into the depth of his soul.

As she grew, she was curious about everything. She never ran out of clever questions and seemed to believe he had all the answers. When he could answer her, it reminded him that he was more than a simple field worker. Sousanna made him feel strong and smart. Brave. He so rarely felt that way anymore. He loved the way she adored him.

Often on his journey home, weary from working in the fields, Niko found Sousanna playing in the street with her friends. When she spotted him she ran to him, squealing with delight, "Papa, Papa!" Gaining as much speed as she could with her tiny legs, arms pumping back and forth, she charged to him.

That was his cue to bend onto one knee and stretch out his arms. She slammed into him and wrapped herself around his chest. He'd fold his arms around her and let out his roaring laugh. Then he'd lift her onto his broad shoulders and carry her toward home. The other children ran to surround him, asking if they, too, could have a ride.

"No," Nikolas would say, "only Sousanna is brave enough to be this high in the sky."

He would do that no more.

Nikolas took a deep breath to stop his tears. He had to think. Morning would come quickly and he had to know what to say to Sousanna. *What does a father say to the child that holds his heart? How can she understand what even I cannot?*

The early light of dawn was beginning to creep in through the window. He buried his hands into his thick yellow hair, pulling it tightly away from his forehead as his eyes traced the outline of cracks in the plaster ceiling. He was a failure. He'd failed to provide for his family as he should.

When he brought Katerina here to Pirgos, shortly after their marriage, he'd been certain it was the start of a good life. The land was flat and there were many fields to work. Fortune smiled on them with the move; he and Katerina both quickly found work planting and harvesting vegetables. Not only that, but, like the other workers in the area, they were given a small home nearby. True, it was only four concrete walls covered by a concrete roof. It didn't even have a floor. But it did have a fireplace. A door, and a window. It was a beginning.

He used to dream that one day he'd be able to build a house with more than one room. A house with so many windows the sun would stream in from every direction. A house with a separate bedroom for his children and a bed for each of them—and another room in which he could lie with Katerina and make love to her without the worry of waking children.

That was before the wars.

German troops appeared in Pirgos out of the blue. They immediately rounded up the townspeople, calling them from their homes into the street. Nikolas and the other men were told to follow the soldiers to the outskirts of town, where they were ordered to clear roads for incoming troops. Uncertain what would happen to them or their families if they did not cooperate, everyone followed the Germans' demands.

Nikolas pulled thorny weeds and heavy brush from roads day after day, until his hands blistered and bled. He didn't dare complain. He'd seen families torn from their houses so the soldiers could use them for their own shelter and comfort. He would do whatever he was told so he and Katerina could keep their home. That's what mattered. His hands would heal.

That didn't mean he wouldn't try to help his beloved country, or his countrymen. Not all of his digging and clearing was for the Germans. His good friend Taki helped. No one else, not even their wives, knew what else they did.

Niko hated that Katerina had to serve these foreign soldiers. Early in the mornings she harvested vegetables or killed chickens, wringing their necks with her hands, to prepare three hearty meals a day for the soldiers. She watched the intruders eat their fill while she and her neighbors went hungry. She never complained, instead telling Niko, "It's better than washing their filthy clothes."

Even with all this, they felt lucky. They were alive. Other Greeks were not so fortunate. Nearby villages were massacred.

In Kalavryta, only a few kilometers to the north, the Nazi soldiers took all the men to the hills and shot them, every single one, while the women and children were locked in the local school, which was then set on fire; and in Thessaloniki, 60,000 Greek Jews had been taken out of Greece to a place called Auschwitz.

On top of these atrocities, famine took its toll. The Nazis swept through the country burning crops and killing animals in an effort to starve the people. The news was that 300,000 of their fellow countrymen died from malnutrition and starvation.

Then one day it all ended. The war was over. The foreign soldiers went home and Greece once more belonged to the Greeks.

Then, as if that war had not been enough to break the backs and the spirit of the Greek people, a civil war began among his own people, as two factions vied for power in the vacuum left by the Germans. Greeks fighting Greeks—it was insanity to Nikolas.

Peace did finally come; but it left its usual companion, prosperity, far behind. The years of fighting had left his people stripped of their dignity, of their soul. Destruction, poverty, and hunger were the new enemy, with everyone wondering how to begin anew.

Nikolas wished he could find the courage to dream again, but the years of war and poverty had taken the last of his hope. Now it was only in his oldest son, Marios, that he saw courage.

"Marios." It was more of a groan than a name. His own anger had caused Marios to leave Pirgos several weeks ago. He and his son argued regularly, but it had gotten worse lately. Marios wanted him to move the family to the city and find work there. Nikolas could not, would not, take that chance.

Why doesn't Marios understand? The security of working in the fields is all I have.

Weeks ago their arguing had become bitter. Marios said to him, "Gregory's family is moving to Patras. His father will work on a ship making lots of money. They'll have a house with two rooms in it." Marios shook his fist in the air. "His father's not a coward." He picked up an orange from the table behind him and threw it across the room. "They'll have a big house and food to eat every day, and we'll still be here, hungry and cold."

Niko's fury filled the room as he shouted at Marios to be quiet. He would never understand what came over him, what caused him to grab a knife from the table and rush to Marios, or grab Marios's frayed collar and push him backwards across the floor. He remembered how Marios's feet shuffled awkwardly in the dirt as he tried to gain his footing, unable to get traction as Niko practically lifted him into the air. What made him slam Marios onto the table and lean over him, brandishing the knife in the air over Marios's throat, as the whole family watched?

Katerina's voice was desperate, pleading. "No, Niko, no!"

Sousanna's scream made him look up. Ilias ran to Katerina and hid in her skirt, and Anastasia froze in place.

Nikolas looked again at Marios. He saw the defiance on his son's face, but he also saw past that to the fear. Though obviously trying not to cry, Marios stared straight into his eyes. He felt Marios's hand on his shoulder, watched Marios's eyes slowly trace up his arm to his upraised hand. He followed Marios's eyes with his own to his fist clenched around the knife. What was he doing? When had he become a father who would hurt his own child?

He jumped back at the pain of his shame. Marios was out the door before the knife hit the floor.

The next day Marios left. Left his home. Left his family. At only eleven years old, he'd walked away from everything he knew, and set out for Athens and the better life he longed for.

Nikolas pressed his eyes shut and covered his face with his hands as if he could block out the memory of that day. *What have I done? Marios is only a child. How could I get so angry with him?*

Of all his children, Marios was the one most like himself. It wasn't only that Marios was handsome and charming. Marios's good looks were different from Niko's. He didn't have Niko's tall stature, or his clear blue eyes. Marios's eyes had so many colors it was like seeing the sun rise and set all at once. His dark hair tasseled this way and that like a piece of silk had carelessly landed on top of his head. No, it wasn't appearance that was similar.

It wasn't even his gregarious personality, his good humor, or his cleverness, though Marios did indeed share all these things. It was something deeper.

His will, that was it. Though small and frail, Marios was strong and determined. He knew what he wanted and nothing was going to keep him from going after it.

Was that it? Was Niko's anger really at himself, because he could no longer do what Marios could—dream, hope, believe? Did he envy his son so much that he couldn't admit his love?

It didn't matter now. Marios was gone.

What a fool I am. More foolish than my son, the dreamer. God help him make them all come true.

As the glow of dawn at the window began to weaken the darkness, Nikolas turned to face his daughter. He wrapped one arm around her and pulled her close to his chest. His last moments with her would be here in bed, just as his first moments had been; Sousanna was born in this bed, as all his children had been.

With each birth, Nikolas waited outside as Katerina's sister Georgia helped bring his and Katerina's children into the world. His first three children arrived quickly and easily. Sousanna's birth had been the difficult one. Through the door he heard Katerina cry out in pain and Georgia's soothing promises. "It won't be much longer. I'm here. All will be fine."

After hours of listening helplessly to Katerina moan and cry out, the welcomed pronouncement finally came. "It's a girl. She is healthy. God is good!"

He rushed inside, almost pushing his oldest daughter out of the way. Katerina held their new little daughter to her breast. The child was still. Katerina was pale and still panting. When Nikolas took the baby into his arms, he felt a special affection for her and knew he would love her the best. Quietly he had vowed, "I will do my best for you, and protect you from harm."

The morning sun erased every trace of darkness. The day Nikolas did not want to come was beginning.

He shook his head against the pillow. *My son who dreams big and cannot settle for a life like his father, and my little girl who I cannot give a decent life. Both will be gone from me, from us. How did I come to this? Driving one child away, and giving away another? God protect them both.*

The deep chime of the church bell startled Niko. It signaled time to rise, time to face the day. On the other side of the bed Katerina stirred, then slowly rose until she was sitting on the edge of the bed. Her head hung loose and low, but her hands gripped the mattress. Her small back stretched open and closed with a deep sigh. When she turned to him, her beautiful olive skin was pale and her eyes red from crying. Just to look at her broke his heart. She said nothing but turned away again and weakly lifted herself from the mattress.

Nikolas felt Sousanna stir under his arm. She rubbed her eyes and looked at him sleepily. "Good morning, Papa," she said. She curled herself up and snuggled deep into his chest.

How had a stranger convinced him to send his youngest child away? Hadn't losing Marios been enough? He blinked quickly. He must not cry; he must be strong. He did this for her. It was the right thing to do, to send her to a prosperous family in a foreign land. This land, this family, could give her nothing. There was nothing left after the wars.

What if they hurt her?

No; in America she will live like a queen, in a nice house with warm clothes and plenty of food. That will be a better life for her, until I can get some money and care for her properly.

What if she forgets us and never comes back?

No; she loves us. She knows we love her. She'll remember.

What if they decide they don't want her and put her on the street alone somewhere?

No. He promised she'll live with a good, Christian, Greek family. They wouldn't do that.

What if...?

What if?

Chapter 11

Sousanna

We don't go in. We keep standing in the yard, just Mama and me, and it feels strange because it's so quiet. Where are the grownups going to the square or the fields? Where are the yiayias looking for something to talk about?

Mama is being still again, like in the house when she didn't move for a long time. She squeezes my hand, tighter and tighter. It hurts.

There's a sound of something crunching rocks on the street. It gets closer and closer until it stops, and in a cloud of red dust a car stops at our gate. Nobody has ever come in a car to our house; I don't even know anybody with a car, and I don't know why this one is coming here. The car is green and white and doesn't have a top.

What if it rains? I wonder, but I don't say it because Mama is still not moving or talking and I don't know if I should either.

Inside the topless car is a man wearing a white hat. He opens the car door and steps into the dust. He is wearing a white suit with white shoes that match the hat. He takes off his hat and waves it in the air, making the dust blow away from him. No one on our street wears a white suit.

Mama finally moves. She brushes her hand across my face, shielding my eyes from the dust and at the same time pulling me into her skirt until I'm buried deep within its folds. She's holding me too close and I can't see anything.

I try to ease my discomfort by breathing in her smell: earth, food, body, but she presses me even tighter against her and I can't take the breath I need. I struggle and pull my head free from her grip but her arm stays around my back, her hand holding my side, keeping me pressed to her.

Sousanna

The man in white is through our gate, walking toward us. He stops only a few feet away and begins to speak. Not to Mama but to me.

"Sousanna, you look very pretty in your dress and red sweater. I am Mr. Bakas."

How does he know my name? He knows me but I don't know him.

"I know you love dolls, and I have come all the way from America with a doll just for you. She is in the back seat of my car. Look, can you see her? She is yours. All you have to do is come with me."

Why is he giving me a doll?

I stretch up under Mama's pressing hand to see the doll sitting straight up in the back of the green and white car. Not one made out of a sock but a real, beautiful doll. She's as big as I am, and looks like a real girl. She's pretty.

I want her. He says she will be mine, just mine, like my red sweater. Two things just for me. But Mama keeps pressing me next to her so I can't go get the doll.

The man speaks again, this time to Mama. He knows her, too, because he says her name. "Katerina, it's time. Give me the letter and let her go."

Mama holds onto me, tight. She's still and straight and quiet. She pulls my face into her skirt again where I can't see anything.

The man's voice says, "Let her go. I will take care of her; she will be safe with me." He doesn't sound nice anymore. I hear him walk closer. "Give me the letter and let her go."

Mama forgets to hold me so tightly. I pull my head out and now I can see her. She feels in her pocket for the envelope from the table, staring at Mr. Bakas with a look I have never seen on her face. She pulls the white envelope out and slowly lifts it toward Mr. Bakas. He quickly grabs it from her hand. Mama releases me, slowly, slowly, slowly, until I am completely free. She still hasn't moved anything but her arms, and she hasn't said anything the whole time. Not to him, not to me.

Mr. Bakas takes my hand and walks me to the car. He smells like the cigars from the stand up the street, and like spice. He opens the car door and pulls the seat forward. "Get in, Sousanna. Sit by the doll; she's yours. Hurry, get in the car."

Sousanna

I crawl into the back of the car with the doll. I've never been in a car. It's roomy and comfortable. The smooth seat is soft against my legs. Mr. Bakas pushes the front seat back into place and gets in the car. He closes the car door and starts the engine. Looking at me over his shoulder, he says, "Everything will be all right now, Sousanna." We drive away.

My doll has short, blond hair like mine. Hers is pinned back on each side with big bows of slippery pink ribbon, like the new blue ribbon tied at the side of my own hair. She wears a pink dress with flowers sewn around the hem, and a white collar with lace all around it, not just bits and pieces here and there like the collar on my own dress. Her white sweater has the most beautiful crystal buttons I've ever seen. It's pretty, but not as pretty as my red sweater Mama made just for me.

My eyes grow as wide as I can make them when I see the doll's shoes and socks. White socks with lace, and shiny white shoes with a buckle. They are whiter than white. I've never seen such beautiful clothes, especially the shoes and socks.

I touch the doll's eyes. "Oh!" They close! I touch her hair, her bows, her dress, her shoes. I try to sit as close to her as I can. I can hardly believe she's mine. I must be a very good girl to have this stranger come all the way from America just to bring me such a doll.

I hear Mama cry out my name, "Sousanna!" She sounds like she's hurt. She cries out again, "Sousanna!" Now I'm sure something is hurting her.

I turn quickly onto my knees so I can look out the back of the car. Mama is running toward me. She's calling my name, running and stretching her arms out to me.

Suddenly I'm scared. Something bad is happening. I don't want the doll anymore; I want Mama. I want the man to stop the car so I can get out and go to Mama. I cry out for her, opening my arms past the back of the seat, reaching for her. "Mama, Mama, Mama!"

The moving car turns the corner at the end of our street. I fall to the side and when I get up and I can't see Mama anymore. I hear her voice screaming my name but she has disappeared. Then I can't hear her anymore either. I'm so frightened I want to jump out of the car.

Chapter 12

Marios

September 1958

Marios felt his father's grip loosen as the knife dropped. He broke free and ran outside, around to the back of the house. How dare his father treat him this way? He couldn't stay here. He wouldn't stay, not one more minute.

I'm getting as far away from him as I can. He's nothing to me. I'll find a better life, myself. He stormed back to the front of the house.

Anastasia was outside with the younger children, herding them out the gate, saying something about a swim at the sea. Papa was walking down the street, toward the square, shoulders slumped and head hanging. Marios stormed into the house and picked up his bedroll. He turned to grab his jacket, and—

Mama.

She was sitting on the bed. Her whole body sagged like an old man's skin. Marios felt the rage drain from him as his heart broke at the sorrow on her face. He sat down next to her and put an arm around her, ready to tell her it wasn't her fault he was leaving; but she spoke first.

"Marios, I know you are leaving. I have seen the stirring inside of you for a long time. When I was your age I was carefree, just as you should be, but our lives now will not allow us such innocence. I know many boys your age—even younger—have traveled far away, looking for a better life. I think I have always known you would be one of those boys. I cannot stop you, but please, wait until morning. Rest tonight so you will have the energy to travel to...where are you going, Marios?"

"I'm going to Athens. I've heard the men talking; there's enough work for everyone there, with good pay. I'll be okay; you've taught me how to be strong. I've watched you work when you were tired, even when you were sick and weak. You're the best mother. I can't stay here and watch you suffer because Papa won't try for something better. Anastasia will be okay—she's older and will marry soon—but I worry for Ilias and Sousanna. I promise, I'll make a better life for them, and for you. I'll wait until morning, if you won't tell anyone."

Mama touched his cheek "You are too young to be so old. Forgive your father and me. We're doing all we know to do. I will say nothing, and tonight I'll boil some potatoes for your journey. They'll be wrapped in a cloth and hidden in the corner. I will pray for your protection every day that you are away from us." She pulled him into her arms, and held him for a long time.

Before dawn the next morning, while the others were still sleeping, Marios quietly got dressed. He rolled up his bedroll and tied a rope around it, making loops to put his arms through so he could carry it on his back. He gathered the hidden bundle of boiled potatoes from the corner, and picked up his jacket.

He knelt down between Anastasia and Ilias and pulled their quilts up over their shoulders. He stroked Ilias's wiry hair and kissed Anastasia's smooth forehead. Then he quietly walked to the bed and kissed his mother's cheek as she slept. Sousanna was buried too deeply between Mama and Papa for him to reach.

At the door, Marios looked back one more time. One little room, with three people in one bed and two others on the floor. Not even enough chairs at the table for all of them to sit down at once. Yes, he was doing the right thing. He was certain of it.

Confidence and hope surged through him as he started out. He reached the next village that morning. It looked like Pirgos, poor and run down. He asked some villagers for a little food, but they had none to spare, so he ate some potatoes as he walked.

None of the villages he passed that day were any better off, and offered him only water. He ate the rest of Mama's potatoes.

Near evening, with all his food gone, Marios came to a house with a tree in front so full of oranges its branches hung over the fence into the street.

"Marios, son, never pick the fruit or vegetables from other people's yards. The people must sell those fruits and vegetables in the market to make money for their families. It's a crime to take food from their yard." Papa had told him this all his life.

Marios desperately needed food. Surely no one would miss just one orange. He reached out a hand and—

"Ouch!" The handle of a broom came down hard on his wrist.

"Go away." An old yiayia shook the broom at him, threatening to beat him with it. He ran away before she hit him again.

Nearby was an open field. He unrolled his bedroll and lay down, but did not go to sleep. At home, Ilias and his sisters would be lying in front of the fireplace, its crackling and flickering comforting them. Out here, it was almost too quiet to sleep.

Marios watched the stars until it was very dark. *It's time; everyone will be asleep now.* He left his bedroll where it was as he sneaked back into the village and gathered fruit. Not just oranges, but apricots and pears from trees in other yards. There was no one to see him as he filled the inside of his jacket and his pants' pockets with stolen fruit, then took as much as he could carry in his arms.

The fruit lasted through the next day. Along with water from the village wells he passed, it was enough to keep him satisfied.

The cool September weather made the journey pleasant during the day. At night, the cold ground was hard, and Marios shivered in his skimpy bedroll. It took a long time for exhaustion to surpass the chill so sleep would come.

The third morning, Marios woke hungry and thirsty. The fruit was gone and there was nowhere nearby to get a drink of water. The pains in his stomach and weakness in his muscles begged him to stay in his bedroll.

"I can't give up. I have to get up and walk. Surely in the next village someone will have food and water to share." His words convinced his body to start walking again.

In the next town an older man sat in his yard. "Please, sir, do you have a bite of bread? I've been traveling for several days and I'm hungry."

"No one here can help you, little boy. We are all hungry; there is not enough for our own families. Go back home."

It was the same story everywhere. Everyone had to feed their own families first.

Marios

How can it be that no one has even a piece of bread to share? Is there no one in Greece with enough to eat? Even Papa shared food with others, and these people can't be as poor as my family.

For two more days there was no food, only a few drinks of water. That night the hunger was so bad he doubled up with pain. He even began to cry, something he never did.

This is all Papa's fault. He's the reason I'm out here alone and sick. I don't even know if I'm going the right way. Only Mama's prayers keep me safe. Someday he'll pay for this.

On the sixth day, Marios barely had strength to walk. He shuffled along slowly. If he could only make it to the next village. There'd be food there, even if he had to steal it.

The sun was high overhead when he reached it. One of the houses had a small vegetable stand out front. A man wearing the same tattered cap as Papa's sat on a stool behind the stand. Surely he could get something here.

"Sir, do you have something for me to eat and drink? I haven't eaten in three days."

The man looked Marios over. "You can drink from our well and eat the food in the rabbit cages we keep out back. I just put out their food; eat all you want." The man laughed. "Or all they will share without biting your hand off. Say, are you alone? You don't look well. Why aren't you at home?"

"Thank you, sir. Yes, I'm by myself. There's not enough work or food at home, so I'm going to Athens." Marios pushed the words out as fast as possible. Each second could be another bite the rabbits ate that he wouldn't have. It didn't matter that it was scraps; it would keep him going.

Five cages sat in a row. Marios grabbed the bits of cabbage scattered in each one and gulped it down as quickly as he could. A partially-eaten apple lay on the ground, and he ate the rest of it.

Thank you for your prayers, Mama; they led me to this food. Thank you. When Marios had eaten all he could find, he thanked the man again, and asked "Can you tell me which way to go?"

"It's too far. You should go back home."

"I can't go home. I'm going to Athens. It'll be easier if you tell me the right way to go."

The man sighed, and gave him the directions.

Villages became towns. The towns weren't as shabby; people weren't as desperate here. He passed a young boy about his own age in the street. The boy stopped him. "Hey, what's that on your back?"

Marios glanced over his shoulder. "That? It's my bed." He laughed. "I'm a turtle. Can't you tell?"

The boy joined in the laughter. "Why do you have your bed on your back, turtle?"

"I'm traveling to Athens to find work."

"Where is your family? You can't be much older than me and my father would never let me travel alone."

"I don't have a father like yours. My father is weak and a coward. I hate him."

The boy leaned away from Marios. "You hate your father? No one hates their father. Have you walked all this way?"

"Yes. I've been traveling many days, finding food and water anywhere I could."

"Come with me; my family will feed you. My name is Ilias. What's yours?"

Marios laughed. *Ilias. It must be fate.* "Marios."

That evening Marios sat down to supper with Ilias and his family. They offered him a beer along with a plate filled with tomatoes, cucumbers, olives, bread, olive oil, and meatballs.

Slowly; don't gorge on it. He forced himself not to stuff the food into his mouth as quickly as he could. What a relief to have a satisfied belly.

The family chattered as his own did at the table. Marios joined in the talk and laughter. Thoughts of dinners at home pecked at his mind. He missed being around the table with his family. There had never been much food on the table, but he was lonely for their company. This family was nice, but they weren't his. He wanted his own gentle mother, his quiet older sister, his shy little brother, and his clever little sister, Sousanna. Maybe even Papa.

That was a good night. Warm and sheltered in a house, with a full stomach. A good night's sleep was just what he'd been needing. His eagerness for the journey returned.

Early the next morning Marios thanked the family and embraced Ilias. The mother gave him a kiss on the cheek and a bundle of food and the father gave him directions, and he set out with a smile.

As he made his way along the edge of another town that evening, he saw an old man along the road carrying small sacks of potatoes, onions, and oranges in one hand and leaning on a cane with the other. The sack of oranges slipped from his hand and landed on the ground with a plop.

Marios ran to pick up the sack and adjust it back into the man's hand. In return the old man invited Marios to come eat supper with him and sleep that night on his porch for shelter. Papa had been right: be good to people and they will help you.

The closer Marios got to Athens, the better off people seemed to be. He didn't have trouble getting food anymore; people had enough to share. He had the energy to greet the people he met and have conversations with them. He could tell people liked him, and that pleased him.

As he topped a hill that evening, he saw it: Athens. It had taken nine days of walking, searching for food and water, and learning about people. Finally, here it was. As far as he could see there were lights and houses and buildings. It was incredible. He'd never imagined a city could be so large.

I made it. He wanted to jump up and down with joy but his body was too exhausted from the last day's travel to do anything but unroll his bed and lie down right there on the cliff. As he closed his eyes and drifted to sleep, Marios thought, *Out there is my future.*

Chapter 13

Sousanna

October 1958

I keep looking out the back of the moving car, wanting to see Mama run around the corner, coming to take me away from this bad man. But we're too far away and I know Mama can't run this fast. All I see is a cloud of red dust.

I stay on my knees for a long time with my face buried in my arms, sobbing. I was a bad girl because I wanted the doll. I should have told the man I didn't want her. I should've held on to Mama's hand and not let go.

When I lift my head, my eyes burn and everything is blurry. More tears spill onto my cheeks and drip onto my folded arms. Where is Mr. Bakas taking me? Is this what Papa meant by a foreign land? How long until I can go back home? What will happen to me? I've never been away from my family.

Maybe Papa is mad at me because I laughed at Marios when he fell in the well. Before he went away Marios was always trying to make me laugh and I thought he was playing a trick on me. I didn't know he was hurt and needed help.

Ilias was the one who ran to our house and got Papa. Together they put a long rope down the well and pulled Marios from the darkness.

Papa was angry with Marios and me. He scolded me. "That was a very dangerous thing that happened to Marios. You should not be laughing, Sousanna."

He scolded Marios, too. "Marios, what were you doing to fall into the well? Do you not have any sense?"

Or maybe they're mad at me because I bite my friends when we play our game and I want to be The American. I bit Christo the hardest of all because he pushed me when he said he wanted to be The American. I made him run home crying. Maybe that's it; maybe his mother told Mama to send me away until I learn not to bite my friends. If that's it I'll never bite anybody ever again.

I'm too tired to think or cry anymore. I turn back around and stare at the back of the seat in front of me. When the car goes around a curve, I slide on the smooth seat. After a while I wiggle over to sit even closer to my new doll. I clasp my hands tightly in my lap. My legs stretch straight out in front of me. I see my scuffed black shoes, then look at my doll's shiny white shoes, and I wonder if her shoes would fit me. I'm too scared to find out.

I lay my head on her hard shoulder to rest until Papa comes to get me. He'll be angry with Mr. Bakas for taking me away, and for making Mama and me cry. He might be mad at me, too, for wanting the beautiful doll and letting go of Mama's hand, but I don't care. He'll give me a hug after he scolds me. I want to go home. I close my eyes to wait for Papa.

The car stops. The air is still. I blink my eyes open to bright sunlight and remember everything: the green and white topless car, the man in white, Mama holding me too tight, the doll, Mama running after the car calling my name.

I look to see if my doll is still next to me. She is. Then I look outside the car and see beautiful flowers and tall trees surrounding a big house. A really big house. The man in white, still in the seat in front of me, has turned and is looking at me. "We're here."

I fold my arms to my chest and talk as mean as I can. "I want to go home. I want my Mama. You're a bad man. I want my mother. Take me home! My Papa will be very mad at you for making Mama and me cry."

I start crying, but I kick the back of his seat as hard as I can and swing my fists in the air so he'll know how angry I am. He doesn't seem to care.

He gets out of the car and leans the front seat forward. He doesn't look at me but at the big house. "Come on, get out."

I want him to look at me so he'll see I have my fists up, but he keeps staring at the house. Releasing the seat, he reaches into his pocket for a cigarette. He lights it, takes a big puff, and blows smoke in the air before he looks at me.

"Come on, I don't have all day. Get out of the car. And stop crying."

I stay next to my doll where it feels safe. "No. I won't. You can't make me. I'm staying here with my doll until you take me back home."

He pulls the front seat forward again, leans in, looks me in the eye, and shouts, "I said, 'Get out,' or I'll pull you out, and you won't like it if I have to do that. Now come on, you're wasting my time. Get out, now."

He might hurt me. I wiggle out of the car and reach back to get my doll. I hold her as close as I can for comfort. Mr. Bakas grabs for her, but he misses and I turn my back so he can't get to her. He grabs at her again, this time yanking her from my arms and throwing her back in the car. "Leave her there; she's not for you."

"No. She's mine. You said she was for me. She's—" I can't control my sobs "—mine." Determined, I reach back into the car. I feel my doll's leg and pull her toward me but Mr. Bakas reaches over me and squeezes my hand, hard.

I want to bite him, but I don't dare. He keeps squeezing my hand. "Let go of her; she's not yours."

I can't hold on. He's hurting me and pulling me away from the car. I have to let go and my beautiful doll falls. She gets stuck between the seats. The ribbon falls from her hair, and one shiny, white shoe drops to the car floor.

Mr. Bakas, still squeezing my hand, drags me toward the big house. I look back and see my doll's head hanging out of the car. My hand is starting to get numb where he's squeezing it, but it doesn't hurt as much as my inside.

"But you said she was just for me..."

I go limp and let Mr. Bakas pull me toward the house.

Chapter 14

Katerina

Katerina stopped running only when she tripped over the broken lace of her worn black shoe and fell onto all fours in the middle of the road. Breathless, her throat raw from calling her daughter's name, she didn't try to get up. It was useless to chase the car anymore. Sousanna was gone.

Never would she forget the look on her daughter's face as she disappeared in the moving car. Even now she heard, in her heart if not her ears, the sound of Sousanna's small voice crying out. Saw her tiny arms desperately reaching back.

Then the silence pressed down on her, and the quiet contrast to the sound of Sousanna's and her own cries made her ears throb and her head pound. The sharp gravel digging into her flesh, piercing her palms and knees, had no measure against the pain cutting into her soul.

America. A strange land, far away. What will happen to my child in that foreign place? Will she be safe? Happy?

Katerina sat back and wrapped her arms around herself, rocking to and fro, sobbing. Why had she agreed to this? Why hadn't she fought her husband on this one thing? Guilt burst from her loud enough for the heavens to hear. "Why did I let her go? Niko, why did you do this? Why?"

She'd failed her daughter; but her prayers could remain with Sousanna. She dropped her head and clasped her hands fervently. "God, protect her. Do not let any harm come to her. And bring her back to me, soon."

Someone put their arms around her shoulders. Katerina knew who it was without looking. Even deep in her mother's womb she'd known this wash of love. Her twin sister, Georgia, was with her, gently drawing her to her feet.

Sousanna

Georgia didn't say anything. Her sister simply held her and walked her back home. Katerina knew the neighbors were watching; nothing was hidden in this close-knit village. They were peering out their tiny windows, watching the horror unfolding on their street. She leaned on Georgia and stared straight ahead until they reached the small cement house where her sister closed the door behind them.

What am I doing? What should I do? Katerina stood inside the door unable to gather her thoughts. Still wordless, Georgia guided her to a chair, then pulled the other chair close, sitting next to her. Katerina sat limply, staring out the window. *How can I escape this nightmare?* No answers came. *I can't do this. I can't...*

Suddenly she is a child again, roaming the hills with her twin. They hold hands and run down the steep path in front of their home, then up again. From the top of a hill they can see distant mountains that go on forever. *This is heaven*, she thinks. She and Georgia pick a bouquet of wildflowers for their mother. On the way home they stop to pick some ripe apricots from the tree in the front yard, and eat them right then and there, juice running down their hands and chins. *What fun to be eight years old again.*

Now it's a cold night. Bedtime. She and Georgia snuggle together under warm quilts and softly sing songs to each other. Beyond the songs, Katerina hears Father telling Mother that he made a marriage arrangement with the Demetriou family. Their son Nikolas is eighteen now, and going into the military. When he returns Katerina will be old enough and they will be married.

She knows who Nikolas is. He's the handsome boy who's so tall and fair-headed. His friends call him Niko, and everyone said he was very clever. He'd gone to school for three whole years, so he could read and write a few words. Such a good-looking and smart boy for a future husband. Everything she could want. She hopes Father will find a boy as good as Nikolas for her sister, too.

Now she's fifteen. She doesn't think of Nikolas or their marriage arrangement. She is enjoying her carefree days, talking with boys who vie for her attention. Some joke with her to make her laugh; others tell her how beautiful she is.

But there's Nikolas. Katerina has all but forgotten about him, but now he's returned home after being gone seven years, serving in the military. He wants to marry.

Katerina

Katerina begs her parents, "Not yet, please. I'm only fifteen; I'm not ready to be married."

"You have been promised," Father says, and she's in the church committing her life to a man she barely knows. Her carefree days are over. Now she must conform to her husband's ways and wishes, just as her mother did with her father.

Suddenly she's in Pirgos, still a newlywed. She and Niko are both working in the field. The owner of the field will let them live in one of the small, one-room houses made of concrete, and let them keep some of the food they harvest to eat.

She doesn't mind the hard work but she doesn't like being so far from her family. She's lonely; she knows no one here. Niko has charmed everyone and made many friends, and his mother and sister and brother are here. He can't understand why Katerina doesn't visit with them more; when he's with them they don't ignore her and speak rudely to her the way they do when he's not there. In the fields her deep sadness causes uncontrollable tears to blur the sight of the vegetables she has carefully pulled from the ground and tied into neat bundles.

Katerina sits at her mother-in-law's table. Niko brought her here to visit, but then he went outside to talk to the neighbors. His mother says, "You have been married almost five years. Why have you not given my son any children? "

Niko's sister says, "God must not care for you or He would let you have a child. He has cursed you. You are cursed and barren."

Niko comes in and doesn't know why she's crying.

The German soldiers are here. They force their way into homes and drag the men and women out. They shout in a strange language that none of the villagers can understand, but their gestures make it clear what they want.

Katerina is with a group of women marched into a house and shown the dishes. The soldiers rub their belly and raise invisible forks to their lips as they point to the dishes and a sack of potatoes. The women quickly begin gathering vegetables to make a soup. Katerina scrubs turnips, and prays. The prayer comforts her; she has found the answer to her loneliness.

Then Katerina sees herself standing in the square in front of the church. There should be people around but she is alone, and she watches herself walk into the church in silence. She kisses the icons and lights candles for her loved ones, then walks to her familiar pew, the one she sits in with Niko every Sunday.

She genuflects in humility to the cross at the front of the church where Jesus hangs, suffering in pain. She gazes up at the ceiling to see the brilliantly-colored glass saints looking down into the church, then kneels on the bar at her feet. She closes her eyes and breaths in the musky smell of incense, puts her hands together, and prays. "God, please give me a child. If you do, I will name the baby after the Saint of this church. I'll love my child with all my heart. Please, God. Please."

Her prayer is answered. She's pregnant, ready to give birth. Her sister is beside her.

Katerina remembers Niko telling her one evening that Georgia was moving to Pirgos and would live only a few streets away.

"My beloved sister, here in Pirgos?" she had said in surprise. "Oh, Niko, how wonderful." And she hugged her husband tightly and danced with joy. Her songs of praise had a new lilt to them, and her prayers that night were full of gratitude.

Now it's time for the baby to be born, and Georgia is there to help with the delivery. The two identical women cry out together as Katerina's child enters the world. Georgia cuts the cord that connected Katerina with her child and raises the new baby high into the air.

"A girl." Katerina names her daughter Anastasia after the saint of her beloved church. Laughter and joy fill the small house. Suddenly there are two babies. Marios has been born, too.

Katerina is looking over the land. The Germans are gone. There are fields of grass and fields of grapes and fields of olives and fields of greens and vegetables. Between all these fields the land is torn and marred, and Katerina sees that these scars are a reflection of the wounds left on the hearts and souls of the Greek people from the wars and famine. Her countrymen appear before her, and they are hollow. She doesn't know how they can be filled and made whole again.

They can't give up; they must all toil on to rebuild their lives. She and Niko especially, because there are now four children to care for. She watches her children troop into the house with some horta and snails they've gathered, and herself boil them for supper. The children suck the meat from the little shells and think they've had a feast. Yanni, who owns the fields they work and the house they live in, gives her some chicken bones left from his meal the night before. She boils them with an onion to make a broth. When the bones are soft Katerina breaks them in half and gives them to the children.

"Suck out all the marrow," she tells them. "It will make you strong and healthy."

Niko comes in and she is glad to see him. She has come to care for him over the years. He's a good husband and a good father. A hard worker. Loved and respected in Pirgos. He hands her a single potato. Katerina asks him, "Where is all the food from the fields?"

"I gave some food to our neighbors. They are hungrier than we are. Sousanna's dearest friend is very ill because she doesn't have enough to eat. I take food to her whenever I can. We'll make it with what we have."

Katerina sees herself shake her head. Her husband has a good heart. "Niko, you're too generous." But he's right; though their family is poor, they have much love, and they are happy.

"Katerina, Katerina." Georgia's gentle voice called her back to the present.

Katerina shook her head. She'd been—not dreaming, but seeing a vision. A vision of her life.

Thank you, God. She'd been on the verge of breaking completely over losing Marios and Sousanna, but God gave her this vision of all she'd survived, to remind her of her strength.

Something stirred in her. Anger? Fear? Strength? Defiance? All of these. She'd forgotten these emotions, accustomed to doing what was expected without thought or complaint. It was the way of her countrywomen: to work hard, care for her family, honor and obey her husband.

Not today. Katerina could not accept this. Would not be silent. Somehow, she had to bring Sousanna home, no matter what arrangement Niko had made.

"Georgia, I have to find Sousanna and bring her home."

Georgia shook her head. "You know Niko will never allow that. You must do as he says and let Sousanna go to a better place where she'll have plenty to eat. You must think of her. This is best, as Niko says."

"No. She's my daughter and I'll take care of her. Sousanna can't have two mothers. No one has two mothers."

Sousanna

"How will you find her? Do you even know where she is?"

"I'll find out where she is and go get her. No matter how far it is, I'll get her. Please, come with me."

Georgia sighed. "Yes, my sister, I will help you. We may both be thrown out of town for going against your husband and head, but we will be together." She went home to prepare for their journey, and to tell her husband that she and Katerina were leaving in the morning to find Sousanna.

Katerina went into the yard to wait for Nikolas. He'd be coming in soon for the midday break. She held her head high, feeling tall and brave. She would not give in.

As soon as Niko and Ilias opened the gate, Katerina confronted her husband. "I'm going to find Sousanna. Where did that man in white take our daughter? You must tell me. Sousanna cannot have two mothers."

Pain was etched on Niko's face. His strong shoulders were slumped and his arms hung heavy at his sides. "Katerina, she is gone. There is nothing we can do now. She's gone. I'm sorry; I made a mistake, letting her go. God will not forgive me, and I cannot forgive myself."

Part of Katerina wanted to comfort him, but determination to find her daughter was greater. "No." She saw the look of surprise on Niko's face, and distress on her son's. She'd never defied her husband, but now she did. "No."

With a start of alarm, Ilias ran out to the street and disappeared. Nikolas shook his head with a sigh. "You can look for her, but I don't think you'll find her. Mr. Bakas said they were going to Patras for only one night. They'll buy new clothes for Sousanna, and she'll be fed well before she goes to America."

"New clothes?" Katerina drew herself up even taller, up on her tiptoes. "What about her red sweater? She loves that sweater. I'm going, Niko. Tomorrow Georgia and I will walk to Patras, and I'll bring Sousanna home."

"I wish I could go, too, but you know it's impossible. We're behind on what we need to gather for the rent. And we need food for Ilias and Anastasia. I must stay and work."

Katerina put her arms around her husband, able to give him the comfort he needed now that he'd given in to her demand. "I know, Niko. Georgia and I will find her and bring her home. I know you wanted to give her a better life, but we are her family. This is where she belongs. We'll leave before the sun comes up to get a good start. You must show me the roads I should take to Patras."

Niko made a map in the dirt to show Katerina the roads. He pointed out landmarks to watch for, and good places to stop and rest. "This is a difficult journey. You'll have to stop and rest several times along the way. The roads are good, but the trip will take a whole day by foot."

Katerina wasn't afraid of the journey ahead. Hadn't she and Georgia spent hours running up and down the rugged hills of Tripoli as young girls and teenagers? And didn't she spend every day working as hard as the men?

Before dawn the next morning, Georgia arrived at her sister's house with a bag of bread and boiled figs. Niko and Anastasia were up. Anastasia had pleaded to go with her mother and aunt. She was disappointed that she had to stay and work, but she submitted meekly and now helped Katerina prepare for the journey.

Ilias had begged his mother, "Please don't go so far away. Stay here with me." Katerina just told him to hush. She had to look for Sousanna. This morning Ilias still lay soundly sleeping on the floor. Katerina patted his head, then kissed her daughter's cheek and hugged her husband goodbye.

She and Georgia set out on the road Niko showed them. Though they were on this journey together, it wasn't like their girlhood days. They were older now, and tired. Soon they were limping along, but Katerina's determination pushed them to continue.

They stopped to rest in the places Niko suggested, and when the sun was high overhead they ate some bread and figs. It was evening when they hobbled into Patras. Tired and thirsty, they walked to the center of town to find a taverna. Not only could they ask for food and water there, but the town's people would be gathered. Someone might have information about Sousanna.

It got quiet in the taverna when they entered. Katerina could feel all of the people's eyes on them as they plopped into chairs at an empty table. A heavy woman wearing a greasy apron approached, carrying a glass of water for each of them.

"I am Hana Mitzou," the woman said. "My husband and I own this taverna. You look thirsty. Please, have a drink. Would you like something to eat?"

"We have no money for food," Georgia answered. "We are here looking for information." Katerina told her story to Hana and her husband.

"You've traveled far," Mr. Mitzou said. "You may have some bread and olive oil."

The twins quickly drank the water and ate the bread, then Katerina stood and began asking the people in the taverna, "Does anyone know about the woman who has several children in her home going to America? I need to find them. They have my daughter, Sousanna. I have to find her and bring her home. Do you have any news?"

Katerina didn't like to speak to strangers, but her desperation made her brave. She would speak to anyone to find her daughter.

A man stood up. "Yes, I heard about these children. They come from families that can't care for them. A man came from America to give them a better life. He brought them here yesterday, but I heard they've already left for Athens, to fly to America. Don't worry about your little girl; she'll be better off now. Go home and pray for her to have a good life in America."

Katerina's knees buckled. Georgia caught her and eased her gently to the ground. Katerina wept in agony. No one made any move to help; they just stared at the sisters as they sat in the middle of the taverna floor.

"Would she drink a beer?" Katerina heard Mr. Mitzou ask Georgia. His voice sounds like it's coming from the bottom of a well. "Maybe it will help settle her down."

"Yes, I think that would help. And maybe some food. Do you have some chicken or eggs we could eat? We're both very hungry."

Georgia helped Katerina back into a chair and pulled her own chair close to her. With her sister's soothing, Katerina slowly took control of herself. Eventually she was able to drink the beer and eat the eggs Hana set before them. When their thirst was quenched and their stomachs full, the sisters offered to pay for the beer and food by cleaning the taverna.

"No, you've been through enough," Mr. Mitzou told them. "You owe me nothing. You can sleep here tonight; my wife will bring some quilts. I'm sorry about your daughter." He shook his head. "There's too much sorrow in our country since the wars. Too much."

Katerina

Katerina and Georgia woke early the next morning. They folded their quilts and left, without Sousanna. As they were leaving they heard the owners call out, "God be with you."

The twins trudged all the way back home without stopping. The pain in Katerina's heart was so great it allowed no room for any other thoughts or feelings. Sousanna was on her way to America where she would have a new mother, and there was nothing Katerina could do to stop it. How could she live with this loss?

Chapter 15

Helena

"I let you stay until the baby was born, but I will not have a bastard child in this house."

"Where will I go? How will I take care of her?" Helena couldn't believe her father was throwing her into the street with a newborn infant. It wasn't her fault her boyfriend ran off when he learned of her pregnancy. Even his parents didn't know where he went—or that's what they said, anyway. They were as disappointed in their son as her parents were in her.

"You should have thought of that before giving yourself to a man you weren't married to. I am shamed before all of Patras. Go now. You are not welcome here any longer."

Helena gathered her little daughter, Abela, into her arms. She longed to give her mother a hug, but it would mean walking past her father, and that she would not do. Her words would have to do.

"Goodbye, Mama. I'm sorry."

Only the soft sound of her mother's weeping answered her. There was nothing left to do. Helena walked out the door and away from her parent's house. She carried nothing but her daughter.

She didn't know where she was going until she was there. Sitting on a hard pew beneath a statue of Mother Mary, Helena nursed Abela at her breast. She studied the statue.

Is this how she felt? Ashamed of having a child before being married but still loving that child with everything in her? Hopeless and alone?

A rustling startled her out of her reverie. "It is an unusual time to see someone in our church," the nun said as she sat down beside Helena.

"My family has thrown me out because I had a baby and I'm not married. I didn't know where to go, so I came here."

"I think I can help you. We have an orphanage for children like yours. It's here in Patras, on the other side of the city. I'll take you there; I know many of the nuns that help at the orphanage. They'll take care of your baby and find a good home for her. That is what you must do. You can't work to make money and also take care of your baby."

Helena couldn't think of any other solution, so she didn't argue. But she wasn't sure she could leave Abela. "I would like to go alone. Can you tell me where I can find this place?"

"If you leave now and walk without stopping, you can be there before night falls." The nun gave Helena directions and sent her off with a "Godspeed."

§

Helena clasped her daughter close to her chest. She wouldn't let go. She couldn't.

Besides, look at this place. It was dirty and it smelled bad. There were so many children they had to sleep three to a bed, and still many were left to sleep on the floor. They were all thin—food was scarcer here than anywhere—and most of them looked sick. Abela would be just one more mouth. The nuns were overworked, hungry and tired themselves; they wouldn't take any more notice of Abela than any of these other children. No, she couldn't leave her baby here.

But it was an opportunity. She needed a place to stay, somewhere she could keep her baby with her. They obviously needed more help.

The arrangements were made. Helena would not be paid for her work, but she'd have a place to sleep and at least a little food each day. Best of all, Abela would be with her.

She worked from the moment the sun sent out its first ray of light until it was too dark to see. Scouring floors, changing diapers, washing dishes, bathing little ones, scrubbing laundry, stopping squabbles among the children, making beds—the work never ended.

Helena found that if she concentrated on whatever task was before her, she could shut out the tragedies all around her. Mothers leaving children who clung to them. Babies left on the doorstep. Deaths from malnutrition or illness. Siblings parted when one was lucky enough to be adopted. That was always the babies and younger children. The older children had nothing to hope for. No one wanted them. As soon as they figured that out, many of them chose to leave and go into the streets, hoping to find work.

Helena had been there about six months when, over the course of several days, official people were in and out of the orphanage. There was lots of talk with the nuns about how to find homes for the children. She overheard some of them talking about the wonderful plan for the British and Americans to take children and give them a good life.

"Good morning. I am Alec Callas."

Helena looked up from the diaper she was changing. It was one of the visitors. She'd seen him several times. In fact, now that she thought about it, every time the officials came, this man seemed to end up wherever she was, watching her. This was the first time he'd ever spoken to her.

"Every time I come here I see you working hard to care for the children. You're not a nun, and you're too young and pretty for this kind of work. Why are you here?"

"My name is Helena and I have a baby. I work here so we can have shelter—a place to sleep and some food."

"You're lucky to have such good fortune, Helena, but I know someone who can give you more than this. You see, I am Greek, but I live in America. I come here to help Americans who want to adopt Greek children from orphanages. They are good people who want to love these children and give them a good life. I must leave now, but when I return, will you talk with me about this, and how you can help?"

"Yes, of course."

What a good man to want to help these children that most have forgotten. What can I do? And how will it give me more? Maybe he wants me to go to America with him. I hope it's not too long before he comes back.

Alec returned in only a few days. He waited until they were alone before he spoke to her. "You work too hard here. You can have everything you want, for you and your baby, if you help Peter Bakas. And the work won't be nearly as difficult."

"Who is Peter Bakas? I never heard of him. What would I have to do for him?"

At the sound of footsteps in the hall, Alec turned in that direction. He spoke over his shoulder as he hurried out of the room. "Meet me in the square tomorrow morning at nine, and I'll explain everything."

"I'll try..." He was already gone.

§

The church bell was just striking nine as she arrived at the square the next morning. Alec stood talking to a man in a white suit in front of one of the cafés. *Maybe they'll get me a meal.*

They didn't even ask her to sit down. Alec introduced the other man, Peter Bakas, and he took over the conversation.

"You may stay in Patras," Peter said. "You'll live in a large home close to the sea, and care for and prepare children that will go to America. You and your daughter will want for nothing—everything will be provided for you. Will you do it?"

The same work she was doing now—caring for children—but in her own home and with plenty of food. Abela wouldn't have to grow up in the dirty, crowded orphanage. So many children got sick from the unsanitary conditions, and there was no money for doctors. It would be much safer for Abela to leave the orphanage. And Helena would have more time to spend with her daughter if she didn't have to work there.

"Yes, I'll do it."

The next day Peter Bakas picked her up from the orphanage and drove her and Abela to their new home. As promised, it was a large house with a big yard near the sea. It was full of beautiful furniture and had indoor plumbing. Cupboards were full of food; closets were full of clothing.

All this, for me? If Father could see me now. Abela will grow up with everything.

"Here's the plan," Peter said. "I'm going to bring some kids here in a few days. You take care of them, but besides that, you have to teach them some things."

"I'm not a teacher—"

"Not that kind of teaching. These kids will be poor. Dirty. They won't have any manners. You've got to get them ready to go to nice homes in America. You'll have three months to teach them to behave, keep clean, use manners, that kind of thing. You can do that, can't you?"

These were things she would eventually teach her own daughter, anyway. It would be good practice.

"Yes, I can do that."

"Good. One more thing. Can you read?"

"A little bit."

"That's enough. Here." Peter handed her piece of paper with a few words and phrases on it. Beside them were strange words. "That's the English words," he explained. "You've got to practice them and teach the kids to say them."

He went over the words with her. *Mom. Dad. Please. Thank you...* Helena hoped she could remember them all.

§

The work was easy. Helena liked helping the children. Most of them were very agreeable. When they first arrived, they cried a lot, wanting to go home, but she soon won them over.

Helena's greatest joy was watching her own daughter. Abela was content and growing into a beautiful child. The children she took in loved to play with her—especially the girls, who acted like little mothers.

Helena set some time aside each morning and each evening for just her and Abela. It was only a few minutes each day, but those minutes made the whole day sweet. Sometimes she blew into her daughter's tummy to make her laugh. Other times she played peek-a-boo or other little games that amused her daughter. Ablela's giggles at these times made Helena's heart sing.

One morning when she went into her baby's room, it was unusually still and quiet. She reached into the crib to wake Abela, shaking her gently.

She would not wake. She never woke again.

Chapter 16

Sousanna

October 1958

A woman comes out of the house to meet us. "Let go; you're hurting her," she says to Mr. Bakas. She takes my hand away from him and kneels down in front of me. Her eyes look all over my face, like Mama's did when she got me dressed.

"My, she's a pretty one."

The woman is pretty, too, with wavy brown hair around her shoulders and red lipstick. Her fingernails are painted pink. She has brown eyes but they don't sparkle or shine like my mama's and sister's.

"Yes, but she's feisty," Mr. Bakas says. "Watch out for this one. We'll have to break that wild spirit." His voice changes for his next words. "Hey, listen, I'm in a hurry, can't stay. You know the plan. I'll be back in a few weeks to take pictures of the children. And by the way, look for the best boy in the group to be a son for my daughter, and a grandson for me."

He walks back to the green and white car without a top and knocks the doll back into the seat. He drives away. With my doll.

The woman says, "I'm Miss Helena and this is my house. There are other children here just like you. They will be your friends, and you can play together. Come inside and meet them." She stands up, still holding my hand, and walks me into the big house.

Peering into each room as we walk by, I can't believe my eyes. There's more than one room in this house. Even more than two rooms.

Miss Helena leads me by the hand deeper into the house. Everywhere I look I see chairs. Big chairs that look so soft I want to touch them, but I don't dare. The walls are filled with beautiful pictures of flowers, and one of Jesus and His mother Mary. I know them from church. There are no dirt floors anywhere, only white marble and rugs like the one we're standing on. I wish my feet were bare, to feel the softness of the rug and the coolness of the white marble. We stop walking when we get to the biggest room I've ever seen.

Voices of children come from the back of the house. "She's here," one voice says. "Let's go look at her." Three boys run into the room. They push and shove and run over each other until they're in front of me.

"Look, she's been crying," one of them says to the other boys. He turns to me and says, "Crybaby, crybaby." They all laugh. One boy even sticks his tongue out me, just like Ilias does.

I hold tight to Miss Helena's hand and bravely stick my tongue back at him. "I'm always The American or I'll bite you." They all laugh and start to run away.

Miss Helena calls after them, "Boys, get the other children to come meet Sousanna in the gathering room. And it's not nice to poke our tongues at people. No more of that or you will be punished."

She lets go of my hand and walks across the room to a big, soft, red chair and pats the seat with her hand. "Come, Sousanna. Here, sit in this chair. The other children will join us in a moment."

I crawl up into the chair. It's soft. I bet this is the kind of chairs Americans sit in. I sink into the seat of the chair. It feels like a big hug. I like it here. Miss Helena is pretty and kind. Not like Mama— she's the most beautiful and the kindest person of everyone.

Is Miss Helena going to be my new mother? It's nice here. I might even like the boys, mostly the one that stuck his tongue out at me. This might be fun until Papa comes to bring me home. I'm not scared anymore.

A bunch of kids tumble into the room. Four boys and two girls. They line up in front of me. They're all wearing nice clothes that look new, and the girls have ribbons in their hair, just like mine. One of the girls smiles at me, but the boys just stare.

The boy who stuck his tongue out wrinkles his nose up and makes a mean face. Miss Helena is standing behind the children so she doesn't see him. But she would see me so I can't stick my tongue back at him.

Sousanna

Miss Helena says, "Everyone, this is Sousanna. She has just arrived from Pirgos. You know how you felt when you first came here. Please help her feel welcome. Girls, I know you will be a good friend to Sousanna."

One of the girls starts crying. "I want to go home," she wails.

The other girl puts her arm around the crying girl. "Me too. I want to go home." She looks up at Miss Helena. "Please, we want to go home. Please?"

The boys start calling out, "Crybabies, crybabies." But one of them wipes his eyes. He's crying, too.

Miss Helena says, "Please don't cry. Everything will be fine. We are all here together and I'll take good care of you. Now, everyone find a place to sit." Her voice makes me think of music.

She sits in the other red chair and lifts the crying girl into her lap. "All of you will go home. You'll go to new homes and have new mothers and fathers. You'll go to America and live in big houses with a lot of food and beautiful clothes to wear. You're all going home very soon."

Why does everybody keep saying that? New mothers and fathers? I want my same Mama and Papa. America? What do they mean? Maybe Miss Helena is like the man in white, and not nice at all. They both want to take us to new mothers and fathers, but we all want to go home to our own mother and father.

I look straight ahead and see a picture of Mother Mary holding her son Jesus in her arms. Mothers should hold their own babies. I won't like Miss Helena anymore. I'll sit in this big red chair and look at Jesus until Papa comes to take me home. Maybe the man in white has taken me too far away, and Papa doesn't know where I am. How will he find me?

The other children go outside to play but I don't go with them. I stay in the chair, and I'm not moving until Mrs. Helena lets me go home.

I sit forever, but I can't wait anymore; I have to go to the potty house. I slide off the chair and look for Miss Helena. She's in the kitchen, fixing something to eat. I don't want to be nice to her so instead of asking sweetly I use a mean voice. "Where is your potty house? I have to go."

Her face looks like she's smelling the potty house from the kitchen. "I don't have a potty house. Here we use a toilet in the toilet room, just like they do in America."

I twist my legs around each other. She better tell me fast. "Where is it? Is it in the back yard? How far away is it? I really have to go."

"You don't have to go outside to find it," she says. I can tell by her voice that she's irritated with me but I can't help it. "Toilet rooms are in the house. It's down this hall. Follow me and I'll show you."

I follow her down the hall to a little room with blue tile everywhere. On the ceiling, the walls, the floors. It's pretty, but I'll have to look at it later because now I really have to go! Miss Helena is still talking.

"In America you will live in a home with toilets like these, that flush, in a little room like this inside your house."

I'm bouncing up and down, barely able to hold the pee, but I have to ask. "Toilets? You mean there will be more than one?"

"There may be. Some Americans have two or three. When you're in the toilet room you must always close the door behind you and keep it closed until you are through. All the other children have learned to use the toilet in my house, and today you—what are you doing?"

Pee is running down my leg and onto the blue tiled floor.

"I can't help it," I say, and start crying. "I told you I had to go. Why did you keep talking? I couldn't hold it anymore."

Miss Helena grabs me by the arm and slaps my wet bottom. Hard. "Never do this again. Do you understand? You're a bad girl, a very bad girl. Now go sit on that toilet right now." She drags me to the toilet and pulls off my wet underpants. "Sit down. This is how a proper young girl goes to the bathroom."

I can't stop crying. Nobody has ever hit me, and it hurt. It hurt a lot. I pull myself onto the toilet seat. I feel like I might fall in, but I don't say anything. I have to be careful what I do and say, or Miss Helena might hurt me again.

As I sit on the toilet hoping not to fall into the water beneath me, I pray in my mind. *Please, God, don't let her be my new mother, please.*

Since I already peed on the floor, there's nothing else to do. "I'm through."

Miss Helena tears off a white piece of paper from the roll hanging on the blue tiled wall and hands it to me. "Here, now wipe yourself."

I know how to do that. Mama taught me to use old rags that she kept piled in the potty house. She told me, "Always clean yourself, Sousanna. It is very important. Then bring the rag to me and I will clean it. Always bring me the rags; we never want to use dirty rags." Now I wipe myself like Mama taught me.

Miss Helena says, "Throw the paper in the waste can beside the toilet. Never put the paper in the toilet, do you understand?"

I just nod my head.

Later the other girls and I go to the blue tiled toilet room because Miss Helena said we need a bath. In the corner is a big white tub. Miss Helena tells us to take off our clothes. She turns the silver handles in the front of the tub, and water comes out. She puts her hand under the running water.

"Just right. Nice and warm," she says.

Warm water. Running right into the tub from the faucet!

I wish Mama could have warm water come into her house, too. We take baths at home now that we have a tub. Spiro brought it to our house one day, a brown, brass tub. He carried it into our shed, and as he left he waved his hand under his nose and said, "Now all of you, take a bath."

Ilias and I laughed but Papa answered in an angry voice, "Go home, Spiro. You make my liver swell. And you could use a bath yourself."

Inside, where I knew Papa couldn't hear me, I leaned over and whispered to Marios, "Even if Papa doesn't like this tub, I do. It'll be like sitting in a tiny ocean."

Marios laughed. "Sousanna, the little fish."

When we bathe Mama has to carry in water from the well. One by one we get in the tub filled with water she brings in. Each time we say, "Time for more hot water," and Mama pours hot water from the black kettle into the tub. That makes it the perfect temperature— for a little while.

In the winter we don't bathe often because the water is freezing before we can finish getting the soap off our bodies. Mama uses a small bucket to pour water over our heads to rinse us off. She does it as fast as she can so we won't get too cold before she's finished. But we always are.

If Mama had running water like Miss Helena, she wouldn't have to carry in the water pail so many times and heat it over the fireplace. And we wouldn't have to take cold baths.

When the big, white tub is full of water, Miss Helena tells Julia and Anna to get in. I follow, cold and ready to get in the warm water. Miss Helena puts her hand on my chest and stops me. "No, Sousanna; you will bathe after Julia and Anna. You're still very dirty and I don't want you in the same tub with the children that are clean."

I've already taken off all my clothes, but I don't argue. I reach into my pile of clothes on the floor and get my red sweater to keep me warm while I wait for my turn.

Miss Helena scrubs me until my skin hurts. After she dries me off, she gives me a beautiful pink gown to put over my new white—really white—underpants. She wants me to wear a long coat she calls a robe over my pink gown.

I ask, "Please, can I just wear my red sweater? Mama worked very hard to make it for me." I don't expect her to say yes, but she does, and I smile at her.

After our baths we all gather in the kitchen around a huge table to say our prayers and drink a cup of warm milk. I don't like milk but I remember the slap on my bottom and don't say anything. Then it's time for bed, my first time ever to sleep away from my family. I try not to cry. If I do the boys will make fun of me again.

Julia and Anna know where to go to sleep. So do the boys. I don't. Julia takes my hand. "Come on, Sousanna, we sleep in here. There's a nice bed with a big pillow and warm blankets for each of us. Don't be afraid; we'll be together. I'll sleep in your bed with you if you want me to."

I do.

When we go into the room where we'll sleep, my eyes open wide trying to see everything. The room is so pretty I couldn't have imagined it. There are three beds, real beds, not bedrolls on the floor. Each one has pink covers and pillows with ruffles. There's a toy bear on each bed and a gold cross hanging over each one. Beside the beds are little tables with books and lamps with pink lampshades on them.

"See, Sousanna," Anna says, "it's nice here. But I still want to go home. My home is not as fancy as this, but I miss my family. I miss them so much."

Julia, Anna, and I all climb into my bed. We sleep together, wrapping our legs and arms around each other to keep from falling off the bed.

Every day I play with the other children. Soon we're all friends. One day I ask them, "Who wants to learn how to play my favorite game?"

They all jump up and down. "Me! Me! Teach us, Sousanna. What is the game?"

I put my hands on my waist and throw out my hip. "Me and my friends made up a game we call The American. Whoever gets to be The American, which is usually me, pretends they are saving everyone else from the soldiers that came to hurt us."

They all cheered. "Yes, we want to play that game. Who should be The American?"

I want to play that part, but if they don't choose me I won't dare bite anyone. No telling what Miss Helena would do to me, especially if I bite Mario. He's her favorite, because he's going to be Mr. Bakas's grandson in America. I don't like Mario. He's mean to me, and tells lies about me to Miss Helena just to get me in trouble. But I have to say he's my friend and be extra nice to him or Miss Helena will be upset.

After we play The American we decide to play Hide and Seek. I see the tree I want to hide behind. As I run to it I look behind me to see if anyone is watching me, and run into the tree. It hurts my nose but I don't say anything because I'm hiding. I want to win the game by not letting anyone find me.

Everyone is found and we're standing together. Suddenly Julia screams, "Sousanna, your nose has blood all over it. Ewe!"

I touch my nose and feel the sticky blood on my face. "It doesn't hurt," I tell my friends. "I promise, it doesn't hurt. Please don't tell Miss Helena, please."

Mario is already calling her. "Miss Helena, Miss Helena! Sousanna ran into a tree and she's bleeding. There's blood everywhere! Come quick!"

"Mario, stop," I beg. "Please don't call her. She'll get mad and spank me again. It hurts when she does that. You don't know because she never spanks you. Please stop calling her."

It's too late. Miss Helena is heading toward us. She grabs me and pulls me inside the house.

"You're the most foolish little girl I've ever had here," she yells. "Look what you've done to your face. Your family in America does not want a little girl with scars on her face. Peter shouldn't have brought you here; you're not worth the money he's getting."

She washes the blood off my nose and paints something red onto the cut. It burns and I kick her.

"Stop it, that hurts," I scream. "I hate you. You're mean to me. When my papa comes he'll be mad at you for making me cry."

By now all the children are gathered around watching. Julia cries out, "On no," and starts to cry.

Miss Helena catches hold of my arm and slaps my bottom, hard, again and again. So hard each slap throws me off balance so I can barely stand. She spanks me so many times I don't think she'll ever stop. It hurts more than ever before and I'm crying so hard it feels like I'll choke and I can hardly catch my breath to tell her, "I'm sorry, I'm sorry, I'm sorry."

I hear Julia plead, "Please, stop; you're hurting her."

Then Anna, crying, says, "Miss Helena, you're hurting her; stop!"

I hear one of the boys, I don't know who, say, "It was an accident. We were all playing Hide and Seek and she ran into the tree. You're going to kill her."

Miss Helena finally stops spanking me. She pushes me away from her and I fall on the floor.

Miss Helena says, "I'm not through with you. I'll break that wild spirit in you yet." She stomps out of the room.

I fall to my knees and cry out, "Mama, Papa! Come get me. She's hurting me, Mama."

Then I feel all the children around me, even Mario. They pat me and stroke my hair. Julia kisses my cheeks and whispers, "Sousanna, we love you. We're here. We'll take care of you." I put my head on Julia's shoulder and close my eyes. My bottom hurts, and so does my arm where Miss Helena pulled it too hard.

Sousanna

I must be a very bad girl. I try to be good, but I'm always in trouble. I don't know what to do.

A boy with the same name as my brother, Ilias, puts his arms around my waist and helps me up. I go lie in my bed until it's time for our nightly routine: prayer, warm milk, and bed. I hope Miss Helena isn't mad at me anymore. But after we finish our prayer and milk and start to our beds in the sleeping room, Miss Helena says, "Sousanna, follow me."

My insides are shaking. What is she going to do to me?

Chapter 17

Helena

The crib was Abela's. No other child belonged in it. But Helena had to do something with Sousanna. Something that would teach her not to fight, that would embarrass her and teach her who was boss. Who did she think she was, anyway? Kicking Helena, when all she was doing was trying to help.

"Break her spirit," Peter said, and Helena would do just that. She'd put Sousanna in the crib and tell her she was a little baby.

Surprisingly, Sousanna didn't fight back. Helena realized she'd wanted her to—she needed a good fight to release the demons tearing her heart apart. But Sousanna just lay down and closed her eyes, immediately asleep.

The next morning there was something different about the girl. She was dejected. Her spirit was gone.

What have I done to the child? Helena had won; so why did she feel like the loser? Seeing the girl so despondent, Helena wanted to hold her close and comfort her.

Instead, she just lifted her from the crib and stood her on the floor. She felt Sousanna wrap her tiny arms around her skirt. Her upturned face was sad and helpless.

"I want you to like me," she said. "I don't want to be a bad girl. Please, Miss Helena, please like me. I'll try hard as I can to be a good girl."

Helena grasped Sousanna's hands and held them gently. She knelt down and looked into Sousanna's eyes through her tears.

"Sousanna, you're not a bad girl. I can only have this house if I do what I'm told." The child would never understand, but the urge to confess was too strong to stop.

"Peter said I should break your spirit, so I tried. But don't let go of your spirit, Sousanna. You're strong. I don't want to break your spirit anymore. I don't want to make you cry or hurt you." Helena hoped her sobs wouldn't frighten Sousanna. It was comfort she wanted to give her, and her spirit back.

"I know you miss your mama, Sousanna. I'm sorry for what I've done to you, to all the children, so many of them. I'm so sorry. I've been unkind to you, but I'm not unkind, Sousanna; or at least, I didn't used to be. I promise things will be better now. I'll take care of you. You'll be safe here. You're a good girl, and you're pretty—and you are strong. Never forget that, and never let anyone take that from you."

Helena took Sousanna into her arms and held her close for a long time. Sousanna returned the embrace, and whispered, "I like you again, Miss Helena."

Chapter 18

Marios

December 1958

Marios had barely stepped off the bus in Pirgos when Anastasia threw herself into his arms, sobbing hysterically. Words spilled from her mouth fast as olives from an overturned basket.

"Marios, Sousanna is gone. They took her to America. Papa sent her away with a man that gave her a doll. I couldn't stop him. I tried, Marios, I tried. He said we'd hear from Sousanna, but we haven't. Mama cries everyday—she even calls Sousanna's name in her sleep. Oh, Marios, I'm so glad you're home. You'll know what to do. You're the smartest of us all; you can find Sousanna and bring her home. You have to find her. She must be scared. She's never been away from us, and they took her so far away. To a place she can't even speak their language."

What was his sister saying? It didn't make any sense. A man with a doll? America?

"Anastasia, slow down; I can't understand you." There was no calming her. Her sobs became wails, her whole body shaking out of control.

He pulled her to the corner, out of the crowd bustling around them, and shook her. "Anastasia, calm down. Stop crying. Look at me. What are you saying? Sousanna is gone? To America? That can't be—she's only a little girl."

"What she says is true." A voice over his shoulder caused Marios to turn around. He recognized one of their neighbors. "I'm sorry," the man said, "but your sister is telling you the truth. Your father sent the little girl to America."

Marios grabbed Anastasia by the arm and pulled her behind him as he strode toward home. His words were more to himself than to her. "How could he do this to her? He'll answer to me for this."

"Marios, I can't walk this fast. Please, slow down." Anastasia was no longer sobbing, but tears still wet her cheeks and her breath was short.

He couldn't let that stop him. "No. Come on. I've got to find Papa. He'll pay for this."

Anastasia's voice pleaded between gulps for air. "That man lied to Papa. I know he did. He came to our house asking for Sousanna to go with him, and Papa threw him out. But he came back, and he said bad things would happen to Sousanna if she stayed here. That she would starve—or be a whore in the streets. That she had no hope here and he could give her hope in America. He promised to send letters and pictures to us every week, but it's been two months and we haven't heard anything." She gasped for breath. "Please, Marios, slow down. I can't walk this fast. I can't breathe."

Marios stopped walking and released Anastasia. She doubled over, grabbing her knees, panting for air.

He felt his muscles tighten and caught his breath in a growl of rage. "He took money didn't he? Bastard. Bastard! He sold Sousanna. Sold her like a goat, or a chicken. I'll kill him for this."

"No, he didn't take money. He didn't sell her. The man promised she'd come back. You know Papa wouldn't do that. He loved Sousanna best. He just wanted her to have a better life than he could give her."

Anastasia was breathing easier now, but her voice still sounded choked. "But he's changed now. He thinks Sousanna will be gone forever and it's his fault because he believed that man. He's broken. He doesn't talk to anyone; he just works and sits in his chair tossing his worry beads. He barely even eats or sleeps. I miss the way he used to be, and I miss Sousanna. It's been so hard since you left, Marios. There's no more fun or laughter in our home. Ilias stays away. He goes to his friends' morning to night so he doesn't have to be in our house."

Marios had nothing to say about that. It was too bad for Anastasia and Mama, and Ilias seemed to be finding his own way, but Papa deserved whatever sorrow he felt.

Anastasia started to cry again. "The man's name was Peter Bakas, that took Sousanna. He lied to Papa and now we'll never find her."

"I swear I'll find Sousanna, Anastasia. I'll find her." Marios gently put his arm around her. He wouldn't mention his thoughts about Papa to her anymore. Instead, he said, "Come on, let's get home. I need to see Mama. She's been through too much."

They walked arm in arm until they reached the familiar gate. The immediate burst of rage was past, but his father's wrongs still sat in Marios's heart.

He's too scared to do what he should. There's no excuse for keeping the family in this poor condition. For attacking me. Now he's sent Sousanna away. I'll never understand him. Never forgive him.

He hadn't always felt this way. He used to admire Papa. The way he knew things, or could figure them out. The way people in town respected him for his opinions. Papa couldn't see that in himself, and never tried to better himself or his situation. He just kept working the fields like everyone else. He didn't respect himself, so why should Marios respect him?

He left Anastasia behind as he crossed the tiny yard and opened the red door of their house.

"Marios." There was no strength in Papa's voice. No emotion. His crystal blue eyes were now a dull gray. Slumped in one of the chairs at the table, he didn't seem as tall as Marios remembered.

"What have you done? Where is she? Tell me what you have done, you coward." Marios marched to him and took hold of his collar, as his father had once done to him, and shook his fist in front of Papa's face.

Papa didn't fight back. His arms stayed hanging at his side. Tears spilled from his eyes. "I deserve whatever you do to me. I have betrayed my family, and lost Sousanna. I'm sorry, Marios. So sorry. I am a coward."

Marios pushed him away. This was not the father he knew. That man would never have allowed his son to treat him this way. This man was tortured and broken. There was still something he had to answer for. Marios had to know.

"Did you take money for her? Tell me the truth; did you take money for my sister?"

"No, Marios," Papa's voice still had no strength, but there was no denying the deep sorrow it held. "You know I would never take money for Sousanna. I love her. You know that. I wanted to give her a chance, a better life. Look around you. What is here for Sousanna?"

With that Papa buried his head into his hands and cried. The sound made Marios think of a wounded or dying animal. He had to get out of there.

Mama was sitting on the ground next to the goat shed. Marios held out his hands. She grasped them in her own, and he lifted her from the ground. "Mama, my dear Mama, what happened?"

She laid his head in her neck and spoke in a whisper. "Marios, my brave son. I have missed you."

She held him in her embrace several moments before stepping back to look at him. He felt the love in her touch as she stroked his face and looked him up and down, then deep into his eyes. "Are you well, my son?"

"Yes, I am well, Mama; but I worry about you, being here with him."

"You can't blame just your father for what happened. I, too, am to blame. I wrote a letter to a woman in America, someone they said would be Sousanna's new mother. But she cannot have two mothers, Marios. I am her mother, her only mother. I will always be her only mother." She lowered her head. "I tried to hold on to her but the man took her from me. He told her she could have the beautiful doll in his car. I ran after them—I tried to catch her. I tried to stop him but I wasn't fast enough. The next day Georgia and I walked to Patras to find her, but she was already gone."

They wrapped themselves in each other's arms and cried. "I swear to you, I'll find her, Mama." Marios whispered his vow into his mother's ear. "I will not marry until I have found her, I swear that to you. I will find a way. I'll bring Sousanna home."

The rest of the day was somber. Katerina prepared a dinner of potatoes, onion, and wild artichokes that she'd picked from the side of the road. When Anastasia had heard that Marios would be coming home, she'd made some goat cheese just for him, and she served it with fresh apples sprinkled with cinnamon for dessert. But it was a quiet dinner. No one had anything to say.

That night Marios rolled out his bed on the familiar dirt floor, between his older sister and younger brother. They all lay close to the fireplace to keep warm in the cold December night. After Ilias and Anastasia fell asleep, Marios reached into his duffel bag to pull out a doll. He'd brought it as a surprise for Sousanna. In glow of the fire, the soft doll was pretty and warm. He wondered if it was as beautiful as the one the man in white had used to lure his sister away.

Chapter 19

Ilias

Ilias didn't know why Marios had even bothered to come home. He didn't help with the work, or tell them about his adventures, or play with Ilias. All he did was hurl vicious accusations at Papa, spoiling for a fight. Papa didn't answer him; he didn't react at all. Just like he hadn't reacted to anything since Sousanna left.

Ilias wanted to go away, stay with a friend, sleep in the shed—anything far from Marios, where he didn't have to hear his brother's cruelty or see Papa giving up on life. But Mama wanted him there. It was her chance to have the family—well, except Sousanna—together again. For her, he stayed.

Dinner should have been a happy occasion, but with Marios being so mean to Papa and Papa just sitting slumped in his chair, there was no laughter and easy chatter like there used to be. Mama and Anastasia were as quiet as he was.

At night, he rolled his bedroll out between Marios and Anastasia, as he always had before Marios left. Just a few more hours. Surely Marios would take his mean self back to Athens tomorrow. For now, at least it was finally peaceful as everyone went to sleep. Ilias snuggled into his bedroll and closed his eyes.

Something rustled beside him. He ignored it and pulled the cover over his face to go back to sleep.

"I'm going back to Athens today and Ilias is going with me."

At his name, Ilias rolled over and opened his eyes. It was barely light outside. It must be morning already, but barely. Why was everyone up so early, and what was Marios saying about him?

"I won't leave him here to starve." Marios's voice was demanding, as usual. As if he was head of the family instead of Papa. "He'll go with me and learn how to work and earn money. I won't see my little brother in the fields, working until he's old too soon. Ilias can stay at Christo's and become a master cabinet maker in Athens, like me. We'll make a good future, for us and for all of you."

"No." Ilias jumped up from his bedroll. "I don't want to go. What if Marios leaves me? What would I do? Don't send me away like you did Sousanna."

"Don't say such things, Ilias," Mama said. "Marios wouldn't leave you. Maybe it would be best for you to learn a trade. What do you think, Niko?"

Papa offered nothing.

"No." Ilias tried again. "I don't want to go with Marios. He's mean to me. I know he won't take care of me. He'll leave me on the side of the road and laugh. I won't go. I won't." He kicked Marios's legs. Maybe if he made him mad enough, he'd wouldn't want to take him.

Then Papa spoke. "Ilias, you will go with your brother. He will care for you." His voice was flat and expressionless, without authority. But Papa's decision would be enforced.

It was just like when he had to quit school. Ilias had loved learning. It was the one thing that made him feel special. He was smart, much smarter than all his classmates, even smarter than Marios. He went to school until he turned eight.

Then one night before everyone went to sleep, Papa announced, "Ilias, you will not go back to school. I need your help in the fields. You will help to plant seeds just as Marios did at your age."

Ilias sat up from his bed roll. "But I like school, and my teacher says I'm smart. Why can't I be the one to learn to read and write? I can already count to 100 and I can do some math. Please, let me stay in school."

Anastasia spoke up. "Papa, he should stay in school. One of us should learn and be smart." She turned over and propped up to her elbows to face Ilias. "I only went to school until I was six, barely a year. I can't read or write anything. Marios can read a few words and write some of them down on paper, but not very good."

Marios sat up. "I can read and write plenty," he protested. "This talk is useless. Ilias, it's time for you to start working. Everyone go to sleep." He threw himself back down and jerked the quilt over his head.

Ilias

A couple of days later, Ilias heard Mama telling Papa that the school teacher came to their home. He asked her, "Why are you not sending Ilias to school?"

Mama said she explained to him that all the children had to work; Ilias was needed in the fields.

The teacher said, "Please Katerina, you must speak to Niko. He is a wise man and must know that school is important for someone like Ilias. He's one of my best students. Please talk with Niko."

There was no convincing his father. Ilias was not allowed to go back to school. There was no convincing him now, either. And it was all Marios's fault.

Ilias ran outside to his hiding place. He kept protesting, even though no one could hear him and it wouldn't matter if they did. "I'm not going. Marios is mean, especially to me. I wish the man in white would have taken me to America. I wouldn't have cried. I'd be happy to go, but it's always Sousanna that gets chosen. Always Sousanna."

Why does everyone love Sousanna best? They always hug her and play with her and carry her around. She gets anything she wants. She's not a baby anymore—she's only a little younger than me. But they think she's so special.

Everybody loved Marios more, too. All the girls—even the old yiayias—were always talking about how handsome Marios was. They liked his dark skin, his eyes with too many colors, and his hair. Everyone put their hands into his hair and bragged, "Oh, Marios, it's so soft."

No one ever said Ilias was handsome or admired his light skin, plain brown eyes, or the hair that stood up from his head like coils of wire. What they said to him was, "You should try to be more like Marios. He greets us in the street and talks with everyone."

Ilias knew another side of his brother, the side that was constantly teasing and making fun of Ilias and putting him down. He always had to be on the lookout for Marios, but other people didn't pay attention to what his brother did to him.

Even his sisters never seemed to notice Ilias. They never included him when they went walking or played with the bubbles from the dish tub. Sometimes he wanted to play with Sousanna and her friends, but none of them liked him.

Sousanna

Only Mama was kind to him. She often found him in a corner or outside playing by himself. She didn't understand why he was alone. "Ilias, you are a sweet child," she would say. "Don't be alone; go and play with the other children."

He'd rather be alone than made fun of. He even had special hiding places where no one could find him. He went there when Marios bothered him, or when Marios and Papa fought. Listening to them argue made Ilias nervous inside. His stomach got all jittery. So he went to one of his secret places and waited until it was quiet again.

This time he hid in the wooden box the dishpan sat on.

The last time he hid in this spot was the day he heard Papa say to Mama, "Spiro told a stranger he should take Sousanna away from us. Never let that man close to this house, Katerina. Never. You will know him because he wears all white clothes. If you ever see him, get the children and run to your sister's house. Do you understand? That man is no good."

Papa's warning frightened Ilias. What would he do if he saw the man? Would he try to take *him* away? It was a good thing he knew where to hide.

The man did come again.

Ilias was playing behind the house, seeing how far he could kick a rock. Out of nowhere he heard Papa start shouting, so he ran to the side of the house to see what was going on.

He peeked around the corner and saw him—a man wearing all white clothes. Papa stood tall over the man, yelling at him, but the man didn't seem afraid. Was he crazy? Couldn't he tell Papa was mad? And so big he could pick the man up and throw him into the street.

The man talked back to Papa. Then for some reason Papa got quiet, and slumped down. The man left, but said he would be back.

Ilias watched Papa drop back into his chair, so heavily one of the legs cracked and Papa ended up on the ground. He started pounding the ground with his fist and yelling, but not words, just a noise that made Ilias's tummy jittery again. But he didn't hide; he had to see if Papa was going to be all right.

Finally Papa lay still and quiet. Then he got up on his knees and bowed his head until his forehead touched the ground. He clasped his hands together over his head and prayed. Ilias could hear his words. "God, help me, help me. What am I supposed to do? What should I do, Lord? Please, help me."

At that Ilias walked over and knelt next to Papa. "It will be okay, Papa. God will help us. You're a good father. I love you."

Papa sat up and took Ilias into his arms, rocking him back and forth. "Ilias, thank you. Thank you, my good son." Ilias smiled to be in his father's rare embrace.

Papa hadn't hugged him since then. In fact, Ilias couldn't remember Papa really even speaking to him since then. Until this morning, when he said Ilias must go to Athens with Marios.

Marios's feet appeared outside the box. "I know you can hear me, Ilias," he said.

How'd he know where I am? Ilias didn't answer. Maybe Marios would go away, maybe even go back to Athens without him, if he didn't answer.

Marios kept talking. "Go pack your bedroll and get ready to go. I'm going to get our bus tickets; we'll leave as soon as I get back."

Bus tickets? Ilias had never ridden on a bus. How could Marios afford that? How did he get the money for all of it—his ticket home, the food he'd brought the family, a doll for Sousanna? And now he was buying them both bus tickets to Athens.

Curiosity got the better of him. He crawled out from the box. "Where did you get so much money? Did you steal it?"

"Of course not. I worked hard for it, and you will too."

"What if they don't like me? Or I don't like them? I don't want to live with strangers."

Marios laughed at him, as usual. "Little brother, you're scared of everything. You better learn to be brave, or you'll end up like Papa. Is that what you want? To always be afraid, and work in the fields forever?"

"No. Mama says I'll be the most successful of all her children, and I will."

"We'll see about that. You'll definitely have to do something about that hair before you find any success." Marios rubbed the top of his head.

Ilias batted Marios's hand down and pulled away. "Do they really have beds for everyone? And eat all they want every day?"

"Yes, we eat three times a day. Don't worry, you'll like them. I met them the first day I was in Athens. There was a woman carrying a bag of food, and she dropped some of it. I helped her pick it up. She thanked me and asked my name and I told her. She said, 'You're very handsome, Marios.'"

Of course she did; everybody always did.

Marios kept talking. "She started to ask if I lived close by but then she saw my bedroll and asked, 'Where are you from?' I told her I just got to Athens from Pirgos. That I'd traveled many days and was tired and hungry. She said I should come with her to her home and get some food. Then she asked how old I was. When I told her I was eleven she almost dropped her bag of food again. I went to her house. Ilias, you won't believe how big it is. At first, she didn't let me in. She made me stay on the porch until her husband came home. But she fixed me lemonade and sweet cakes. I couldn't believe my luck."

"That's—wait a minute; you're trying to trick me, aren't you? You didn't really have lemonade and sweet cakes."

Marios laughed again. "Yes, I swear. I'm telling you the truth, just like it happened."

Ilias wasn't entirely convinced, but Marios did seem different. He wasn't acting like he did when he played tricks; he was talking to Ilias like he did to other people. Maybe he was telling the truth, after all.

"So how did you get to sleep in the bed? And how did you become his apprentice? Didn't he know you're poor, and only know how to work in the fields?"

"When her husband came home she explained everything to him. He asked if I had a place to stay. I told him no. He said I could sleep on the porch until I found a place, and they'd give me food and blankets. In the morning she brought me milk, cheese, toast, and a boiled egg for breakfast. I thanked her and asked her name. She said she was Stathoula and her husband was Christo, like your friend's name. When I finished eating, Mr. Christo asked me to go with him to his work. He said I could be of help to him. That's how it started. I went to work with him every day and helped. After a few days they invited me in and gave me a room all to myself. With a bed that's not on the floor."

"Will I have to sleep on the floor in your room? Do you think they'll really want me? What if I can't do the work as well as you? Will they send me away?"

Marios actually put his arm around Ilias. "You're smarter than me. You'll do fine." His voice was teasing, but in a nice way, when he said, "But, remember, I'm your big brother and I'll always be more clever than you." Then his voice got serious again. "Now go get ready. I'll be back in a little while and it'll be time to go."

It didn't take Ilias long to pack his few possessions. Anastasia helped him roll his bedroll, crying as she did so. When they were finished, she put her hands on his shoulders and said, "Goodbye, little brother. What will I do now, without my sister or brothers? I'll be all alone, and very lonely. But I will pray for God to watch over you."

Ilias turned to Mama. She took his head in her hands and kissed both his cheeks and his forehead. "Ilias, you are too young for this adventure, but I will pray every day for your protection. Marios will take good care of you." She started crying, making it hard to understand her words. "I'll miss you, my sweet son; I'll miss you very much. Go and learn, so you can have a good life." She picked up his small bag of belongings and placed it over his small shoulder. "I love you, my child. God be with you and Marios."

Papa stood still. He didn't move toward Ilias, so Ilias walked to him and wrapped his arms around Papa. "I love you, Papa. I know you are a good man and have tried hard for our family. I will miss you."

Papa did not return his embrace. He just said, without emotion, "Goodbye. Work hard."

Marios returned with the tickets. He ignored Papa but spoke his goodbyes to Mama and Anastasia. Ilias followed him out the door and down the street to the bus. Maybe it wouldn't be so bad. Maybe Marios really would be nice to him now. Maybe in Athens people would like him, and he wouldn't have to find places to hide.

Chapter 20

Sousanna

Every day at Miss Helena's house the other children and I learn how good American children behave. I won't have to play the part anymore; I'm going to *be* the part.

The hardest thing we have to learn is stopping what Miss Helena says are "unacceptable habits." My unacceptable habit is burping after eating a meal.

I don't mean to burp, but the food hurts my tummy. It's all so different from what I eat at home. Miss Helena fries our eggs instead of boiling them. She fries fish, too, and puts thick red sauces and lots of cheese on our vegetables. She always fills my plate full. I like it, and I'm not hungry anymore, but it hurts my stomach. Burping makes me feel better.

The first time I do it Miss Helena says, "Sousanna, that is not a nice sound to make at the table. Or anytime, for that matter. In America people do not burp."

"Okay."

"Not 'okay,' Sousanna. Say, 'Yes, ma'am.' Use your manners. Always use your manners."

"Yes, ma'am, Miss. Helena."

But I can't stop. After dinner I let out a loud burp. One of the boys burps, too, to make fun of me. Then the other two boys join in. We all laugh.

Miss Helena doesn't laugh. She frowns and stands up. "Sousanna, boys, that's not funny. And it's not how good American children behave. All of you follow me. Anna and Julia, stay here at the table."

The boys and I follow Miss Helena into the gathering room. "Each of you go face a corner and stay there until I come back. If I come in here and you're not facing the corner, you'll have to spend more time standing there. And no stories or warm milk for any of you tonight. When I come back, it will be a bath and to bed. You must learn not to burp. Do you understand?"

"But, Miss Helena, the food hurts my stomach. I try not to burp, but I just have to," I try to explain.

"Tomorrow I won't give you as much food, and you'll eat very slowly."

"Okay—I mean, yes, ma'am, Miss Helena."

As soon as Miss Helena leaves the room Mario burps into the corner and we all laugh.

We learn lots of other things, too, like table manners, and how stay clean, and how to dress neatly. We learn new words. Miss Helena calls them "necessary words" because they are words we will say in America. They sound funny, but I like learning them anyway. Sometimes we practice the new words when we learn to answer the telephone. It's fun to learn so many new things, now that Miss Helena doesn't get so mad at me since the time I had to sleep in the crib.

No matter how fun it is here, I still want to go home. I cry for Mama and Papa every night, and so do Julia and Anna. They want to go home, too. I never see the boys cry, but I know they do because I hear them sometimes.

Miss Helena tells us almost every day, "You must forget your families. Your mothers and fathers have given you away to live with people in America. They were too poor to care for you, but your mothers and fathers in America will give you a good life. You'll have everything you want in America. You are very lucky children."

I know that can't be right, because all I want is to go home, and that's not in America. Someday Papa will come get me. But it might take him a long time to find me in America.

I try to imagine the new family I'll have until Papa finds me. Will my new father be tall like Papa and carry me on his shoulders? Will my new mother be beautiful and kind and soft like Mama? Will I have brothers and sisters? Will they tell me stories and snuggle with me at night? Will their food hurt my stomach?

There's so much to wonder about.

§

Miss Helena takes extra care combing our hair and tying our bows. The boys have to tuck their shirts tightly into their pants. She says, "Mr. Bakas will be here today to take your pictures with his camera."

"What's a camera? Does it hurt?"

Miss Helena laughs. "No; it's fun. You look at the camera and smile really big. Then in a few days you can see a picture of yourself. In America you'll get your picture taken many times by your new parents. You might even get your own camera so you can take pictures of others."

"I've seen a camera before," Mario says. "Once someone came to our street and took a picture of my whole family in front of our house. He said it was for a newspaper story he was writing. But I never saw the picture."

When Mr. Bakas comes he's still wearing his all-white clothes. He still acts mean. "Let's get this over with. I have to catch the boat for the Islands. Who's first? Which one is my grandson?"

Miss Helena nods toward Mario.

"Mario, you'll be first," Mr. Bakas says. "You look very handsome."

Then he points at me. He gets a funny look on his face. "I remember you," he says. "You're Sousanna. You're next."

I stand at the wall under the picture of Jesus in his mother's arms.

"Smile," Mr. Bakas demands.

I grit my teeth together and opened my lips as wide as I can. My cheeks push my eyes almost closed.

Mr. Bakas lowers his camera. "Not that big. Just think of something happy." I think of the bubbles from the wash tub floating up in the dark sky.

"Better, much better."

Chapter 21

Anastasia

January 1959

Anastasia roamed the hills overlooking Pirgos, searching for greens to add to the supper pot. It was her favorite chore. Up here in the fresh air and sunshine, gathering wild plants didn't seem like work at all. Nothing like the drudgery of working in Mr. Yanni's fields.

Maybe it was because all she harvested from the wild went to nourish her own family instead of someone else's. Or because it was so beautiful up here, with the bees and butterflies hovering over wild orchids and sweet-scented flowers. From here she could sit and watch the sea below. Gentle waves rolling in and out on the shore somehow calmed her.

Or perhaps it was because gathering horta had started out as a special time with Mama. She'd been—what, five? six?—when Mama first brought her up into these hills surrounding the village.

"You must learn to find food from the earth," Mama said. "I will teach you what is good to eat and what is not."

Anastasia never thought to complain about no longer going to school. That was something else she learned from Mama—to work hard and without complaint at whatever needed doing. And what needed doing, always, was getting enough to eat. It had been so since the wars.

So she'd eagerly hiked up the hill with Mama and paid close attention to her guidance. Even though Mama never complained about any of her work, Anastasia knew she liked being in the hills best, too; she could tell by the way Mama's voice got excited when she found something to add to their basket.

"Oh, look, Anastasia," she'd exclaim. "This is horta, the most delicious thing. Can you find some?"

Or, "Look, a dandelion flower. Pick it and blow away the fuzz—but make a wish first. Then pull the leaves off and put them in the basket; they're good nourishment."

Another time, "Over here, Anastasia. Under the trees, see this? These are the good mushrooms. See the color and how small they are. But never pick the big white mushrooms, or we'll all be sick."

And again, "Here, where the soil is moist, you can find snails buried in the dirt. Those are the best prize of all. They're good with wild artichokes. Oh, let's find some of those."

Was it any wonder Anastasia loved to go up in the hills with Mama? There'd been much to learn. Mama came with her many times, teaching her, until she was able to harvest more than Mama. Now people said she was the best forager in the village. It was embarrassing to hear the villagers speaking of her this way, but it was true.

Picking greens to nourish her family wasn't the only reason Anastasia loved going to the hills. Up here, away from the cramp of their small home where there were always chores to do, away from the toil in Mr. Yanni's fields, she could dream. She could pretend that maybe, someday, her life would be different. Maybe she could have a life like the one she imagined Sousanna was living in America.

As Papa always said, "It won't always be this way. Things will get better, you'll see. Someday you'll have a better life, I'll make sure of it. I'll find a man to take care of you."

Maybe somebody rich would fall in love with her.

Anastasia stretched her arms out wide and tilted her head to the sun. "Oh, you can kiss me on a Monday, a Monday," she sang. "A Monday is a very, very good day..." Feeling the cold air swirling around her, she twirled round and round as she sang, until she fell to the soft ground.

It was a nice dream, but it was just a dream. Why would a rich man fall in love with her? She was uneducated. And always covered in dirt. If not from the hills, then from the fields. She'd worked in Mr. Yanni's fields since before she learned to gather greens. Since she could walk, really. Something else Mama had taught her.

At first she just walked by Mama, taking bundles of vegetables and placing them in a basket. Even this had to be done a certain way.

"Always put them the same direction," Mama said. "Keep them neat, and don't let the leaves tear or the stems break."

Anastasia carefully placed the bundles of vegetables just so. There was pride in Mama's voice when she said, "Look at you. My little field worker," as she handed Anastasia another bundle. Mama repeated the words often over the years, and had unknowingly sealed Anastasia's fate with them. A field worker was all she'd ever be.

Once, Anastasia, hungry, had raised a turnip to her mouth for a bite. Mama snatched it from her before she could sink her teeth into it.

"No, Anastasia. These are not for us, my sweet girl. Put it in the basket. These vegetables are for Mr. Yanni. They belong to him, not to us."

And for all this work, since she was a small child, Anastasia had never been paid any money. Neither had her brothers. Even her parents received only a few coins. Their payment was the single room they lived in and a few vegetables offered by Mr. Yanni from the crops they harvested.

Enough dreaming and reminiscing. Her skirt and pockets were full; it was time to head home. For dinner, Mama was making stifado stew, with rabbit and seasoned with onions, garlic, allspice, oregano, cloves, and cinnamon. The aroma of the delicious seasoned rabbit would radiate from the fireplace into the whole house. The greens Anastasia brought would be boiled in salt water and served alongside. It was her favorite meal. The kind they'd only dreamed about just a few months ago.

Marios made it possible. He sent money every month from Athens. With three less mouths to feed, Mama had managed to save enough to buy a barrel of olive oil, some spices, and four chickens for eggs. Aunt Georgia gave Mama a gift of two rabbits. Did they ever have babies! Now there was plenty of meat.

They finally had enough to eat every day, and Papa wouldn't eat it. He refused to come sit at the table for a meal. "Katerina, leave me alone. Don't bother me with your food. Can't you see I don't want to eat?"

"Niko, please, you have to eat," Mama begged, every day, every meal. "We have to stay strong so we can make things better for when our children are all home again."

Sousanna

It was no use. He just sat outside in his broken-down chair, his broad shoulders slumped over, tossing the amber worry beads. Regardless of his protests, Mama took food out to him. He'd eat only a few bites, then put it down.

Anastasia hardly recognized this man as her father, he was so different. The villagers thought so, too. They didn't respect him anymore. Neighbors stopped visiting. What was the point? He didn't greet them, or answer when they asked his advice. The children, who used to follow him around and beg for a ride on his big shoulders, didn't even notice when he walked by.

He still went to work every day, but he spent all the rest of his time sitting, staring at the gate, waiting for news of Sousanna. Three months had passed since her little sister was taken away by the man in white. The man who'd promised, "You'll receive letters and pictures of Sousanna in America. She will keep her Greek language and go to the Orthodox Church." But they heard nothing.

What if Sousanna never came back? What if she forgot them? These questions pecked at Anastasia's mind most when she washed dishes. She couldn't help remembering that last night together, back in October, when she put extra soap in the dish tub at the side of the house to make the water sudsier.

"Sousanna, let's wash the dishes and blow bubbles," she'd coaxed. "Tonight we'll make more bubbles than you've ever seen." She scooped up a handful of suds and blew them into the air over Sousanna's head.

Her sister's face lit up with delight. "You made so many bubbles!" She giggled and blew her own handful of bubbles into the darkening sky. "Look, look. This one is so big—oh, there it goes." She jumped up and down, pulling on Anastasia's skirt and pointing at the giant bubble as it floated away. "See it, see it. It will fly all the way to the sea."

When they finished the dishes, Anastasia took Sousanna into her lap and sang all their favorite songs, until it was time for Sousanna to run and jump into the bed. Then she sneaked Sousanna's black shoes out and took them behind the house. She wanted her little sister to have clean shoes for her journey. She spit onto the little shoes, and rubbed them all over with her skirt to try and remove the scuffs. They were too old to look truly clean and shiny, but they did look better.

That was all she could do for her little sister. She still ached with missing Sousanna's little face. Her chatter and laughter. Even her mischievousness. What was it about Sousanna that captured her heart? It wasn't fair, but she loved her sister better than her brothers. Was it just because they were both girls? Because Sousanna was the baby?

Maybe it was because Anastasia had helped deliver Sousanna. When Marios and Ilias were born, Anastasia was still a small child herself, and she'd stood outside the red door with her father, waiting to hear the news of a brother or sister.

She heard the groans and cries from inside and thought Mama must be dying. *I'm never having children*, she thought.

But when Sousanna was born, Anastasia was eight years old. It was time for her to help Aunt Georgia, who acted as midwife for Mama.

Anastasia thought seeing Mama in so much pain would make her sick or faint, unable to help, but it didn't. She felt very grown up, and was able to follow Aunt Georgia's directions quickly and efficiently.

"Get the knife from the table. Don't touch the blade; it has to be kept clean," Aunt Georgia told her. "And bring me those rags off the cord." She pointed to where their clothes hung across the corner.

Anastasia quickly gathered the knife and rags and handed them to Aunt Georgia. Mama lay sideways on the bed, with her feet on the edge of the mattress so the baby would drop easily.

"Come here." Aunt Georgia beckoned to her. "Stand close to your mother's legs and help me catch the child."

Anastasia stood next to her aunt, between her mother's legs, holding her arms out. She could see the exhaustion and pain in her mother's face as Aunt Georgia encouraged her, "Push Katerina, push." Suddenly, there she was. In her arms was a slippery new baby sister. Anastasia couldn't breathe; excitement galloped through her veins.

The baby cried out as Aunt Georgia used the knife to cut the cord that connected the baby to her mother and tied it in a knot. Anastasia felt a tenderness flow through her as she held her tiny new sister.

I will have children. Many of them.

Anastasia gingerly placed the baby in Mama's arms. There were many things she could do to remain helpful. She gathered up the bloodied rags and put them in a bucket of water to soak. She used the broom to rub some drops of blood into the dirt floor until they disappeared.

When all was tidy, Aunt Georgia opened the red door and announced the birth. "It's a girl, and she is healthy. God is good."

Anastasia smoothed the bed coverings around Mama, and kissed her forehead. Her skin was cool and white.

"Mama, you don't look well; you're so pale."

"I'll be all right. I just need to rest. This birth was not easy."

Papa burst into the room. He brushed by Anastasia and hurried to the bed. When he lifted the baby from Mama's arms, his gaze seeming to be far away. It was the expression he got when he was contemplating something. The expression lasted only a moment, then he cuddled the baby close to his chest.

"She is our special child," he said.

Can I be your special child, too? Anastasia had thought. But she didn't say anything.

A bubble floated up from the dish tub. How could she bear this ache in her heart? Her tears splashed into the dish pan.

What did her future hold? She'd overheard a boy from the field telling his friends, "My mother says Anastasia's father is desperate to marry her off. They're so poor she needs a husband soon. And she'd make a good wife because she's a hard worker and knows how to cook good meals from very little food. Besides, I think she's really pretty."

Was Papa really looking for a husband for her? Would he pick the man, or would she be allowed to choose for herself? Would her husband love her, or just marry her for a good wife who could work hard and make do?

Would Sousanna truly come home one day? If she did, would Mama forget about Anastasia?

Chapter 22

Nikolas

Nikolas tossed his beads softly so he could hear his wife and her sister gossiping in the house. Well, really all the gossip came from Georgia; Katerina listened quietly, as usual. According to Georgia, Spiro was still trying to convince everyone in the taverna that he, Niko, had taken money for Sousanna.

The anger Nikolas once felt, should now feel, at such an insult, was no longer in him. Let the people think what they want. He deserved it. No, he hadn't taken money, but so what? He'd let Sousanna go off to a foreign country with a stranger, and his sons, both so young, go off to work like men in the big city.

When did I get to be such a fool?

Now Georgia was telling Katerina that Taki had stood up for him against Spiro. He'd reminded the people of all the times Niko had helped them. Like when little Emilia was so malnourished they all feared she'd die, and every day Niko took her what little food he could, even though it left his own family with nothing.

Here Katerina spoke up. "I was angry with Niko when he gave away our food. Our own children were so hungry. How could he take food from our children's mouth and give it to someone else? But he saved the little girl's life."

"Yes, that's what Taki told them," Georgia said. "Then he looked straight at Spiro and told him he was a liar."

Wish I'd seen that, Niko thought. *Everybody knows you can't trust Spiro, but nobody's ever said so. Leave it to Taki.*

Georgia was still talking. "Then he said Niko works as hard as anyone; it's not his fault things are so bad. And that he showed the greatest love a father can: he did whatever he had to, to give Sousanna the best life she could have, even though it broke his heart."

Katerina murmured a reply but it wasn't loud enough for Niko to make out what she said. He did hear the two chairs scrape in the dirt and Katerina tell Anastasia to get her gathering basket. They must be through with their coffee.

Sure enough, a few minutes later all three emerged. Georgia said good evening to him as she passed, but he didn't answer. She turned toward town; Katerina said something about dinner, as if he cared about that, and headed the other direction, arm in arm with Anastasia.

He should be teaching his sons to be men. Or lifting Sousanna up on his shoulders and going to town to visit with friends. But here he sat alone. There was no one for him to teach or lift onto his shoulders. All his children were gone.

"Mr. Demetriou?"

He raised his head. A girl he didn't know stood outside the gate. What could she want from him? He looked away.

"Mr. Demetriou? This is from Marios." Without turning his head again, he slid his eyes toward her. She held out an envelope.

She must be the girl that brought the money from Athens. Katerina had said something about that once, some girl Marios had met in Athens that came to visit her aunt in Pirgos. She brought messages and money for them when she came. Katerina always dealt with her.

"If you could just take this," the girl said. When he didn't respond, she came in the gate and dropped the envelope in his lap. "It's for your wife, from her sons." Scorn tinged her voice, and she left with her nose in the air.

For my wife? From her sons? Who is she to say it's only for Katerina? And they're my sons, too.

It's for your wife. Her tone still irritated him.

Katerina used these precious drachmas to put good food on the table. But maybe this time he'd walk to town and use the money to show Spiro he could buy a pint of beer or a glass of wine now. Shut him up, him and his bragging. Him and his fabrications, spreading lies about Niko. Yes, that's what he'd do. He tore open the envelope and threw the note inside to the ground, putting the money in his pocket. He'd buy a glass of wine. No – he'd buy the whole bottle.

The taverna got quiet when Nikolas walked in the room. He spotted Spiro sprawled in his chair. All the other eyes turned with

Spiro's to stare at him, but no one greeted him. So what? He had no need of them. Idiots, that's what they were. Idiots who listened to Spiro's lies.

"Get me a bottle of wine." He made his voice loud so they all could hear. They'd all be talking about him after he left, anyway— might as well let them know what to say.

The owner brought out a bottle of the cheap local wine and a glass.

"No glass," Niko said. He threw his drachmas on the table, grabbed the bottle, and left.

Back at home, Nikolas settled into his chair and opened the bottle of wine. He didn't bother to get a glass but raised the entire bottle in a mock toast.

"To hell with you," he shouted. "To hell with men that wear white clothes. To hell with smart men that can teach my sons what I can't. To hell with Spiro. To hell with all of you—and to hell with me." He took a long drink. The liquid slid down his parched throat, leaving a warm trail behind as it coursed into his stomach.

He took another drink. The warmth spread. It eased the tightness around his middle. A few more drinks and his muscles and mind relaxed. The worries about his children slowed their swirling and torment. He closed his eyes and tipped his chair back so he leaned against the wall. He could remember Sousanna laughing...

§

"Niko! Niko!"

"Papa!"

The voices of his wife and daughter seemed to come from far away. Nikolas felt his head being lifted. When had he come to bed? No, it was too hard to be his bed. *What...*

"Niko, speak to me. What's wrong?" Katerina's voice was in his ear, shouting.

He tried to speak, to ask what was happening, but his mouth was so dry. His tongue stuck to the roof of his mouth and nothing came out but a croak.

He felt Anastasia kneel on his other side. She made a disgusted noise. "Eww. What's that smell?"

Niko tried to open his eyes, then snapped them shut again as the setting sun stabbed his eyeballs. He turned his heavy head and lifted his eyelids a tiny bit, squinting through them just in time to see Katerina's own eyes widen as they spotted the wine bottle a few feet away. He let his eyelids drop again, shutting out the scene.

"A bottle of wine..." Katerina sounded like she didn't believe her own words. "You're drunk?"

Niko's head fell with a bang as Katerina suddenly stood.

"Nikolas, you're drunk." Katerina's voice was no longer wondering, but bold. Angry. "You drank a whole bottle of wine. By yourself. Well, you can just lay there in the dirt until you get sober again." Her steps into the house were firm and even. Anastasia's steps followed, softer and hesitating.

A few moments later the soft steps returned. Anastasia's skirt rustled as she knelt beside him. A warm hand slid beneath his neck, lifted his head. "Here," she said, "I brought you some water from the well. Take a drink."

As he sipped the cool water, his daughter whispered, "Why, Papa? Why did you do this? You're not the father I know."

§

Niko rolled over, his joints creaking in protest. The ground... *The ground? What the...*

He looked around with bleary eyes. His chair was on its side. A wine bottle lay near it. Vague flashes of the evening before tried to work their way into his mind, but, like fragments of a dream, slipped out of reach before he could assemble them into a full memory.

Fighting the bile rising from his stomach, he sat up and righted the fallen chair. Using it as a support, he heaved himself to his knees. *Just a little bit more...*

Niko found himself face-down on the ground again. Determined, he spit the dirt from his mouth and slowly, deliberately, hoisted himself up and stood.

If this is what drinking a bottle of wine did to him, he'd never have another. How could he work? Every movement made his muscles ache and cramp.

Somehow Niko got through the day. He drank lots of water, and by the time he trudged in from the fields that evening, he'd worked out most of his aches. Perhaps he'd be able to sleep tonight; he was so tired. Since Sousanna had gone, his sleep was punctuated by bad dreams, and fits of tossing and turning. He never felt rested.

As soon as he settled into his chair again, worry for his sons and youngest daughter assailed his mind. What if Marios or Ilias got hurt, working with the carpenter's tools? What if Sousanna got sick? What if...what if...

Niko reached into his pocket for his amber beads. A few drachmas, left from last night, jingled together under his fingers. He could get another bottle of wine...

No; it made him feel too bad. And to pass out in his yard, where all the neighbors could see? How could he have disgraced himself like that? He, Nikolas, once the most respected man in town?

He wouldn't have to drink that much. He could take it inside the house, where no one could see him. He'd just have enough to ease his troubled thoughts. To remember Sousanna's laughter.

He headed to the taverna.

§

Another long day in the fields after another sleepless night. Another day with no word from Sousanna. Niko had found only one way to ease the pain: his nightly wine. He shouldn't spend money for it; food was more important.

But it was so cheap. Hardly anything, really. Since the boys were sending money, he might as well use a few of his own hard-earned coins for a bit of comfort.

At first it didn't take much. After that first night, he didn't drink so fast, and a bottle might last several days. As the weeks went on, it took more and more to achieve the numbness he desired.

Katerina didn't even try to stop him anymore. She didn't bother to fix him supper or help him when he passed out on the floor from drinking too much.

Anastasia did. She brought him water every evening, and always coaxed him into eating at least a bite or two. Through the winter, he found a bit of comfort and warmth in his nightly wine by the fireplace.

As spring came, Niko took to drinking while sitting outside. He didn't care if the neighbors saw him. What did they know of his pain, anyway?

One such evening Anastasia walked through the gate with a basket filled with herbs and snails just as Nikolas was sitting down with a new bottle of wine. She dropped her basket, spilling its contents all over the ground, and ran to Niko. She grabbed the bottle from his hands and wrenched it back.

"Please, don't."

"Give it to me." He swiped at the bottle but missed as she pulled it further out of reach. "I need it to make my thoughts go away. I don't want to think. All my children are gone; I've sent them all away."

Anastasia pulled herself up straight and held her head high as she spoke clearly and boldly. "I am one of your children. And I'm still here." She paused, swallowed back her tears, and lowered her voice. "I should have begged the man from America to take me instead, so you could have Sousanna."

Does she think I wouldn't care if she was the one taken away? Is that what she thinks?

Nikolas stood and pulled her into his arms.

"Yes, Anastasia, you are still here. My oldest child, so quiet and gentle, I forget you are still only a child. I do miss Sousanna; but I would have missed you, too. I love you, my daughter."

Anastasia squeezed him tightly, then pulled away. She looked Nikolas in the eyes. "Papa, I understand why you chose to send Sousanna to America and allowed Marios and Ilias to go to Athens to learn a trade that will give them a good life. But it changed you, and I don't like what you're becoming. Remember, Papa, that I'm still here, and I need a father. I need you." She set the bottle of wine on the ground beside his chair and went in the house.

Niko looked at the bottle. His daughter deserved better.

There would be no more drinking. After a moment he picked up the bottle and followed Anastasia into the house. He set the bottle on the table. No, that wouldn't do.

I'll pour it out. He picked it up again, almost dropping it as a knock at the door startled him. *Who can that be?* No one came to visit them anymore. He looked at Katerina, but she shrugged her shoulders and raised her eyebrows, questioning.

Niko didn't expect to be so pleased to see his good friend standing outside. The wine had deadened his morale along with his memories. He opened the door wider. "Taki, my friend. Will you come inside?"

Taki looked surprised at the invitation. "I will, thank you. I was afraid you'd tell me to go away. I've missed you, my good friend." He put his hand on Niko's shoulder and gave it a squeeze to emphasize his feelings.

Niko saw Taki look at the bottle still in his hand. He quickly set it on the table and pulled out a chair for his friend, taking the other for himself.

Taki's brow was furrowed as he sat. "I'm concerned about you. Look at your wife; she's a good woman, but you're embarrassing her. The neighbors won't talk to her anymore, because of you. Did you know that?"

Nikolas shook his hanging head.

"And your daughter, Anastasia," Taki continued. "She's the age for boys to look at and consider for a wife, but they don't want a father-in-law who's a drunk."

"I'm not a drunk!" Nikolas jumped up and stalked to the other side of the room. But all the times he'd woken up on the floor after a night of drinking teemed into his mind. It was time to admit the truth.

"I did drink too much. Letting the wine turn off my mind was easier than living with the guilt. I destroyed my family. I sent my children away. I'm no good. I'm nothing."

"That's not true." Taki crossed to him, again clasping his shoulder. "You are Nikolas. Do you not remember who was the first man in Pirgos brave enough to defy the Nazis and join the resistance? Who dug tunnels under the soldiers' very noses to carry supplies and arms to our brothers, our fellow countrymen fighting the invaders? Who was the only man to lead our brothers to and from the tunnels so they wouldn't be detected by the German soldiers?"

"That was long ago. Now I am a coward who has lost honor in my community and betrayed my family."

"You're the smartest man in the fields. You're loved and respected for your ideas and opinions."

"Bah! Not anymore."

"You love your family and friends. You help all your neighbors. And even though it hurt, you were strong enough to do what you had to for your children. Don't you see, my friend? That is the greatest love a father can have. So come now, straighten yourself out. Remember your courage and your love. No more drinking all that wine. Besides, it's making you ugly."

Niko turned to face his friend. "You will not believe this, but I was going to pour out that bottle. Now I know I won't buy another." He teasingly slapped Taki's cheek. "I can't be ugly, because you're ugly enough for us both."

The men laughed together. Niko pulled Taki into his embrace, kissing his cheeks. "Thank you, my friend; thank you." He'd laughed, for the first time since the stranger in white showed up at his gate.

But as Niko walked Taki out to the gate, he turned serious again. "Taki, am I a fool for believing Peter Bakas? It's been months and we've heard nothing. Do you think we'll ever see Sousanna again?"

Taki had no answer.

§

March 1959

Nikolas wandered around the square, looking at the colorful market stands. There were greens and vegetables, of course, and fruits and fish. His brother George sold honey, and nearby was a flower stand. The tables of spices and olive oil were always crowded. Gypsies sold colorful clothing and jewelry.

Most people didn't look at all the stands; they knew what they needed and went to their favorite vendors to get it. But Niko liked to visit with people, and hear the chatter and laughter around the market. It was a happy place, a reminder that there was joy and contentment in the world. He was in no hurry to buy the fish he came for.

Children running by almost knocked Niko over. He grabbed a table and caught himself just in time. As he took a moment to get his feet under him again, the aroma of roasting meat seasoned with lemon and oregano caught his attention.

A new stand on the corner was selling goat meat. A fire behind the stand roasted skewered pieces of meat customers could purchase to eat immediately, without waiting to go home and cook it. Niko watched the goat-meat seller pull a piece of meat from the fire and set it out to cool, then skewer more meat to roast. The man looked frustrated as the souvlaki stick splintered and broke in two instead of poking through.

His stick is too blunt. And too thick. Someone should make some souvlaki sticks that are thin and sharp.

It was the kind of idea he used to have, when he was a still a young man with dreams.

He'd never acted on those dreams. But what if he did? What if he did what Marios always challenged him to do: find something to do other than field work to earn his living? He hurried to the warehouse behind the square, then home.

"Katerina! Katerina!" He started calling her name as soon as he entered the gate.

"What is it? Are you hurt? What's wrong?"

"Nothing is wrong. Come, sit with me. I want to talk with you."

Katerina sat across the table. "Where's the fish? And what are you doing with those useless pieces of wood?"

"They may be useless now, but when I have whittled them into good, sharp souvlaki sticks they'll be worth something. We can sell them, and soon our children can come home."

"Souvlaki sticks? That's a wonderful idea. How can I help?"

"You and Anastasia may bundle the sticks as I whittle them. On Saturday, we'll go to the market together and sell them."

Each evening, after a long day of work in the fields, Nikolas sat by the fireplace and whittled wood into sharp-tipped souvlaki sticks until his hands ached and shook.

It gave him hope for a better future. A time when his sons could return home and not have to work so hard. A time when Katerina and Anastasia could stop working in the fields like men. Maybe even a time when his sons and Sousanna could come home.

Is all this possible? Or am I just an old fool after all?

Chapter 23

Sousanna

*M*iss Helena gathers all of us around the table. "Tomorrow you will leave for America," she says. "Mr. Bakas and Mr. Callas will come in their cars to drive you to Athens. It will be a long ride. In Athens you'll get on the airplane. Remember the pictures I showed you? The plane will take you high into the sk—"

Julia starts crying. "Please, Miss Helena, I want to go home. Please? I'm scared to go up in the sky." Anna and I put our arms around her.

The boys tease her. "Crybaby, crybaby."

Anna shouts, "Stop it. You're scared too, so stop it." They do.

"Come here, girls. You, too, boys." Miss Helena reaches out her arms to us and we gather close to her. She takes Julia onto her lap. "You cannot cry for your old families anymore," she says. "It will upset your new American families. They will want you to be happy with them, and to forget your life here in Greece. So no more crying. I want everyone to have a good night's sleep so you'll be ready for your adventure to America."

She sets Julia on the floor and leads us to our beds, tucking us tightly under our quilts. She kisses our foreheads one by one and whispers, "I love you. God be with you."

When she gets to me she says, "Sousanna, be brave. I'll miss you. God bless you, my spirited little girl."

"Be brave." That's the last thing Papa said to me. I will. I will be brave.

I dream of Mama. She's in the field bundling vegetables, and I'm sitting in the back of the green and white car without a top and my big doll is next to me. The car is moving but no one is driving; it's just me and my doll in the car. We pass the field where Mama is working. She stands and waves.

"Be well in America, my dear Sousanna," she says. "Be brave, and remember your mother until I see you again." I wave back, and so does my doll. I wake up.

After breakfast Miss Helena tells us we all have new clothes waiting for us on our beds. "Make sure your clothes are neatly buttoned and smoothed out. Fold your socks down. I'll comb everyone's hair. Your new families will have more clothes for you in America, so you don't need to take anything with you. Now quick, Mr. Bakas and Mr. Callas will be here soon."

"Miss Helena, may I take my red sweater?" I plead. "Mama knit it just for me; it's all I have that's just mine. Please?"

"Yes, Sousanna. Put it on under your jacket. You should have your sweater."

When Mr. Bakas comes he says, "Look at these fine children. Are you ready to fly over the ocean?"

Julia starts to cry. "No. I'm scared." No one goes to comfort her. We're too scared. We all just stand there.

Mr. Bakas says, "Don't cry; it'll be okay. I'll be with you. Let's get in the cars. We need to hurry." He takes Mario's hand and leads him out.

Outside I see the green and white car. It has a top on it now. It scares me and I run back to Miss Helena.

"Please, Miss Helena, will you be my new mother? I want to stay here with you. Please, please." I start crying. I can't stop, and I cry so hard it hurts my chest.

Miss Helena kneels down in front of me. "No, Sousanna, you can't stay here. But don't worry; you're going to a good family that will love you, and you'll have everything you ever dreamed of."

Mr. Bakas comes to take me to the car. As he reaches for my hand Miss Helen says, "Peter, wait."

She changed her mind! She's going to keep me with her!

"I need to tell you something," she says. I hold my breath, waiting for her to say I can stay.

"Don't bring any more children," she says instead. My breath slowly seeps out of me. "I won't do this anymore," Miss Helena continues. "I can't do this anymore. You can have the house back, but don't bring me any more children. I'm so ashamed..."

Her voice trails off in sobs. I remember the morning after being put in the crib. Miss Helena said something like this. I'm still not sure what she means.

Mr. Bakas steps closer to her. "You may keep the house; it's yours. I, too, am done. This is my last trip." He looks down at me. "Come, Sousanna, we must go."

I get in the car next to Anna. Mario is in the front next to Mr. Bakas. All of us are crying as we drive away from Miss Helena. I see Mr. Bakas wipe his hand under his glasses. Could he be crying, too?

We drive a long time. Eventually we run out of crying. I can't see Mario's head in the front seat anymore; he must be lying down, asleep. Anna sits very close to me, asleep on my shoulder, pushing me into the side of the car. I stare out the window watching trees, cars, houses, and, every once in a while, a beautiful flash of sea.

§

Anna shakes me. "Wake up, Sousanna. Wake up, we're here."

I sit up and look around to see what's happening. I can't believe my eyes. The airplanes are huge. They didn't look so big in the pictures Miss Helena showed. And there's so many of them. Rows and rows. Some have big doors open with stairs going to them.

There's a roaring sound, louder than thunder, as one plane leaves the ground. I lean into the window to watch it disappear into the clouds.

Mr. Bakas leans the car seat forward for Anna and me to get out. "Mario, hold my hand," he says. "Anna, you hold my other hand. Sousanna, hold onto Mario's hand. We're going inside to get ready to get on the plane." I see Mr. Callas doing the same with the other children.

I'm scared again. *Papa, please come get me. I don't want to go in the sky away from you and Mama.* My tummy is shaky, and all of a sudden my breakfast jumps out of it. It goes all over the floor, and some onto Mr. Bakas's white shoes.

I don't remember what happens next but now we're inside the airplane and Mr. Bakas is holding me. He's being gentle and kind, not like the day he made Mama and me cry, and lied about my doll.

"You'll be okay," he says. "I'll watch over you." He sits me in the seat beside him and pulls a strap around me.

"No, take it off. Take it off, it's too tight, it hurts, I can't move, I have to get out, take it...." I throw up again. It goes all over the seat in front of me. A pretty lady with a hat comes and asks us to get up so she can clean the seat.

My tummy is still sick and I'm scared. What if Mr. Bakas is mad and leaves me outside the plane all alone?

He doesn't seem mad. He helps me go to a place where another pretty lady with a hat cleans my face and hands me a glass with something fizzy in it.

"Here, sweetheart, drink this," she says. "It's ginger ale, good for upset tummies." She looks at Mr. Bakas. "You need to sit down, sir, it's time to take off."

I tug the pretty lady's sleeve. "Help me. He's putting a strap around me, so tight I can't move. Please, can you make him stop?"

The lady laughs. "Sweetheart, that's just a seat belt. Everybody has to wear one, but just for a little while. It's to keep you safe. Mr. Bakas cares for all his children. He's traveled with us many times, so I know he'll take good care of you."

I let Mr. Bakas pick me up and carry me back to my seat. Is he really going to take care of me? Has he turned into a nice man? I look into his glasses. His eyes are as crystal blue as Papa's.

This time when he puts me in a seat and pulls the strap around me, I don't fight back. I don't want to fall out.

Mario and Anna are sitting on the other side of Mr. Bakas. I wonder where the other children are. "Mr. Bakas, where are—"

There's a lurch as the plane lifts off the ground. I throw up again, this time all over Mr. Bakas.

Mario yells, "Eww. That stinks. What's wrong with her?"

Anna asks, "Sousanna, are you dying? What's happening to her? Put the plane back down on the ground; put the plane down."

The plane keeps going higher and higher. There's no stopping it. Or me from throwing up. My stomach hurts and I'm scared and I can't stop crying.

Mr. Bakas says, "Hold on, Sousanna. You'll be okay, just hold on."

"Please, can I go home now? I want my mama, she helps me when I'm sick. Please let me go home."

He doesn't answer, just strokes my hair until another pretty lady with a hat comes. She takes the strap off me and helps me out of the seat. She says to Mr. Bakas, "You may go to first class and use the bath there to clean yourself off. Do you need anything?"

"No, just help her. Clean her up and give her something to eat; she's weak."

The lady hands me something she says I should eat, and I do even though I don't know what it is. When my tummy is full, I burp. Then I throw up again, this time into a bag the lady gives me.

The plane finally goes down to the ground again, and stops. We get off the plane into a crowd of people.

I should start looking for my new mother. There's a pretty woman; she's smiling and she looks nice. "Will you be my new mother?"

The woman looks confused. She says something to Mr. Bakas with words that don't make any sense. Maybe she's crazy. I don't want her to be my mother.

I look around the crowd of people and see another woman that looks nice. "Will you be my new mother?" She barely glances at me before she turns away. I don't want her to be my mother, either.

Anna laughs. "You're funny, Sousanna, trying to find a mama."

Mr. Bakas stops and kneels down. "This is not America; we're in Italy. We're getting on another plane, and that plane will take us home."

Mario gets excited. "It will take us home?" he says. "Back to our houses and our families?"

"No, Mario; home to America. That will be your new home. You'll be my grandson in America, and you'll have a wonderful life." Mario doesn't say anything.

"And, Sousanna, stop asking women to be your mother," Mr. Bakas says to me. "Your mother is waiting for you in America."

"My mother is not in America. She's waiting for me at home, at our house." Mr. Bakas ignores me.

We get on another plane.

§

"Wake up children, we're here," Mr. Bakas says. "We're in America. Your new mothers and fathers are waiting for you. Let's go meet them."

Chapter 24

The Browns

Excitement. Resentment. Anticipation. A mix of emotions potent as anything in a laboratory bubbled in the usually-placid Brown household.

Margaret's practiced composure hid her eagerness for the last, missing piece to complete her perfect family: a darling daughter. A little girl she could dress up and show off, spoil with concerts and lessons and all the things she'd missed out on as a child. A complement to seven-year-old David, a daughter to sit beside their son for Christmas cards and family portraits.

David didn't think he needed a sister sitting beside him. He liked his family just the way it was, himself and two parents. He, the center of attention, the recipient of all.

Jack wondered how it would all work out. His wife seemed to think the little girl would enter their home as if she'd always belonged there; his son acted like she'd never belong. It would take patience and understanding—things not always abundant in the Brown home.

"David, are you ready?" Jack asked his son. "We don't want to be late."

David was dressed in his best suit, complete with bowtie and wing-tip oxfords. "Yes, but these shoes hurt my feet. Can I just wear tennis shoes?"

"No; you know your mother would never allow that."

Margaret joined them in the foyer. "How do I look?" She ran her hands down the front of her perfectly-smooth dress.

"Like a beautiful mother ready for her beautiful new child," Jack answered.

"I can't believe we're going to get a daughter. We'll be the perfect family."

Neither of them noticed the scowl on David's face.

Margaret was so elated Jack hated to bring up the subject, but he felt she must be prepared. He tried to explain on the drive to the airport.

"You know, Margaret, this'll be different from when we adopted David. This little girl—"

Margaret interrupted. "She's not just a little girl; she's Nita Marie."

"Yes, well, Nita Marie hasn't been languishing in an orphanage like David was. Mr. Bakas promised she'd be healthy and cared for. If she remembers her family she might not be happy about coming here."

"Of course she will. Look what we're saving her from. She'll be happy to have a family that's not poor. Trust me, I know what I'm talking about. I hated being poor. It'll be fine, you'll see. What little girl wouldn't want to have everything we'll give her?" Margaret spoke with confidence, leaving Jack quietly uncomfortable with her expectation.

What Margaret expected was a perfect family. She and her husband, parents to one little boy and one little girl. The boy would be smart and athletic; the girl, pretty and sweet. Both children would adore their new mother and give her all the love she didn't have growing up. None of them would want for anything. This had been Margaret's dream since she was a young girl.

Her own family had left much to be desired. She and six older brothers, children of poor parents who made up in strictness what they lacked in money. Their entire family was looked down on, both for their penniless condition and for the Native blood that ran in her father's veins. Her brothers used that as an excuse to run wild. Margaret tried to be the ideal daughter her mother wanted her to be, but somehow trouble always found her. And since no one wanted their children to be influenced by the wild Indian kids, she hadn't had many friends growing up.

Margaret vowed at a young age it wouldn't always be that way. She determined to rise above her circumstances and make good. When she was successful and had her own perfect family, the community would have to accept her at last.

The Browns

Jack Brown came from a prominent family in a small town outside of Tulsa. His father was an award-winning architect, and Jack and his older brother Ted were expected to be equally successful.

The Brown brothers were known as good boys. Their life was comprised of family, friends, church, sports, and education. After college, Jack returned home, staying with his parents while looking for his own place. Rather than hang around watching television, he liked to go out at night, get out of the house.

One night when he reached the counter at a local bar, he found himself standing next to the prettiest woman he'd ever seen.

"Hi, I'm Jack," he said. "I see you're almost through with that; can I buy you another?" He flagged the bartender.

She shrugged. "Sure. I'm Margaret. Are you from around here? I don't recall seeing you before."

"I grew up here, went from elementary all the way through high school."

"Me, too. Wonder why we never met. You know the Johnson boys? I'm their sister."

Jack had never been friends with the Johnson boys, but he knew exactly who they were: the wild troublemakers. He'd heard stories of their escapades. Kind of envied them, truth be told. They did whatever they wanted, other peoples' opinions be damned.

So this is the sister, he thought. She was supposed to be a wild one, too, a real party girl who loved to drink and really got around with the male population. *No wonder; she's a knockout. Probably has guys hitting on her all the time.*

He said, "I remember the Johnson name. I think we ran in different circles; you're a little younger than me, I think."

Margaret laughed. "Oh, I'm sure we ran in different circles. Yours higher and mine lower, those circles?"

Jack hadn't meant to be insulting. He stumbled over his words. "No, that's...I didn't...I meant just because we're not the same age, that's all. So what have you done since high school?"

"I went into the Army."

"The Army? Wow. What'd you do there?"

"Get me that next drink and I'll fill you in."

"Sure. Where is that bartender?" Jack flagged the guy behind the counter again, more insistently this time. He ordered them each a beer, and they watched in silence as the bartender filled the mugs.

Margaret took a long drink before telling her story. "I took pictures. I loved photography, guess I had a knack for it. They put me in the field with the troops. I took the pictures that told the real story about what the soldiers were going through. Up close, right in the action, where other photographers with families didn't want to go because it was too dangerous."

"Wow," Jack repeated. It was hard for him to think of the lovely young lady next to him trudging through the mud and blood of war. He remembered a hoopla over some pictures in the town paper back during the war. He'd read something about a local taking them, getting to be a famous, hot-shot photographer. The photos impressed him.

"I've seen some of your pictures in the paper. You've done some incredible work."

"Thanks. I'd rather you think of me as a war photographer than a Johnson kid." Margaret laughed but Jack heard a grim note in it.

"So what'd you do after the war ended?"

"Before it ended, you mean." She forced herself to speak lightly so the conversation wouldn't turn dark and depressing. "I met a soldier and fell madly in love. We got married, but I lost him only a year later. He was killed in France." She couldn't suppress a sigh, but continued on.

"I couldn't face the war again, seeing what happened to the soldiers...couldn't even pick up a camera. Had to finish my stint in the Army in an office, bookkeeping. Then came home. Been here ever since. Got married again, but he was a real loser, and we divorced. Now I'm free. That's my story. What's yours?"

Jack liked the way she answered. She didn't try to hide anything but didn't try to use it to get sympathy, either. Just told it like it was. He could tell there was more to this woman than her looks. She wasn't like the socialites he usually dated, who didn't know anything about the world and were used to everything revolving around them because of their fathers' money. Margaret was smart and strong. She'd had to make her own way, and she'd done it. He liked that, and thought it probably meant she was a bold lover, too. He wanted to find out, but it was too soon to mention his desires; he figured he ought to at least answer her question before bringing that up.

Before he could say anything, Ted walked up. Unlike Jack, Ted had immediately recognized the Johnson girl. He was also well aware of her reputation, and felt it was his duty to rescue his brother from her clutches. He decided to act like the two men had previous plans to meet for a drink. It wouldn't be as rude, he thought.

"Hey, Jack, there you are," Ted said. "There's an empty table, let's grab it while we can." He pointed over several nearby available tables to one clear across the room.

Margaret turned her back to the men and lit a cigarette. She knew exactly what Ted was doing and didn't want to give him the satisfaction of being the one to break up the conversation.

Jack put an elbow on the bar, leaning on it purposefully. "No, thanks," he said. "I'm talking to the lady." He turned to Margaret. She still had her back to them but he knew she could hear him. "Margaret, this is my brother Ted. Sorry for his lack of manners; he must have been raised in a barn."

Margaret turned to face them, her glance at Ted telling the men exactly what she thought of that brother. "I can tell."

Insulted, Ted left without another word.

Jack picked up where they'd been interrupted. "So, my story. After the war I went to the university and got a degree in chemical engineering. I've been home almost four months. A few weeks ago I landed a great job with an oil company in Tulsa. Think I'm going to move there; this town's a little too small for me."

"Chemical engineer? Congratulations. You're a smart one. Handsome, too, I must say, with those blue eyes of yours."

That's when Jack knew for sure Margaret was as interested in him as he was in her. After visiting over a few more beers, he was pleased but not surprised when she invited him back to her apartment to spend the evening. He didn't go home until the next morning.

His father was waiting for him. "What the hell do you think you're doing, spending the night with that girl?"

"What do you mean, 'that girl'? What do you know about her?"

"She's a Johnson, isn't she? I know their reputation. And she's already been married twice. That's not the kind of girl for you."

"I guess Ted told you who I was with. I'm a grown man; I don't need my brother supervising me. Or you either. I like Margaret. A lot. I'll see her if I want to."

"That would be a big mistake. If you insist on seeing a girl like that, you'll have to do it from somewhere else. I won't have you defying me in my own house. Understand?"

Jack understood. He moved out and continued to see Margaret. There was a determination in her that he admired, and he didn't mind the wild side that kept life interesting.

Margaret liked Jack just as much. He had the steadiness she craved, and he was already well on his way to being successful and prosperous. She could finally have the life she always wanted.

Except for one thing. The day they were to be married, she confessed. "Jack, there's something I need to tell you. I should have told you before..."

§

When Jack read about the crisis in Greece and the overflowing orphanages, he immediately showed the article to Margaret. It could be the answer to their prayers. They tried not to get their hopes up—after all, they'd been turned down once already.

Margaret had confessed to Jack on their wedding day that she was unable to have a baby. He didn't care; she was all he wanted. But she wanted children. She longed for her perfect family, and Jack wanted to give her one. They tried adopting a baby, but Margaret was not approved to be an adoptive mother.

Jack called the agency listed in the article to see if there was a chance. He was surprised at how easy it was. There were no background checks this time; they had only to provide proof of Jack's employment and a couple of letters of recommendation.

"The boy we bring you will be in dire need of medical help," the agency liaison told them. "Food and medicine are both in short supply in the Greek orphanages. You should be ready to take him directly to a doctor or hospital."

"He won't be deformed, or anything like that, will he?" Margaret asked.

"No, of course not. He'll be malnourished. Very thin, and possibly ill. He'll need the devoted care of his new parents and their doctor."

But nothing could have prepared them for the condition David was in when he arrived. The bald, toothless, skeletal, three-year-old placed in Margaret's arms was close to death. His pitiable state stirred Margaret's maternal instinct immediately; he needed a family to care for him as much as she needed a child to care for. The boy clung to his new mother, craving the attention he'd been denied so far in his short life. Margaret finally had the complete devotion she longed for.

A dentist made a special, tiny set of false teeth for David so he could eat. Several doctors attended his various medical needs. With this care, and the loving attention of his new parents, David regained his health and grew into a hardy, handsome, bright young boy.

Now seven years old, he had no memories of those sickly days, or his existence before adoption. All he knew of life was as the healthy son of affluent parents in America. He was especially close to Margaret, who felt personally responsible for his outcome and thought it proved she was a good mother.

But David no longer needed his mother's undivided attention. He was beginning to seek independence. Margaret felt him pulling away. She yearned for another child to save. Another child who depended on her for everything. Who adored her.

Jack called the agency they'd used to adopt David, only to be told that couples who already had a child couldn't adopt another. He consulted his priest, who put him in touch with someone who knew a local Greek-American attorney named Peter Bakas that could arrange adoptions.

Jack called the number he was given and spoke with an office girl named Sabrina, who asked him a few questions about what kind of child he wanted.

"A little girl," he said. "One that's healthy." He didn't want to repeat the anguish of wondering if the child would live. "And we'd like her to have blond hair, if possible." That was Margaret's request; she thought blond was prettier and more socially acceptable.

Sabrina confirmed they could provide a healthy, blond girl, then explained that the cost was five thousand dollars, with half paid now and the other half when the child was delivered. Jack took Margaret when he went to pay the first half, expecting that they'd have to sign a bunch of forms. They were surprised but relieved to find that there were no forms to sign, no letters or documentation to provide.

Sousanna

§

Inside the airport, the Browns found Sabrina standing with a group of people. Jack called to her across the concourse, waving.

Sabrina waved back. "Come this way. The plane just landed; we're going out to greet the children."

Margaret and Jack each took one of David's hands and hurried to catch up. Out on the tarmac, Margaret tried to keep her hat from blowing out of place in the cold January wind as they watched some men push a set of steps up to the plane. When the door opened all the parents stretched and craned to see over each other, trying to be first to see the children and guess which would be theirs.

All the regular passengers disembarked first, but at last a line of young children dressed in beautiful clothes appeared. They were helped down the steps by the stewardesses. Parents began to cry and wave with excitement.

Sabrina knew exactly which child to take to each family. Plump envelopes like the one in Jack's pocket disappeared into Sabrina's purse as she traded children for money.

Peter Bakas exited last. He carried a little blond girl and led a young boy by the hand.

When David saw them, he jumped up and down, pulling on Jack's jacket and pointing to the boy. "Can we have him? I want a brother."

His parents didn't notice him. They were too busy waving at the girl.

Margaret called to her, "Nita! Nita Marie!"

Jack laughed at his wife. "She doesn't know her name."

Peter carried the blond girl to the Brown family. He said to Sousanna, "This is your new mother, father, and brother. Be a good girl and they will love you and take good care of you."

Jack held his hand out to Peter. As they shook, Jack said, "Thank you. We're grateful to you for bringing us a daughter. You're a good man, helping all these children."

"You're welcome," Peter answered. "This one's a little feisty, but clever. She doesn't understand English yet, so be patient." He tried to hand the girl to Jack, but she clung to him, her little arms and legs like tendrils of a vine around a stake.

Jack wrapped a gray wool blanket around her and plucked her from Peter's arms. He reached into his pocket and pulled out the plump envelope containing the rest of the money he owed for the adoption. It quickly vanished into Sabrina's purse. Then Jack and Margaret were left alone with their two children.

The new parents looked the little girl over. She was limp and expressionless.

"Why isn't she smiling?" Margaret asked. "Why doesn't she hug you? What's wrong with her?"

"This is all new to her. She's probably scared." Jack turned to his son and bent down. "David, here's your new sister."

David took one look at his new sibling and surprised his parents by sticking his tongue out at her. "I don't like her. Give her back," he said.

Even David was surprised when the little girl giggled. Then, to their shock, she stuck her tongue at David before quickly tucking her head into Jack's shoulder. She started crying, saying something none of them could understand.

Chapter 25

Sousanna

When the plane stops again, Mr. Bakas makes us sit still so all the other people can get off the plane first. The pretty women help us put on our coats and comb our hair. One of them says, "You must look your best," and I'm happy to understand her because a lot of people around us are saying funny words that don't make sense.

Anna starts crying and says she wants to go home. I start crying, and so do Julia and Ilias and Mario because we all want to go home, too. Mr. Bakas says, "Stop crying. We're in America and your new parents are waiting outside the plane to take you to your new homes."

That's not what we want. We want our own mothers and fathers. I make a fist and hit Mr. Bakas in the arm.

"We want to go home," I tell him. I say it very loud and mean so he'll hear me and pay attention. "Take us home. We want to go back to our real home. We don't want new parents." I keep hitting him until he grabs my arm like when he took my doll away from me.

"All of you, stop crying." Now his voice is mean, too. "We can't get off until you stop. Do you want to live on this plane forever?"

Mario yells, "No, I don't want to live here. I'll stop." We all try to stop crying and wipe our eyes and our noses. I hit Mr. Bakas again because I don't know what else to do, but not as hard this time because what if he gets mad?

Mr. Bakas picks me up and tells Mario to hold his other hand. The women in hats lead the other children by their hands. Mr. Bakas lets all of them go in front of us, so we are the last ones off the plane. The wind blows my hair over my face. I push it back so I can see America, but it's not very pretty.

There's a lot of people waving their hands and calling out words I don't understand. It's cold and I'm scared and it's no fun being The

American in this place and I don't like it and when I go home I will tell all my friends I don't want to be The American anymore, they can be it. I'll be a Greek soldier.

Mr. Bakas carries me to a man holding a gray blanket. He's standing by a woman with round cheeks wearing a funny hat that has a feather in it, and a little boy that looks familiar. They talk to each other using the strange words.

Mr. Bakas says, "This is your new mother, father, and brother. Be a good girl and they will love you and take good care of you." He tries to give me to the strange man but I hold on tight because Papa knows I'm with Mr. Bakas but he might not know if I go with this man.

Besides, I don't like Mr. Bakas but at least I know him and he might go back to Greece and then I could go with him. I wrap my arms around his neck and my legs around his middle and hold on as hard as I can. He tries to pry me loose, but I won't let go. The strange man puts the blanket on me and pulls me away from Mr. Bakas. I cry and reach for Mr. Bakas.

"No, Mr. Bakas, don't leave me here, I want to go home—" But he just turns his back and walks away.

I'm exhausted and I can't go home and I don't know what else to do. I remember what Papa said, and Miss Helena, too, and even Mama in my dream. "Be brave, Sousanna." I'm still scared but I'll try to do what they said. I lay my head on the man's shoulder. He pulls the blanket tighter around me and I'm glad because it's really cold. He says something and I lift my head to look at him. He has blue eyes. Not as blue as Papa's, but I like his eyes.

The woman looks at me but doesn't touch me. The boy looks like my friends back in Greece. He sticks his tongue out at me and I think it's funny and stick mine back at him, but then I get scared because no one kisses me or strokes my hair. They must not like me very much.

We walk away from the crowd. The woman that's my new mother holds the boy's hand, that's my new brother, and talks to him. He laughs and as we walk he tickles my leg hanging out of the blanket. I kick his hand away.

After a long time we come to a place where there were so many cars I can't see them all at once. We go to a pink and white car, just like the one Mr. Bakas has except his is green and white, and this car's top doesn't come off. Are they all going to Greece to take children away from their families and bring them to America?

The man that's my new father puts me in the back seat of the pink and white car with the boy, and he gets in front with the new mother. I'm trying to be brave but I'm scared and I want to be close to someone because it feels safer, so when the car starts moving I wiggle across the seat close to the boy. He tries to push me away and says something to the woman and she says something back but I don't know what so I just stay close to him until the car stops.

The woman turns around to look at me and talks for a long time but I can't understand her. She says one word a lot, "Nita." Then some of her words seem familiar; they're some words Miss Helena taught us. I know one of them—*name*. I try to remember how to say the right words so I can say them to the woman. *I know.*

"Hello my name is Sousanna."

"No. Nita."

I know what "no" is but why is she saying no? My name *is* Sousanna. And what is "Nita" that she keeps saying? I don't know that word.

Maybe I didn't say it right so I try again because I want to please them with my new words.

"Hello my name is Sousanna."

The woman says something to the man. It sounds mean. She glances back at me, a look like I'm in trouble.

We get out of the car and the woman takes my hand and the man takes the little boy's hand and we walk through more cars, just like the place where the planes were, until we reached the front of... Is this our house? It's too big, I don't want this for my house. I'll get lost in it.

I start to cry. The woman bends down and for the first time kisses my cheek. "Nita..." She says that word again and then her lips keep moving for a long time saying a bunch of other words I don't know. But her voice is nice.

Finally she quits talking and stands up. The man picks me up as I wipe away my tears. We go through big glass doors into the biggest house I could ever imagine. How big will my room be?

Inside there are people everywhere and things all over the place. So many kinds of things. Pillows and blankets and pots and pans and dishes and lots of things I don't know what they are. Rows and rows of things.

We keep walking through things until we come to some stairs that move down by themselves. We don't even have to step; they carry us to the ground below.

I can't believe my eyes. Dresses everywhere. Beautiful dresses. And shoes. Shiny, shiny new shoes. Everywhere I look, everything is beautiful and new. But I still don't know why all these people are inside our house.

The man sets me down. The woman says something to him and he and the boy walk away. I reach my hand for the boy but he doesn't see it and keeps going away from me.

The woman takes my hand and leads me through the dresses. Each one is more beautiful than the last. She takes them from the place they're hanging and carries them with us.

Something dings and a voice is talking in the air. Is it God? I grab onto the woman's legs for protection, but she just laughs and pulls my hands away, saying something I don't understand. I look at the other people. None of them are scared so it must be all right; but what was that voice talking in the air?

Now we're looking at petticoats. Miss Helena made all of us girls wear a petticoat under our dresses. These petticoats are bigger, with layers and layers of stiff fabric making them stand out so they barely fit in the racks. The woman points to them and says something, then puts my hand on one of the petticoats. There are so many colors: red, yellow, blue, white and pink.

The woman points to me and then the petticoats. I think I know. She wants me to pick a color I like, so I pick red. She pulls it from the rack and piles it on the dresses she's holding over her arm.

We go into a room with a lot of little rooms inside it. There are still people all around. Maybe this isn't my new house. I think it's like the market Miss Helena took us to one time, where people go to buy things. This one is a lot bigger. It must be as big as Pirgos.

Inside one of the small rooms, the new mother takes off my clothes and puts the other dresses on me, one at a time. She turns me this way and that, making noises that mean she likes it or she doesn't like it—that's something I understand. After trying on all the dresses, and the red petticoat, the woman dresses me and we take all the clothes to another woman behind a counter.

Sousanna

We go back where all the shoes are. So many shiny shoes and so many colors. I jump up and down I'm so excited to see them all. The new mother laughs and for the first time gives me a hug, saying that word again, "Nita."

I try on lots of shoes. Black ones and white ones and pink ones and red ones and some soft shoes like the boys wear called sneakers. We take all of them. And new white socks with lace to wear with my shiny new shoes. Socks that won't be itchy or have lines of mending that hurt my feet. It's just like Miss Helena said, I have beautiful clothes in America. I hope she's right about having good food, too.

The new mother puts the shiny new shoes and lacy socks on our pile at the counter, along with underwear that has lace around the legs, undershirts, a blue coat, white gloves, a white hat, and a shiny black purse. The lady behind the counter puts them in bags, and there are so many we can't carry them all, we have to wait for the father and brother. This family must have many cords hanging in the corners of their house.

We carry the bags to another part of the market, and there are toys everywhere. Toys and dolls. Beautiful dolls, more beautiful than the one Mr. Bakas took away from me after he said it was all mine, just for me.

I run to the shelf of dolls. I look at them all and I see her, the doll I love most of all. She's tall with blond hair like mine, and like the doll that got taken away. She's wearing a wedding dress and veil like the women in the village wear when they go to the church and get married, parading down the streets in their beautiful gowns for all to see.

I reach for the doll and pull her off the shelf. Three other dolls fall on the floor. I cling to the wedding doll and stand still to see what's going to happen to me for making the other dolls fall. The new mother puts her finger right in front of my face. She shakes it and I don't know what she's saying but I know she's unhappy with me. But she doesn't slap my bottom. She takes my wedding doll and hands it to the new father. The boy, my new brother, looks at me and rolls his eyes.

One by one the new mother picks up the dolls and hands them to me. She gestures for me to put them back on the shelf. When they are all neatly back on the shelf, we take my doll and a stuffed bear that the boy got to the woman behind the counter. My new mother is saying something to her that makes her look at me with a sad face, and instead of putting them in a bag she hands them to us. As she gives me my doll she bends down and pushes my hair behind my ears. There are tears in her eyes but she smiles. She says something to me. I don't know what, but it sounds nice.

It's hard to carry my new doll because she's so big her white shoes drag on the floor. The new father reaches to take her from me, but I pull my hand from my new mother's and wrap both arms around my doll, turning away from my new father so he can't take her away. I turn so fast that I fall down, but I keep hold of my doll. I'll fight for her and this time I won't let go no matter what. Nobody is taking her away from me!

The new father gently puts his hands under my arms and helps me stand up. He smooths my doll's dress and veil, and adjusts her in my arms so I can carry her without her feet dragging behind. I'm glad my new father is nice.

I remember some of the strange words that Miss Helena taught us to say when someone does something nice for us, and say them to the father. "Thank you."

They must be the right words because everybody gets a big smile, even my new brother.

We walk out the glass doors of the market. The man stops us and gathers me and my new brother on each side of him. He points to big, blue shapes over the top of the glass doors. As he points to each shape he makes a sound. He looks at the boy and then me, and points to a shape and says the sound. He wants us to say the sound. The new brother knows it the same time as me. In unison we repeat the sounds the new father says as he points to each shape.

"S...E...A...R...S."

"Yes," the father says when we've repeated them all. I know that word, it means we it did right. He hugs my new brother, his bear, my new doll, and me all at the same time. The brother and I have made him happy. The new mother just watches.

We walk through the sea of cars until we find the right one. My new father opens the back part and puts our packages into the open space but I hold my doll tight in my arms until he closes the lid. We get in the car and my doll and my new brother's stuffed bear sit between us.

Sousanna

Maybe I will be okay here until Papa comes to get me and take me home. Does he know where I am? Can he find me in America? What if he can't get here? But Papa can do anything.

The new mother and father keep talking their strange language. Sometimes the new mother turns to look at my new brother and me and says things and he answers in the same strange language.

I don't know any words they say until I hear the new mother say something with the word "name." Then my new brother turns to me and slowly shouts, "MY...NAME...IS...DAVID."

I can understand! I know what he said. I shout back, "MY... NAME...IS...SOUSANNA." We both laugh.

I like him even if he's not really my brother. Marios and Ilias are my brothers. But this boy is handsome, with dark skin and hair and his eyes that are almost black. He looks like the boys in my village. Did he come from Greece in an airplane, too? Was he taken from his family?

When the car stops, the new father helps me get out with my doll. I say "Thank you" again.

My new father smiles and says, "You're welcome, Nita."

I know all the words but the last one, "Nita." They say that word a lot so I'll have to figure out what it means soon.

Outside the car is a beautiful white house with three steps up to a black door that has four little windows across the top of it. There's giant windows across the whole front of the house, not like our one tiny window at home. The top is not flat like my house, but tall and shaped like the tents gypsies live in. I hope this is my new house; it's so pretty.

There are trees in the yard, and even though they don't have any leaves or fruit on them and the grass on the ground is brown, it's still beautiful. The tiny white flowers along the front look like little white bells hanging from green stems.

Americans really do live in pretty houses; they must own a lot of fields to have such nice houses. I know this because I heard Papa telling his friends when I would ride on his shoulders, "If only we could own our own fields, we could live in nice houses too. We were cursed to be born poor."

My new mother and father each take one of my hands and walk me up the three stairs to the front door. David follows us. But the new father lets go of my hand and runs back to the car to get something out. I know what it is: a camera.

The new mother moves David and me close to each other and walks back to where the new father is standing with the camera over one eye. She says something and I don't know the word but her voice sounds just like Mr. Bakas's did when he said "Smile!" so I do, as big as I can. Maybe they'll send this picture to Mama and Papa, and I want them to know I'm not crying and I'm being brave and a good girl so they can come get me now.

Or maybe my family can come live with me in America. They'd like it here. We could all live with this family. Their house looks big enough for many people to live in.

After we take so many pictures my face hurts from smiling, the new mother opens the door and guides me inside the house. We walk into a big, open room with a big chair on either side of one long chair that many people can sit on together, just like at Miss Helena's house. She called the long chair a sofa. There's a round table in the middle of all the chairs with books on it, and some pretty bowls with many colors. In one of the bowls is a box of cigarettes like the ones in Mr. Bakas's car. I know what all these things are, but I don't know what the big box is that has a window in it, but the window is dark and I can't see through it. Why would anybody have a window you can't see through? Maybe Americans aren't very smart.

I don't move but stretch my head so I can see into the next room and there's a long table, as long as Miss Helena's was. It has a beautiful blue cloth over it with a jar of pink and red and yellow flowers in the middle.

There's a good smell coming from that way. I don't know what it is but it reminds me that I'm hungry. The new mother takes my hand and says that word again, "Nita" and keeps talking as she leads me into the kitchen. I know what many of the things in here are: a stove, a refrigerator, a place for water to run in the house, doors that I know have dishes and glasses behind them, and drawers full of forks and spoons and knives to eat with. Miss Helena had all these things in her house, although her stove and refrigerator were tiny compared to these.

I jump and grab the new mother's leg when the telephone hanging on the wall makes its loud ringing sound. The new mother says something to me and pushes me away to answers it. She seems happy while she talks into it.

When she hangs up she takes me back in the big room where David is sitting on the sofa and the new father is in one of the big chairs. The box with the dark window has a man in it. He's looking right at us and talking with the strange words. Who is he and how did he get in the box and why does he keep looking at me? I start crying and run to sit by David, as close as I can. It's hard to talk while I'm crying but I can't stop crying so between sobs I ask him, "Please, David, will you help me? I want to go home."

He puts an arm around me and looks at the new mother and doesn't say anything. I don't think he knows how to help me.

The new mother says something to the new father and he goes to the box with the man in it and pushes a button on the side. The man disappears and the window is dark again.

I stay close to David because it feels safer next to him. The new mother sits in the other big chair next to me.

She leans toward me and says, "No, Sousanna. Nita...name Nita. No Sousanna."

What is she saying? Is she telling me that has to be my name? No, I don't like that word "Nita." *Don't take my name away, don't call me that word!*

I stand up and put my hands on my hips and puff out my chest and say the words Miss Helena taught me. "Hello my name is Sousanna."

"No. Nita."

I'm still crying but I shout anyway. "HELLO MY NAME IS SOUSANNA HELLO MY NAME IS SOUSANNA HELLO MY NAME IS SOUSANNA—!"

The new mother stands up. She looks mad, and even though I don't know all her words I know she's scolding me and she keeps saying, "Nita...name...Nita...no Sousanna."

I fall on the sofa and put my head in David's lap, sobbing. He tries to push me away. There's something different here and I'm more scared than ever before because what's different is that there's nobody here to care for me or love me. I'm all by myself here even with this new family.

Sousanna

The new father picks me up and holds me in his lap. I don't know what the new mother is saying but I can tell she's not happy. She goes into another part of the house.

I feel a little better in my new father's arms, and even though my tummy is hungry I must have fallen asleep because David is shaking me and I wake up on the sofa with my doll lying next to me. I rub my eyes and look around hoping I'm home with Mama and Papa and Anastasia and Marios and Ilias, but instead there's my new brother and now the box has not only a man in it but also a woman and two boys and people I can't see laughing. David looks around the room then whispers something to me. I don't understand most of his words but he uses my name, my real name. "Sousanna..." and he takes my hand and leads me to the long table.

It's covered with food. So much food, more food than I've ever seen. There's a big piece of meat on a platter with carrots and potatoes and onions around it. There's bread with butter, and green beans in a glass bowl. Beside my plate is a big glass of white milk.

Yuk. I hate milk. I had to drink it every night at Miss Helena's even though I didn't like it but I didn't complain because she might slap my bottom if I did. I'll have to drink it here, too, because the new mother might spank me if I don't.

My new father lifts me into one of the chairs and puts a white napkin in my lap. Miss Helena showed us how to use napkins when she taught us American table manners. He pushes my chair close to the table. After he sits down, he lowers his head and so do the new mother and David. He's saying a prayer.

When he finishes talking to God, the new mother picks up my plate and fills it full of the wonderful food. I gobble up every bite and drink the milk even though I don't like it because I'm thirsty. It tastes different from the milk at my house and at Miss Helena's, but it's still nasty.

When my plate is empty, I burp. I can't help it, my tummy is so full. I hope they won't slap my bottom. But they just laugh. At least the father and David do. I put my hand over my mouth and laugh, too. The new mother says something I don't understand but sounds like Miss Helena did when she told me not to burp. We all stop laughing.

Then they all get up and gather the plates and take them away, leaving me at the table alone. While they are out of the room

I quickly burp again. When they come back, they're each helping hold a large plate with a cake on it. They set the cake in the middle of the table in front of me, saying their funny words and the word that's supposed to be my new name, Nita.

The mother cuts the brown cake and puts a piece on a small plate that has beautiful flowers painted all around the edge. It makes me think of the flowers on my yellow dress from home. She hands the plate with the piece of brown cake to me and cuts pieces for the others.

I bite into the cake and a satisfied sound comes out of my throat. "Ummm." Everyone laughs again. I eat all the cake and all of a sudden I feel sick to my tummy—really, really, sick. I have to find their toilet room, fast.

I push out of my chair and run to the part of the house I haven't seen, looking for the toilet. I hope I can make it before I have an accident. There it is. I open the toilet and pull down my underpants and hoist myself up just in time.

The new mother follows me into the toilet room. She looks worried. David comes in behind her but makes a disgusted sound and runs off holding his nose.

I still don't feel well even when I'm finished using the toilet. The new mother puts her hand on my forehead and calls out. The new father comes in and does the same thing with his hand on my forehead and then my cheek. They talk to each other and she picks me up and takes me deeper into the new house.

She carries me past some rooms with beds in them to a last room. She clicks on the lamp sitting on the small table next to a bed and sets me in a white wooden chair while she pulls back a pink cover with tiny ribbons all over it. Under the cover a lace ruffle hangs down to the floor. The bed has four pillows but the mother takes away the two with lace and flowers sewn into them and sets them on top of a white chest that has tiny flowers painted all over the front of it.

Two dolls sit on a shelf with other toys I don't know and lots of books. Two pictures hang on the wall, one of girls playing in a field of flowers and the other of a little girl and a yellow duck. Over the bed, just like at Miss Helena's and over Mama and Papa's bed, is a cross. On the floor is a rug with flowers like the ones the girls in the pictures are in. It's more beautiful than anything I ever imagined.

The mother takes off my shoes, then gently pulls my dress and slip over my head.

Oh, no! Where is my red sweater? I don't remember where it went, so much was happening. They took off my coat when I got here; was my red sweater underneath? Did I leave it at the market when I put on all the dresses? I can't remember. I have to find it.

I try to ask the new mother. "Where is my red sweater? I don't remember. Mama made it for me, just for me. Please help me find it." She looks confused. Why doesn't she understand? "Please find my red sweater, please."

I start to cry again but she doesn't seem to notice, she just puts me into a long pink gown, lays me in the bed, and pulls the beautiful cover over me. She doesn't kiss me or stroke my hair like Mama always does after I jump into her bed. She just clicks off the light and walks out, leaving me all alone in the big, dark room and I'm not brave. I'm scared and I want to go home. I feel sick and I don't understand anything here. I can't stop crying. I want Mama and Papa. I want to go home.

Chapter 26

Katerina

August 1959

Katerina stretched her back and wiped her brow. The chime of the church bell signaled the end of her day in the field. She carried her basket of vegetables to the warehouse, scanning the throng of workers for Anastasia and Niko.

She found Niko when she heard someone call out, "Niko, what do you think of this Economic Community that Karamanlis is trying to get Greece into?" A group of men gathered around him to join the discussion. No use waiting on him, then; he'd be talking politics with the men all the way home.

Gaining back the good opinion of the townspeople helped Niko. Katerina could see him walk taller, like he used to. He called greetings to their neighbors, and they sought him out for his opinions, just like in the old days. Even the old yiayias fawned over him again. Katerina teased him, "Niko, you still have the charm to make yiayias giggle like young girls," and they laughed together.

Still, he didn't have the same strength and vigor he once had. It seemed to Katerina that the guilt he felt for the loss of their children weighed not just in his heart, but on his whole body, making him slower, stiffer. It was a pain that would never release him.

That pain sunk its talons into her, too. Marios and Ilias were making a life far away; how many months would pass before she'd see them again? Or would it be years? And Sousanna—too many months had gone by without any word from her youngest child to expect that she'd return home anytime soon, if at all. Katerina hadn't known that heartbreak was something physical, but the ache to hold and care for her sons and her daughter was a pain no doctor could heal.

"Do you want me to carry your basket home so you can go to the church?" Anastasia appeared at her side. Her daughter knew where her heart was.

"Yes, please," Katerina answered. "I will be home soon to help you prepare supper." She kissed her daughter's cheek and hurried to the church.

In the church she knelt before the statue of Mother Mary. If anyone could feel her loss, her pain, it would be the Lord's mother. She'd lost her Son, too. Katerina asked God and the Blessed Mother to watch over her children until they could be together again.

They would be together again. Katerina would not accept anything else. She didn't know when, or how; but, Lord willing, it would be so. Katerina knew that faith is the power of life, and she kept the faith that one day she'd have her family all together again, laughing, playing, celebrating. That faith kept her strong.

When her supplications were complete, Katerina returned home. She and Anastasia prepared the evening meal together, as they did every night. Her daughter brought Katerina great comfort and joy. Day after day, they worked side by side at their many tasks, talking about the war and how it had changed everything, about husbands and children, and about the day Anastasia would one day marry.

After supper, as they were washing dishes, Anastasia confided, "Mama, I see some boys looking at me. They whisper to each other then look at me and smile. It makes me feel special."

Katerina laughed. "You are very beautiful, with your dark hair and eyes. And you're a good girl. Everyone knows how kind you are. Of course the boys will admire you. You will make a good wife one day. But, my sweet daughter, do not wish it too soon. Be young and enjoy your life as long as you can."

"Enjoy my life? You know there's too much work to do for that. The only time I enjoy my life is when I go to the hills alone."

Katerina pulled her close into her arms. "I'm sorry you never had a chance to be a child. Too much has been expected of you; but things are better for us now. You go to the hills and sing and dance, anytime you can. Go there and be free from all your work, at least for a little while."

"Mama, I try to be happy when I'm there. I try to forget the work that's always waiting to be done; but I've always worked and don't know anything else."

The words were a fist to Katerina's heart. Would Anastasia's life be the same as hers, working always for others, no joy of her own? She grabbed her daughter in a tight embrace, not caring that the dishwater dripped from her hands down Anastasia's back. She had no words of comfort for the girl, but hoped Anastasia could feel her desperate wish for something better radiating from the core of her being through her arms.

They finished the dishes in silence. By the time they wiped them all dry and carried them into the house, Niko had several souvlaki sticks ready to bundle.

Katerina was pleased with his efforts. Every evening, after a long day in the fields, he sat with his knife and whittled the sticks. He used only fine hardwood, and worked them until they were sharp and tapered just so, making them stronger and easier to use than the thicker, blunter souvlaki sticks available elsewhere. Now all the café owners wanted only Niko's sticks.

"The wood does not break or splinter when we skewer the meat onto them," they told him appreciatively. Katerina had never imagined that something so ordinary as souvlaki sticks could make such a difference in their lives, but so it was.

She and Anastasia had just settled themselves near Niko to bundle his newly-carved sticks when she heard Georgia calling, running through the yard to their house. "Katerina, Niko! Help! It's Ellis! He can't breathe. Come, help me!"

The three of them jumped up and ran for the door. They hurried as fast as they could, following Georgia back to her house. They ran in the door just in time to see Georgia's husband struggling for his last breath. He had fallen out of his chair by the fireplace and was lying on the floor, gasping for air and holding his chest. Niko knelt beside him.

Niko will know what to do; he must. He was in the military, they must have taught him what to do.

Katerina watched Niko lay Ellis on his back and try to breathe life back into him; but after a few minutes he sat back and put his head in his hands.

"Georgia, he is gone. I'm sorry."

Georgia ran to Ellis and wrapped her arms around his lifeless body. She lay her head close to his heart, quietly sobbing. Katerina knelt and folded her arms around her sister, holding Georgia silently, just as Georgia had done for her the day Sousanna was taken.

Katerina was not surprised when, a few days after the funeral, Georgia said she was leaving Pirgos.

"With Ellis gone, I have no way to care for our children," Georgia told her. "In Tripoli I can live with Mother. I can help her, and my children will have a place to live. But my days will be lonely without you."

Katerina held her tears inside, as she'd taught herself to do. "I understand. You must do what is best for you and your children. We don't live lives that give us choices; we must simply do what we can to survive our circumstances."

Katerina helped her sister pack her things into a truck that would take Georgia and her children to Tripoli. "Kiss our mother many times for me," she said. "Tell her I am strong and well. My prayers will be with you every day. I love you, my sister, and I will miss you."

The truck driver honked and waved his hand for her sister to get in the truck. They embraced one more time, and for a moment, Katerina felt so connected to her twin sister she did not think they could part. The two women had started life as one being and belonged together.

At last Georgia climbed into the truck and it pulled away. Katerina waved goodbye as her twin sister disappeared down the road, yet another loved one lost to her.

§

With her sister gone, Katerina began to spend more time with her friend Sofia. She'd let that friendship stale in the past few months. It hurt to see Sofia still with her daughter Emilia, who had been Sousanna's best friend, while Katerina no longer had her own young daughter.

Time eased the pain, and evenings spent with Sofia, Emilia, and Anastasia became the time Katerina cherished most. It felt good to remember happy days, when she used to watch Sousanna and Emilia play or draw pictures in the dirt under the big lemon tree at Emilia's house.

The women and Anastasia would tat or do other handwork while Sofia shared the local gossip. Inevitably conversation turned to their families. One evening Sofia mentioned how tall Emilia was growing.

"Do you think Sousanna will be tall like Niko?" she asked; then quickly added, "Oh, I'm sorry. I wasn't thinking."

Katerina's needles stilled. "It's okay. That's a question I ask myself. Will I ever know how my Sousanna looks as a young girl? As a young woman? A wife, a mother? I wonder if she'll be tall like her father or a small woman like myself."

Suddenly Emilia spoke up with a tone of defiance. "Why did you take me into the hills the day they came to take Sousanna? Why did you do that?"

"I didn't want you to cry when you saw Sousanna taken away. I knew how much you loved each other, and I wanted to protect you."

"But I didn't get to tell her goodbye. You took me away so I wouldn't cry, but when we came home I cried the most I ever cried because she was gone, and nobody told me she wouldn't come back."

"Sousanna loved you very much," Katerina said. "We are all praying for the day she will be home again." She picked up her needles and resumed tatting.

Chapter 27

Sousanna

February 1959

The new father is talking to me but all his words are jumbled sounds and I don't know what he's saying. He looks serious, like Papa does when he didn't get enough food to bring home after working in the fields all day. Maybe this father didn't get enough food.

When Papa looks like that, sometimes I act funny to make him laugh. Will that work with this father? I jump around with my hands over my head, the way my uncle George does when he dances at home. Mama and Papa and Anastasia always clap with the music when Uncle George dances. If they could see me dance, they would be cheering and clapping. I pretend they're watching me while I dance around.

The new father smiles, then laughs at my dancing. But he doesn't know how to clap while I'm dancing He waits until I'm finished to clap. He seems happy now.

I don't understand most of what the new family says to me. I try to use the words Miss Helena taught us: yes, no, mother, father, sister, brother, good morning, good night, thank you, please, bathroom please, hello my name is Sousanna. But they're not enough. The new family doesn't know most of what I say, either.

Everything, and everybody, is so different from my home. I feel strange all the time and I'm never sure how to act. There's only one thing that's the same. America has church day, too.

When that day comes, my new mother dresses me in a beautiful dress, lacy socks, and shiny shoes. I even get to wear soft gloves and carry a purse. She puts my favorite lace doily on my head. It's fun to dress up so pretty, but I want to wear my red sweater. I ask for it, but my new mother doesn't understand my words, and I don't know where it is to show her.

My whole new family walks into church together, just like my family in Greece does. The church feels familiar. It has all the smells and sights of the church at home. Incense and ladies' perfume. The pictures of the saints and of Mary, and Jesus hanging on the cross up in the front. I'm comfortable in church because I know what everything is, and I know what to do, even if I don't understand all the words the priest says.

Mama and Papa love God and Jesus, and they like to go to church. I can tell because when they go in, their faces relax and look happy, even though they don't laugh in church. Mama's face gets soft and peaceful. They listen closely to the priest chant and read the scripture. Lots of times Mama puts her hand on her heart, and I think she loves God extra then.

Mama taught me to love God, too. I remember when she taught me how to cross myself correctly.

"Sousanna, you are old enough to learn this now," she said. "When we pass a priest or a church, and when we enter the church, you must cross yourself to show God you love Him."

She took my hand, the one I use to hold my spoon or a stick to draw with, and arranged my fingers, then moved my hand to make the ends of my fingers touch my forehead, my chest, one shoulder, and the other shoulder. "Now you try."

I put my fingers the way she showed me and touched my forehead and one shoulder. "I forgot which shoulder is first."

"Forehead first, chest next, then shoulder to shoulder. Right shoulder first, the same side as your hand. Try again; you must do it correctly."

Forehead, chest, shoulder—"Oh, no; this shoulder first."

I practiced many times until the motions came easily.

"That's my smart Sousanna." Mama gave me a big hug. "I'm proud of you, and God will be pleased when we go to church tomorrow and you cross yourself."

It was Papa who taught me, as I sat in his lap for one of our talks, how to pray.

"Papa, in church why does the priest close his eyes and talk to God? You and Mama do it, too. I know you are praying, but why? What does that mean?"

"We pray to ask God for His help, Sousanna. We also thank Him for our blessings. We close our eyes so we can concentrate and not be distracted, and we lower our head because we love God and want to be humble before Him."

"What is humble?"

"It's showing God we know He is greater than we are. The thing you should remember is that when you pray, God will hear you. Just tell him what you are thinking."

Every Sunday my new family goes to church. I know to kneel, cross myself with my right hand—forehead, chest, right shoulder, left shoulder—and wait in the long, wooden pew for the holy parade to come in, led by the altar boys carrying a tall pole with a golden cross on top and followed by the priest dressed in his beautiful robes with the Bible in his hand. I know when the priest closes his eyes he's praying to God.

The priest says one prayer the same every time we come to church. All the people say it with him. I hear it so often that I think I can say some of the words.

"Our Father in Heaven...will be done...heaven...give us...bread ...as we forgive ...Amen." I did it! Now I know some more American words.

I'm glad Papa taught me how to pray. And I'm glad because now I remember that I can talk to God and ask Him for help, like Papa said.

At night, after I put on my nightgown and get in bed, my new father brings a book to my room. While he says the words in it I look at the pictures to see what it's about. When he turns the last page, he says, "Good night, Nita," and turns off the light and goes away.

That's when I close my eyes and talk to God. First I say the American words from the prayer at church. Then I say my own words, in Greek. "God, please show Papa how to come here and get me. I want to go home. I miss my family."

Then I always think of my Papa and Mama, and my sister and brothers. I remember them hugging and kissing me, and saying, "I love you, Sousanna." I miss them. It hurts my inside to be away from my home and family. It aches so much that I cry every night.

Sometimes I cry in the day, too. "Thélo ti mitéra mou. Thélo na páo spíti," I say.

Sousanna

The new mother seems to know I'm saying I want my own mother, my home. She shakes her finger at me and scolds me. I don't know all the words she says, but I can tell it's bad by the mean sound of her voice and the scrunched-up, scary look on her face. When she gets like that I can't even move.

I understand some of the words, though, because she uses them over and over: "Stop crying. I'm your mother now. Stop asking for your mother."

I remember what Miss Helena said. She told us not to ask for our families in Greece once we got to America, because it would make our new parents very sad, and maybe even angry. She told us to treat the new families like they're our real family, and like we don't have any other mama and papa.

I don't want to treat the new mother and father like my mama and papa, but this mother might spank me if I don't behave. I don't want a spanking. They hurt.

There's something else Miss Helena said, words to make the new parents happy. Special words we're supposed to call the new parents. To keep from getting in any more trouble, I look up at the mother and say, "Mom."

Immediately her face straightens into a satisfied look and she says, "Good girl."

I know those words, and that's what I want to be. I want to be a good girl. I don't want to make trouble or to get in trouble. I don't want to hurt my new family's feelings, even though I don't love them like I do Mama and Papa. I'll call the mother and father the special words, "Mom" and "Dad." I won't ask to go home anymore, at least not out loud. But I will not forget about Mama and Papa. Not ever.

§

March 1959

Mom tells David and me to put on the clothes she laid out on the bed for us; we're going to have company. I put on my slip, my crisp, blue dress, and my socks and shoes, and go find Mom.

"Please," I ask, holding the two long pieces of fabric out from the back of my dress.

She puts her hands on my shoulders. "Nita, I want you to say, 'Please tie my bow.' Say it. 'Please tie my bow.'" She lets go of my shoulders and pulls the pieces of fabric to the front to show me. "This is a bow."

She's being so nice to me, I get excited. I say, "Please, tie my boo." It doesn't sound right, like she said it, so I can't believe it when she laughs.

"Good enough," she says, "but the word is 'bow.' Let me tie it and then we'll comb your hair and put a ribbon in it."

I know most of what she says. I can understand a lot more things than I know how to say in American.

After we're dressed David and I sit like two little grown-ups, he in his suit and me in my beautiful blue dress. Mom takes a picture. We smile, and I hear the doorbell ring at the same time the camera snaps.

Dad answers the door. "Lucy, Ted come in, come in." He hugs the thin woman and shakes the round man's hand.

Mom puts the camera down and waits for them to come to her. She gives the woman a half-hearted hug, and only says, "Hello, Ted" to the man. I can tell by the way she says it that she doesn't like him.

David runs to them. He wraps his arms around the man's legs and shouts, "Uncle Ted!"

The man reaches down and lifts David into his arms. I watch them all as if they're in the television set.

Holding David, the man says to him, "Hey, there's my pal. How ya doing?" His words end with a chuckle.

"Good."

The man sets David down and the woman bends down to give him a hug. "Look at you," she said. "You're getting so big and handsome."

Then Dad gestures his hand toward me. "And this is Nita," he says.

Sousanna. I know better than to say it out loud.

Everyone looks at me. I'm still, not knowing what to do. Nobody tells me, so I'll do what David did. I run to the man and hug his legs tightly.

I don't know why everybody laughs.

The man and woman both kneel in front of me. The woman's smile is so big it seems to go all the way across her face. The man has kind blue eyes, like Papa's. The woman reaches her arms out to me and I fall into them. The man wraps his arms around both of us and says in a soft voice, "Welcome, Nita. Welcome."

"I'm your Aunt Lucy," the woman says. "That's your Uncle Ted. He and your father are brothers. We're happy you're here, and we're happy to meet you."

Chapter 28

Nikolas

June 1960

Niko watched the young man mindlessly fiddle with souvlaki sticks. He made a pretense of possibly purchasing some, but it was clear what he was really interested in, as his eyes were not on the wares he handled but something else entirely: Anastasia. Niko shook his head, chuckling to himself. If he had a drachma for every boy who came to flirt with Anastasia, he wouldn't need to sell these sticks.

But which one was the right one for his daughter? The one now talking to her was a possibility. Vaso was educated and successful. He'd gone to the university in Athens and become an accountant. He would have a good living. And he was certainly interested; he came by their stand every time they opened it, spending more time talking to Anastasia than making his purchase.

Anastasia seemed to like Vaso, too. She didn't stand back quietly as she did when some men came to chat with her, but stepped aside with him to talk and laugh.

Suddenly Vaso turned away from Anastasia to face him. "Mr. Demetriou, I would like to take Anastasia for a walk into the square. May I have your permission?"

The boy was finally making a real move. From the corner of his eye Niko saw Anastasia grab Katerina's arm, bouncing up and down with a huge smile.

"I think she would like to go for a walk with you. But only to the square, and just for a short while."

"Yes, sir." Vaso held out his elbow for Anastasia. She placed her hand lightly on his arm and together they turned toward the square.

Sousanna

For several weeks, each time Anastasia came to help her father at the market, Vaso appeared, and took Anastasia walking. Then one evening he came to their home and took her walking in the hills. Suddenly it seemed he was always around.

It was time for Niko to make a decision. Vaso was kind, smart, had a good job, and seemed to care very much for Anastasia. He would be a good match for Anastasia. Niko decided to make the arrangements for his daughter to marry Vaso.

To do this, he and Katerina would go to Vaso's home and talk with his parents. But, Niko decided, he would not rush the young ones. Next year would be soon enough for them to marry. Anastasia would be sixteen then, and Vaso twenty-three.

Sunday, after church and the noon meal, was a good time to go to Vaso's. He and Katerina wouldn't be tired from working all day, and they would already be dressed in their Sunday clothes. He had nice black pants to wear with his new white shirt and black tie, and his brown jacket was still good. He wore the same tattered cap that had marked the years of his life since he was a young man.

Just a few weeks ago Katerina had purchased a new dress—the first she'd gotten since their marriage. She had new shoes, too, with big square heels, and stockings without any tears or mending.

"Katerina, I remember when you were a young girl and I learned our parents had arranged for us to marry. I was happy to hear the news. I thought you were very beautiful, and today, I still think you are very beautiful."

"Thank you, Niko." Her voice was distracted. "I pray we'll be well received by Vaso's parents, and that this will be a good match."

"Don't worry, Katerina. They went through hard times just like the rest of us. But our lives are better now, and their son will be marrying a good girl with a good family."

At Vaso's home, Theo greeted Nikolas with a hug and Litsa kissed Katerina on both cheeks. "Welcome Niko, Katerina," Theo said. "Vaso told us you would be coming to see us. Please, come sit."

Litsa brought coffee and spoon sweets. They all nibbled and sipped, talking about the local news. Finally enough small talk had been made and Niko broached the reason for their visit.

"Theo, you must know our children care for each other. Katerina and I think they would be a good match for marriage. I'm sorry that we don't have a dowry for Anastasia, but you can be assured she will be a good wife for Vaso. She'll treat him well and make a good home. But she's only fifteen so we'd like them to wait another year to marry."

Their hosts didn't look pleased. Theo stared at the floor with a grimace for a moment before he answered. "Yes, we know our children care for each other. Our son has spoken to us about Anastasia. He is very angry with us, but I pray you will understand. Vaso is educated and has found good work. He needs a wife who will help him become respected in the community. Not just someone who can care for a home, but someone who can also read and write—"

Niko sprang up so quickly his legs almost buckled. "Are you my neighbor? Did you not suffer as the rest of us? You think my daughter is not enough for your son, is that what you're saying?"

Theo spoke with a smooth voice, gesturing Niko to sit back down. "No, no. We know Anastasia is a good girl—"

Litsa interrupted. "She's too young. And she's not educated. No. My son will not marry your daughter." She stood deliberately and walked away with her chin thrust out.

Niko took Katerina by the arm and marched her out the gate, ignoring Theo and his pleas for understanding. Niko would not look at him or his son again. The arrogance. They weren't good enough for Anastasia, anyway.

Niko was still angry and humiliated on Thursday, when they went to the market again, but he tried not to show it for Anastasia's sake. After she'd cried all night at the news he and Katerina brought back, she'd quietly gone about her business as she always did. It would be best for her if they all carried on as usual.

He carried his small folding table and set it up next to his older brother George, who made a place for them next to his honey stand. Katerina and Anastasia carefully displayed the sticks on top of it.

"Niko, my brother," George exclaimed, giving him a hearty slap on the back. "What a beautiful day it is today, yes? A day for dancing."

Niko smiled at his brother's exuberance. Leave it to George to lift his mood. They hadn't been close growing up due to the difference in their ages, but these days Niko liked spending time with his older brother. George had managed to keep his lighthearted attitude even through the hard years. He didn't take life too seriously, but lived by the familiar Greek saying, "This is our life! Save your tears for what matters!" He was always laughing and carrying on. It was hard to stay upset around George.

Now George pranced to the middle of the aisles. He raised his arms and began to dance, snapping his fingers to some rhythm in his own mind. The other vendors began clapping in time to the rhythm of George's snapping.

"Nikolas, little brother, come. Come dance with me."

Niko waved his hands and shook his head. "No, no."

"Oh, come, Niko," his brother coaxed. "Tall, handsome Niko, come out here where everyone can see you. I want everyone to see my little brother who is not so little by my side."

The vendors cheered and called for him until Niko slowly walked out into the aisle and began to dance with his brother, both of them snapping their fingers over their heads to music no one could hear. Seeing George, almost half the size of Niko, and Niko towering above his older brother, everyone burst into laughter, some calling comments about their height.

George joined in the joking. "This is my little brother. I have never seen the top of his head he is so tall. All I can see is up his nose." He jumped and slapped the bottom of his shoe with the back of his fingers. Everyone cheered at his display.

Niko was thankful for his older brother. The anger and disappointment, though still there, no longer threatened to overcome him. And for a short time at least, his secret worry was relieved.

He hadn't mentioned it anyone, not even Katerina, but something was happening to his body. Maybe it was the long periods of time he spent sitting and whittling that caused his legs to get rigid and his hands to shake. The fatigue was surely from the years of work in the fields. But the lack of balance? The buckling knees and the need to brace himself when rising? Even more disturbing was the way his head sometimes dropped or nodded uncontrollably. It didn't happen all the time, and so far no one had noticed.

Every night he prayed, "Please, God, keep me strong. Now I have work, and I can care for my family. Keep me strong so I can make up for all the years of hunger and poverty to my wife and children, and bring the young ones home."

Nikolas

August 1960

"Hello. I would like to try your sticks in the new restaurant I'm opening." The speaker was a stranger, new to town evidently. He had some sort of hump on his shoulder.

"They are the finest souvlaki sticks in Pirgos," Niko said, picking one up to show him. "I whittle them myself so they are very sharp, and they won't splinter or break."

"I have heard that," the man said. He was answering Niko, but his eyes were on Anastasia. It was eerily similar to another time one of his daughters had been admired by a stranger. "If they work as well as everyone says, I'll offer you a deal to make them by the hundreds," the man said.

"Why don't you buy a few, try them out," Niko offered. "I think you'll be pleased and we can talk. Are you new here? I don't recognize you."

"My name is Nedtarios. I've just returned home from the army. I was wounded and I'm using my compensation to open a restaurant."

Niko sold a handful of sticks to Nedtarios. *He'll be back and I'll make a deal for enough money to build a house. A real house, with more than one room.*

Sure enough, the next week Nedtarios was at the market waiting for him.

"Nedtarios, my friend, you're back. Are your pockets lined with money for me to make you hundreds of souvlaki sticks?"

Nedtarios didn't laugh at his joke. "Your sticks are good. Let's have a drink and discuss how we can work together. I have an offer to make to you...for your sticks, and something more."

Niko set up his stand before answering. Katerina and Anastasia arranged the sticks on the table. He noticed that Nedtarios watched Anastasia intently, but she didn't seem to notice him.

"I'll meet you in the square at two o'clock," Niko said. "There's a yellow café with tables outside. We can have a drink and talk."

§

"Beer or ouzo?" Nedtarios asked. "I'm buying."

"Beer."

Once the drinks were ordered Nedtarios said, "My restaurant will be the best in Pirgos. It will have nice tables and comfortable chairs with clean, white cloths on the tables. I want to treat the people here well and offer good souvlaki to my customers. I plan to be very successful and will need at least a hundred sticks each day."

"A hundred sticks a day? Do you not know where you are? Things are better, but we are all still poor."

"I understand." Nedtarios sat back, relaxed. Confident. "It'll be nice, but I won't charge any more than anywhere else. I want to treat people well. We've all been through too much. The war did terrible things to people; believe me, I know." He pointed to the lump on his shoulder. "A bullet went straight into my shoulder. This hump is from the infection and torn muscle. It will never be healed, but it's nothing compared to the things I saw. But, I'm getting a nice compensation." One side of his mouth lifted in a cynical half smile.

Niko didn't know what to say. He took a drink of beer to cover his discomfort, but Nedtarios didn't seem to notice the awkwardness. He kept talking.

"The girl you call Anastasia, she's your daughter, yes?"

Niko nodded. "Yes, she's my daughter." *But she's not going to America.*

"She's very beautiful." Nedtarios leaned forward again, speaking intently. "I want to marry her. I can give her a good life. I'm thirty-five years old, ready to settle down. I get a lot of money from the army, and I'll have the restaurant. I can take good care of her. Not just her, but you and your wife, too."

Niko took another drink of beer. It was too soon. He just met this man. But Nedtarios was going to live here; Anastasia would be nearby, where he could make sure she was treated well. Niko's head started to drop; luckily he was able to make it stop this time. *What if I don't get better? What if I get worse, or something happens to me? Who will care for Katerina and Anastasia?*

He heard himself say, "Okay, yes."

Nedtarios looked surprised. "'Okay, yes?' To what? The sticks? Or Anastasia? Or both?"

"Both. You've served the Greek people in war, even been wounded. You want to offer people good food they can afford. You're a good man and will take care of my daughter. So yes, both."

Chapter 29

Anastasia

Anastasia carried her basket full of freshly-dug horta at her side as she ambled home. Knowing she was bringing a treat for her family's dinner that evening should make her happy, but the sadness she'd felt since Vaso's parents rejected her left no room for joy. Seeing Vaso had been something Anastasia looked forward to each week. Now that was gone.

Even in the hills she could no longer sing or dance. Now she was only there to forage food for her family. She knew Mama worried about her—she'd always been quiet, but now Mama said even her soft laughter and smiles were gone. Anastasia didn't think there was anything to laugh or smile about. Her chance at love and happily ever after was gone. Would she ever be good enough for anyone? Or for anything other than working the fields?

As Anastasia approached home she saw Papa at the front gate of their home. He was leaning on the gate with an odd look on his face. Pain, and something else she couldn't define. His head was trembling.

"Papa, you don't look well. Let's go inside so you can lie down and rest."

He leaned, almost fell, onto the gate as he pushed it open. "No, we must talk," he said. "I have news for you and your mother. Go inside and empty your basket, then bring your mother and come to my chair."

Anastasia took his arm to walk with him across the yard. Before he sat down, he turned to her and clasped her hand with his.

"Once I said Sousanna was the best of my children; but you, Anastasia, have proven to be the best of my children. You are here, taking care of your mother and me, and you have endured our years of want while staying kind and gentle. God blessed me the day you were born, my sweet daughter." He stopped talking as his arm tensed and dropped. He had that odd look on his face again, looking at his hand as if it belonged to someone else.

"I can see you're not well. Let me get Mama."

He held onto the outside wall of the house and eased himself into his chair. Thank goodness he'd fixed the broken leg so the chair was steady once he was able to sit. Anastasia ran to get Mama.

"Anastasia says you are not well. What happened? Are you ill? And she says you have news for us; have you heard from Sousanna?"

"No, Katerina, I'm sorry. There is no news from America, or from our boys in Athens. My news is for our daughter here."

"Me?" Anastasia asked. What news could there be about her?

"Yes. Do you remember the man at the market that offered to buy our sticks for his restaurant?"

She shook her head. "No."

"I think I remember him," Mama said. "He was the man with the mustache. He seemed to have something wrong with his back; a hump, maybe? Yes, I remember him. He was very serious. Even your brother could not make him laugh."

"I met with him today in the square," Niko told them. "We made a deal for the souvlaki sticks. We will have to work extra hard; he wants a hundred sticks a day, and he will pay us well for them."

Mama gasped. "A hundred sticks a day?"

Anastasia could hardly imagine anyone needing that many souvlaki sticks. "That's the best news. We can do it. Maybe we'll make enough from the sticks that we won't have to work in the fields."

"No." Niko sighed. "We have to work Mr. Yanni's fields to stay in our home. But that is only part of my news. There is more. Anastasia, I have arranged for you to marry this man. His name is Nedtarios—"

"What? I don't even know him. How could you do this to me? It can't be true."

Niko started to stand but sat back hard into the chair. "Listen to me," he said. "Nedtarios is a good man, and he will provide a good life for you. This is how we do things. Your mother and I did not choose each other; our marriage was arranged by our parents."

Anastasia's thoughts were reeling so fast she couldn't speak. She just watched as Katerina leaned close to Niko's face and spoke with a voice Anastasia had never heard from her.

"You have done what? Again, you have given a daughter away? You barely know this man. No, you cannot do this to Anastasia."

Niko pushed her hands away. "You must trust me," he said. "I believe Nedtarios is a good man. He'll take good care of Anastasia. He will give her a nice home, nice clothes, good food. And she will remain in Pirgos. I have decided, and I will keep my promise to him and to our daughter."

"To me? What promise have you made me?" She couldn't stop the tears flowing down her face.

Niko didn't answer. He just walked into the house and closed the door. Anastasia fell into her mother's arms and sobbing.

She didn't speak to Niko for weeks. At the market, when Nedtarios came to buy sticks, she intentionally ignored him. Then one day she thought, *If he's going to be my husband maybe I better pay attention.* She watched him from the corners of her eyes.

He was handsome. Very handsome, in fact. The hump on his shoulder was not as obvious as she'd feared. How old was he? He was not a young man, certainly not anywhere close to her age.

Niko waved his arm. "Anastasia, come meet Nedtarios."

She took a deep breath and walked toward the man that would be her husband. The father of her children. Her future.

"Good morning, Anastasia. I am Nedtarios. I hope you have received your father's news for us as good news."

She burst out laughing. She couldn't help it. It must be nerves. Papa and even Mama scowled at her. She covered her mouth with her hand and tried to control her laughter.

"I'm sorry. My father's news was a surprise to me."

"Maybe we could go for a coffee in the square and talk."

"I don't drink coffee."

"Maybe lemonade?"

Papa answered before she had a chance to turn him down again. "Yes, Anastasia would like to have a lemonade with you. Only for a short time; I need her back to work with us."

Though reluctant, Anastasia did not argue. Neither of them said anything on the way to the café. She was glad he was polite, not trying to take her hand or put his arm around her.

The square bustled with people gathering to visit after the day's work. They found a café with places to sit and Nedtarios ordered a coffee and a lemonade. Finally he spoke to her.

"Anastasia, I know you are only fifteen. We can wait until next year to marry..." He stopped and cleared his throat, looking suddenly awkward. "Forgive me, I am not thinking. Of course we should get to know each other before we discuss serious things like marriage. Let me tell you about myself, and my family."

Anastasia nodded her head as she sipped her lemonade from a straw.

"I have a good family. My parents were both killed during the atrocities of the war. Now it is only my sister and me. My sister is a nun at the monastery outside of Pirgos. Do you know it?"

A nun? Anastasia felt her eyes widen. "Your sister is a nun? Yes, I know the monastery. Mama took me there once. It's the most beautiful place I've ever seen."

Nedtarios smiled, the first time she saw him do so. "Yes, it is. My sister and I were very close growing up. When I left to go fight in the war, she prayed to God for my safety. She vowed that if I came back alive, she would go to the monastery and become a nun, and serve God the rest of her life. As you can see, I did come back alive." He glanced toward the hump on his shoulder. "Wounded, but alive. The day after I returned home she packed her bedroll and some food and walked two days to the monastery. She is very content there. We can go visit her one day, if you like."

There was a tenderness in Nedtarios as he spoke of his sister. Maybe she could get used to the idea of him as her husband. Eventually.

"Now will you tell me something about yourself, Anastasia?"

"There's not much to tell you. I have lived with my parents and worked. I have two younger brothers living in Athens. They are working to become furniture makers. And I had a sister—"

"Had?"

"Yes; her name is Sousanna. She was taken to America many months ago. I miss her, but I hope she has a good life in America. That she is being well cared for."

"You're very grown up for a fifteen-year-old girl. I hope to make your life a good one, too, and that you will feel as well cared for as your sister in America. Come, it's time we walk back."

There was one more thing Anastasia had to know. "How old are you?" she asked boldly.

"I am thirty-five."

Chapter 30

Sousanna

September 1959

"May I wear my red sweater to school?" I ask Mom in perfect English as David and I carry our empty breakfast plates and glasses into the kitchen.

"No, it's too hot for a sweater today." I understand all her words, but don't like her answer. I don't complain. There are too many other things to think about.

Today is my first day of school. I'll get to do all the things Mom has been telling me about: meet new friends, learn to read books and write words, color pictures, sing songs, and "so many other fun things."

Yesterday, as she hung up my new school clothes in my closet, Mom told me about lunches. "Nita, when you and David leave on the bus in the mornings, you will each take your lunch with you in a lunch pail," she said. "Your teacher will take it and put it away until it's time to eat."

She called David, who was in his room across the hall. When he appeared at my bedroom door she said to him, "Get your lunch pail from last year so Nita can see how it works. It's in the bottom drawer in the kitchen."

David came back holding a tin box with a cat and mouse on the front. I recognized them from the cartoons we watched on the TV in the front room. Tom and Jerry.

Mom opened the box to show me a container inside that would hold my milk and how the rest of my lunch would lie beside it. "Today we'll go to Skaggs and pick out your lunch box," she said. "There are many pictures on the outside you can choose from. It'll be fun."

"I want a new one too," David said. "Can I get a new lunch box, too?"

Mom laughed. "Of course you can. We'll all go together."

I picked out the lunch box with Barbie on the front and around the thermos. David's has Roy Rogers sitting on his horse, waving.

I set my plate and glass on the counter and look to see what Mom is putting in my new lunch box. She's pouring milk into the Barbie thermos. She screws the top on tightly and puts it sideways inside the box. Then she takes potato chips from the bag and wraps them into a piece of plastic. I watch her wash and dry an apple. There's a chocolate Hostess cupcake wrapped in the package it came in. She puts each item neatly inside my new lunch box.

She puts two pieces of bread on another piece of plastic and gets out the peanut butter. I jump up and down clapping my hands. "Yummy, a peanut butter and jelly sandwich. My favorite."

Mom looks down at me and smiles. "I think you're going to like your new school. I met your teacher, Mrs. Semeras, and she's very nice. Today you won't ride the bus; I'll drive you and David to school in the car so I can go in and help you get settled."

Her face turns stern. She bends down so she's close to my face. "Nita, listen to me. I don't want you to talk about where you came from, or that family, do you understand? People don't want to hear about that; they won't like you if they know how you came here. You must forget all that. And only speak English words. If you say any Greek words I'll punish you."

Out loud I say in English, "Yes, ma'am." But in my mind I answer her with Greek words: *I will never forget my family. You're not my real mother, and my Papa is coming to get me. He won't punish me for using any kind of words.*

"And don't do strange things. Watch the other children and do what they do."

I know why she says that.

In the yard, mixed in with the grass, are tiny, bright green plants with little leaves. Once when no one was looking I picked off some of the leaves and ate them. They were a little bitter but they had a fresh taste, like the horta Anastasia and Mama gathered. I wanted to keep tasting them, and thinking about home.

One day I wanted to make a sandwich from the tiny green plants. When I thought no one was looking, I took two pieces of bread outside to the back of the house, where the big yard was turning green. I picked a bunch of the plants and stuffed them between the two pieces of bread.

I just took a bite when I heard someone yell, "Put that down. Put it down." It was Dad, and he was marching toward me with a mad look on his face. I dropped the sandwich but his voice scared me so much I couldn't move. He kept yelling.

"That will make you sick. Do not eat grass. You are not an animal. You do not live where people eat grass. Don't ever do that again." He grabbed my arm, just like Miss Helena did once, and slapped my bottom hard.

It hurt. I pulled loose before he could do it again and ran into the house to my room. In my mind with Greek words I yelled, *I hate you. You hurt me. You're not my father. My real father would never hurt me. I hate you. Papa will be mad at you for slapping my bottom.*

Dad came into my room. "Nita, you have to understand, there are things that we do not do here. We do not eat grass. I don't want you to get sick. I spanked you so you would remember not to do that again. Not to hurt you but to teach you. There is so much for you to learn so you can be like other children here. I love you, Nita."

His words were soothing, and I decided not to hate him, but he's still not my father. He walked away without touching me or kissing me or holding me in his arms so I would feel safe.

I remember this when Mom tells me not to do strange things. I say "Yes, ma'am" again and she stands up.

"Okay, kids, time to get in the car. First I want to take a picture of you together. Go sit on the sofa and straighten out your clothes so you'll look nice."

David and I climb on the sofa. I look down to see if my socks with the lace are folded neatly over my ankles, and smooth out the full blue skirt of my dress over my white petticoat. I reach up to touch the blue ribbon tied around my head to be sure it hasn't slipped and pat my hair so none of it sticks up out of place. I put my hands in my lap, cross my ankles the way Mom likes, and smile. In my mind I think about how Mama and Anastasia would like to see me in these beautiful clothes. Maybe when they come to get me we can go to the Sears store and buy pretty clothes for them, too.

Sousanna

On the way to school David and I sit in the back seat of the car holding our new lunch boxes. I'm so excited my tummy starts to feel sick. I tell Mom and she pulls the car over quickly. I get out and throw up over and over until all my breakfast is all over the ground. Mom cleans my face with some tissues.

"You smell awful," she says. "We'll have to wash your face before you meet your teacher." Her voice is mad but she doesn't spank me.

"I'm sorry, I couldn't help it."

"I know you're nervous, but you have to control yourself." I don't know that word, *nervous*. I hope it doesn't mean I'm sick and have to go see the doctor. I don't like doctors.

When I get back in the car David looks away and holds his nose the rest of the way to school.

The school is a big building with lots of rooms. We find a toilet room where Mom washes my face and I rinse my mouth out. Then we go to David's classroom. I stand by the door while Mom goes in to talk to David's teacher. They both look over at me and the teacher nods her head to something Mom says. Then Mom kisses David good bye and says, "Be good, David. Listen to your teacher."

She takes my hand and we walk down the hall to my classroom. It's full of kids. No one notices me. I hold on tight to Mom's hand as we walk to the front of the room where the teacher is standing.

The teacher leans over close to my face. She holds out her hand to me and says, in a quiet voice, "Hi, Nita. I'm Mrs. Semeras. Welcome to our class. I'm happy you will be one of my students. There are many nice children in this class and I know you will make friends with all of them."

I take her hand; it's very soft. When I look at her I feel something good inside my tummy. She's beautiful, almost as beautiful as Mama, with dark skin and hair, and eyes that, like Mama's, are not brown or green but somewhere in between. Standing next to her, I feel safe for the first time since Mr. Bakas took me away in the green and white car.

Mom leans over to hug me. "Nita, I hope you're a good girl," she says. "Do your best for Mrs. Semeras. I'll be back to get you this afternoon."

Mrs. Semeras walks with Mom to the door and I hear her saying I will be okay.

Sousanna

What now? I stand perfectly still to see what will happen next. Mom told me to watch the other children and do what they did, but they're all doing different things and I don't know which ones I should follow.

Mrs. Semeras comes and puts her arms around my shoulders. She leans into my ear and whispers, "Nita, I have a secret. Can you keep a secret? You must promise to not tell anyone."

I turn so our faces are almost touching. "Yes, I like secrets. I promise I won't tell anyone."

"I am from Greece, too. My family still lives in Greece, and sometimes I go there to visit them, and they come here to visit me. I read about you in the newspaper many months ago when you came here with the other children, and when I learned you were coming to our school, I asked for you to be in my class. I will take good care of you and help you learn many things. And, my dear Nita, you can tell me anything. I will keep your secrets as you have promised to keep mine. You are safe here."

I look right into her eyes and put my arms around her so tight and lay my head into her shoulder. She holds me, and I don't want to let go.

I love her.

Then she looks at another girl that has curly red hair and freckles all over her face and says, "Joni, will you be a friend to Nita? She is new to our country and is still learning many things, including our language. I think you two would make nice friends."

Joni takes my hand. "Yes, ma'am," she says. We look at each other and giggle. She has a little gap between her front teeth that looks funny but her green eyes are friendly.

When Mrs. Semeras asks us to sit on the floor in a circle, Joni sits next to me and takes my hand. I like her. I look at her and think she's like my friend Emilia in Greece. They are both fun and funny, and nice.

Joni leans over and whispers in my ear, "Nita, you must look at the teacher, not stare at me."

I lean to her and whisper in her ear, "My name is not Nita; it's Sousanna."

Joni giggles. Mrs. Semeras looks at us and puts her finger to her lips. "Shhhhh."

At lunch Joni stays by my side. We sit together at a long table. Two other girls come sit at the table with us.

"That's Laura and Cindy," Joni reminds me. "This is Nita."

"Sousanna," I say. They don't answer.

"Joni, are we still playing after school today?" the girl called Laura asks as she opens her lunch box. It has the same Barbie on it as mine.

"Sure. Nita, ask your mom if you can come over to my house and play after school today."

"I think I can come, too," says Cindy, also arranging her lunch from her box. "Let's all bring our Barbies to play with."

After school Joni walks to my car with me and I ask Mom if I can go play with the girls at Joni's house.

Joni sticks her head through the open window of the car. "Hi, Mrs. Brown. I'm Joni Meyers. I got to be Nita's friend all day today. She's funny. She tried to trick me, saying her name was Sousanna. Can she come to my house and play?"

Mom looks angry. "Not today, Joni. Nita, get in the car, now. And, Joni, her name is Nita."

Joni slowly pulls herself away from the window. She looks at me and whispers, "Sorry if I got you in trouble." She squeezes my hand. "I'll be your friend again tomorrow, for as long as you want me to be." She lets go of my hand and walks away toward the yellow school bus, but she turns around and waves. "Bye. See you tomorrow."

I get in the car. Mom doesn't look at me or talk to me. She doesn't ask me if I like school or if everybody was nice. She just stares straight ahead with her eyebrows pulled together and her lips pressed together.

After supper she calls me from my room. She's in the living room, sitting in one of the chairs. Dad is sitting in the chair on the other side of the sofa.

"Nita, we've told you over and over not to say your old name ever again," Mom says. Her voice is hard. "You belong to us now and you must obey our rules." She looks at Dad. He's looking at the floor. "Jack, she needs to be spanked for disobeying. It's the only way she's going to learn her lesson."

Dad glances at her, then me, then back to the floor. "I don't know, Margaret. She's still trying to adjust."

"She's trying to adjust? What about me? What about my adjusting to this girl crying for her family day and night? She has to learn her lesson. She needs to be spanked."

Dad slowly stands up and unbuckles his belt. He pulls it out of its belt loops and looks sorrowfully at me as he folds it in half.

All of a sudden I know what he's going to do. He's going to hit me with that belt. I run screaming to my room and slam the door shut. I lean against it so he can't open it.

The door pushes against my back.

"Nita, let me in."

"No, you're going to hurt me. I want my Papa. He'll get you if you hurt me."

The door pushes against me so hard I fall forward and land on my knees, like Mama did when Mr. Bakas took me away. Dad comes in the room and stands over me. "Get up and go lean over the bed."

I'm shaking and I feel sick but I go to the bed because he might hurt me worse if I don't do what he says.

"This is for crying for your mama and papa," he says. "Don't do that anymore."

I shriek when the belt comes down across my bottom. "Ow, it hurts! Don't do it again, please," I beg through my sobs.

But the belt burns across my bottom again. "And that one is for saying your name is Sousanna. Your name is Nita now. Do you understand?"

I bury my head into the mattress, crying as much from shock and betrayal as pain.

Dad sits on the bed next to me. "Nita, you must forget your old family and home. This is your life now. We are your mother and father, no one else." He strokes my hair, only once.

After a while my wails become sniffles, and he says, "Hey, I want to know about your first day at school. How was it? Did you like it?"

I answer without looking at him. "I like Mrs. Semeras. She's nice. And I have a new friend, Joni. She helped me all day and invited me to play at her—"

"What's going on in here? Did she learn her lesson?" I startle, but don't look at my mother.

"Yes, I think she understands," Dad says.

"Good. Nita, get ready for bed. Come with me, Jack; I need to talk to you." She walks away.

Sousanna

As I lie in bed I think of Joni. She's tiny and delicate like Mama, and she's kind. I try to go to sleep quickly so I can wake up and be back at school with Mrs. Semeras and Joni. I'm going to tell them both what Dad did to me.

The next morning David and I ride the bus to school. When I see Joni get on the bus I stand up in my seat and wave to her. "Joni, come sit by me."

She waves back and hurries to my seat. She sits in the empty space next to me and I hug her, happy to be together again.

On the ride to school I tell Joni everything that had happened last night. I tell her my name really is Sousanna, and my real family is in Greece but they're going to come find me and take me home.

"I think you should not talk about that to anybody else so you don't get in trouble again. But you can tell me everything, and I won't tell on you again. I promise. Let's be best friends."

I think of Emilia again. I miss her a lot. She's my best friend at home; but Joni can be my best friend in America. "Yes, I want to be best friends. You're nice to me. I'm glad Mrs. Semeras asked you to help me and be my friend."

Joni holds my hand. "We can have lots of friends, but we'll always be the most special to each other, and tell each other all our secrets."

Chapter 31

Ilias

"Ilias, you're a smart boy and you have a real talent with numbers and shapes. You'll be very successful one day," Christo said one afternoon as he studied the sketch of a rocking chair Ilias drew.

The warmth of appreciation flowed through Ilias. "My mother said I would be the most successful of all her children."

Christo patted his head. "I think she's right. Mothers usually are, you know."

Ilias enjoyed designing furniture. Seeing the shape of it in his head, figuring out exactly how to build it so that it turned out like he envisioned. Christo helped him learn the math and geometry he needed, and the rest seemed to come naturally. He now did most of the design work. Christo constructed the furniture according to his plans, and then Marios finished it by carving intricate patterns into the pieces and staining the wood a magnificent mahogany, pine, or maple.

Ilias finally belonged somewhere. Christo and Stathoula had welcomed him into their home, just as Marios had promised. They treated the brothers well, and Christo patiently taught them everything they needed to know about furniture making. He wasn't stingy, either, in his commendation or his payment for their work.

"You boys may be young," he often said, "but you're fine apprentices. One day you boys will own your own furniture shop and put me out of business."

It was embarrassing at first; no one had ever praised Ilias that way and he blushed with awkwardness. He got used to it quickly, though, and now it was pride that warmed his face at the compliments. Christo was like a father to him. Ilias hadn't hated

Papa the way Marios did; but now, the way Christo treated them made him understand Marios's feelings. Papa was never like that.

Mrs. Stathoula was good to him, too. Nothing like Mama, of course; she was the best in the world. He'd give anything to be able to see her, feel her warm hand on his cheek, hear her say his name.

Even Marios didn't tease him as much as when they were back in Pirgos. Not that he'd quit completely. If he thought Ilias was being noticed more than he was, he'd still make jabs, saying things like, "Hey, Ilias, are you still scared of the dark? Have you found a corner in this house where you can go and hide like you did in Pirgos?" But Ilias didn't care.

Another good thing about living here was that Ilias was able to learn all the things he missed from not going to school. Besides the math for their work, Christo taught him how to read a little bit. One book on Christo's shelf fascinated him: *How to Make, Use, and Save Money*. He spent hours trying to work through it, but there were so many words he didn't know.

One evening Christo and Marios came in and saw Ilias studying the book. "Can you read that?" Christo asked.

"I don't know most of the words, but I want to learn how to make a lot of money."

Christo chuckled. "How about we read it together, and I'll help you with the words you don't know. Maybe we'll both learn how to make a lot of money."

"If you're going to be the money genius, you can manage our pay," Marios said. Ilias grinned. He was made for this.

Each week, he paid their expenses and divided what was left between his brother and himself. Then, taking the advice of Christo and the book, Ilias put most of his money aside in a box under his bed. He just shook his head as Marios spent his wages as fast as he earned them.

His brother had no responsibility with his money; he wasted it on his playboy life. Then he'd ask Ilias to lend him money. If Ilias didn't want to, Marios would act like he used to in Pirgos when he teased and embarrassed him. But Ilias didn't want to give away all his money. Now, after reading the money book with Christo, he knew exactly what to do.

He was ready when Marios came to him the next weekend and said, "Ilias, my little home-body brother, why won't you share your fortune with me? I know you're saving your money and hiding it under our bed. You stay in this room and never go out. Let me have some of your money and I will have a good time for both of us."

"Sure, Marios," Ilias answered. "You're a big playboy now and need a lot of money. Here, take these drachmas; but for every two I give to you, you owe me those plus one more back on pay day."

"Sure, sure. It's a deal." Marios's answer was so cavalier Ilias wondered if there'd be a fight over it come pay day, but Marios kept his promise and paid him one extra drachma for each two he borrowed. Ilias watched his money grow and began thinking. How could he get other people to do what he had bargained with Marios? He liked money; it made him feel important and safe.

Even though Ilias had control of the money, Marios still tried to tell him what to do with it. Ilias argued when Marios insisted a small portion of their earnings was to go to Pirgos to help their family. Finally Ilias decided it wasn't worth fighting over. Marios could have his say on this, but the portion would be small. At least it gave him a reason to write to Mama.

Dear Mama... Ilias painstakingly formed each letter. Then he handed the pencil to Christo. It felt good to write those words, but they'd be there all day if he had to write the whole note. So he and Marios told Christo what to write in the message home. Marios added their money to the envelope, then ran to give it to Angelia.

Marios was always meeting girls, but Angelia had an aunt who lived in Pirgos. She rode the bus there every month to visit, and offered to take letters from Ilias and Marios to their family. It was their only connection with home.

When Angelia returned to Athens, she brought back news of home and messages from Mama. Always, Mama said she was praying for them each day. She sent her sons her love, and told them to take care of themselves and wished them health and success. Rarely did she mention her own life or how she and Papa and Anastasia were doing; her messages were all about the boys.

So the photo included with this letter was a double shock. The fact that their parents had even gotten a picture of themselves made was a surprise. It showed Mama standing with her hand on Papa's shoulder as he sat in his broken chair, leaning over a cane.

A cane? That was the second shock. Mama and Papa both looked so much older than just a few months ago, and Papa didn't look hearty and well but like a broken-down old man. Their faces were sorrowful.

Marios asked Angelia, "What's happening with our family?"

"I'm sorry, but things are getting worse for your family," she said. "They were doing well for a while, selling souvlaki sticks your father made. But now he's ill and your mother worries all the time for him. Anastasia is engaged, but not to the man she wanted."

Ilias felt the old quivering in his stomach. He would be sick with worry if he didn't figure out a way get over it. He looked at Marios, hoping for guidance from his older brother.

"We can't concern ourselves with these problems," Marios said. "We have our work here now. Papa will have to take care of them. It's his doing, anyway. We're doing all we can, sending money."

Yes, let Papa take care of himself, Ilias thought. Marios wasn't worrying himself sick over them, so Ilias wouldn't either.

Ilias kept the photo under his pillow. After Marios fell asleep, he talked to Mama. "I think you would be proud of me, Mama," he whispered to the paper face. "I'm doing what you said. I'll be the most successful of all. I love you and miss you. Keep praying for me. I'm lonely without you."

§

June 1961

"We want to be on our own. I'll be 14 next month and it's time for me to take care of myself and my brother. Will you help us find a room to rent?" Marios said to Christo.

Christo scratched his head. "Boys, I know you want to be independent but you're both still too young to be on your own. Stay here a while yet."

"No, it wouldn't be right. We must learn to rely only on ourselves." Marios's insistence paid off. Christo told them about a friend with a room they could rent for a small fee. It was close to the center of town so they could continue working for Christo.

Was it just to have the freedom to run around town chasing girls that Marios had wanted their own place? Ilias wasn't sure, but he didn't really care. The more Marios was gone, the more quiet time he had to think and study and plan.

Chapter 32

Anastasia

Anastasia was pleased that Nedtarios didn't wait until they were married to begin caring for her and her parents, but began building his future with them immediately. First he paid Mr. Yanni for the house and land her family had worked for and lived on through so many years. Then he hired builders to add two bedrooms, a kitchen, and a bathroom. They now had a real house. Finally he had running water installed, and marble floors. Anastasia had never imagined living in such luxury. Last of all, a telephone.

She couldn't enjoy it as much as she thought she would. She was too worried about her father. His health steadily worsened. No one knew what was wrong with him, only that his tremors grew progressively worse. He often fell off balance, so he began using a cane to steady himself. He was always fatigued, but kept pushing to work just a little more.

Two months before she and Nedtarios were to be married, Papa got suddenly worse. One morning he couldn't get out of bed. His body became stiff like a board and shook uncontrollably.

"Anastasia, run get the doctor, run!" Mama yelled. "No, no—call him, call him on the telephone. Hurry." Mama tried to hold Papa in her arms to calm his body, but he was too big for her to contain, so she laid on top of him to keep him from falling out of the bed while Anastasia fumbled with the telephone until she was able to dial the number she knew to be the doctor.

"This is Anastasia Demetriou, my father is ill and shaking. Help us!" With the doctor on his way, she dialed another number she had memorized. "Nedtarios, please come. Papa is very ill. Come quickly."

The doctor and Nedtarios arrived at the same time. The doctor walked into her parents' room, took one look at Papa, and said to call for an ambulance.

Anastasia watched, helpless, as strangers barged into their home and carried her father out. There was nothing she could do to help, and everywhere she went she seemed to be in someone's way.

"I must go with him. He is my husband; I have to care for him." It was Mama, pleading to go in the ambulance. Anastasia hurried to her.

"Come, Mama, Nedtarios will take us in his car."

At the hospital, they spent a long time waiting in a small room until someone came to tell them that Papa would need to stay there several days so the doctors could treat him.

"Go home," they said. "Come back Friday. We'll take care of him; there's nothing for you to do here."

Mama refused to leave, and Anastasia stayed with her. Nedtarios had to go back to his restaurant, but whenever he could he came to be with them.

On Friday, the doctors said Papa could go home. There were so many other patients in the large room that Anastasia held up the blanket from Papa's bed to give him some privacy while Mama helped him get dressed. When Nedtarios arrived, the doctor called all four of them into his office.

"Niko, you are very ill," the doctor said. "You have a condition called Parkinson's Disease. Unfortunately, we have no cure for this disease. It will get worse. You will slowly lose control of all your muscles, until you are completely bed-ridden. I am sorry to tell you this, but you and your family must be prepared."

Anastasia felt tears gather in her eyes. She looked over at her parents. Their eyes were dry; their faces were set. Determined.

Mama patted Papa's hand. "Don't worry," she said. "I will take care of you. We'll survive, just as we always have."

Anastasia blinked back her tears. She would be strong, like Mama. No words came from her mouth, but in her heart Anastasia vowed to care for both of them.

§

August 1961

Anastasia felt beautiful in her long gown covered with lace and beads and a veil that trailed on the ground behind her. She held onto her father's arm as he leaned on his cane. They walked slowly through the streets of their village in the traditional wedding parade, so all the neighbors could see the lovely bride and throw her white carnation petals as a wish of happiness.

Standing at the threshold of the church, Anastasia tried not to think about being in love, about happily-ever-after with a man she wished to marry, a man who adored her as she adored him. Her life was doing what others said, doing what was best for everyone else instead of herself, working for others. That had always been her life, and it did not change now.

It was best to focus on the good in the arrangement. Nedtarios may not be the husband she'd have chosen, but he was a good man and a hard worker. He'd provide for her and her parents, give them a good life. She was thankful for the security and comfort he could give her parents. Perhaps love would someday come to them, as it had to Mama and Papa.

There was something else to be grateful for, too. Marios had returned to Pirgos for her wedding. He didn't seem to carry the anger in him that he did as a young boy. He was playful and good-natured, and brought a lightness that had been missing from their home for many months.

Anastasia knew it was a shock to Marios when he first saw the condition their father was in. Papa had still been robust when Marios left; her brother hadn't witnessed the gradual decline, so the difference was stark to him. She'd seen it in the way Marios stopped still for a moment when he first saw Papa.

She'd seen Marios surprised again when Nedtarios told him of Papa's involvement with the resistance fighters in the war. He'd looked at Papa with new respect after that, and treated him with the honor due a father.

It would be hard to say goodbye to Marios again; his coming home had been exactly what the family needed. It was the first step to healing the rifts among them and bringing them all together again.

Now she could enter the church with a contented heart.

Chapter 33

Sousanna

December 1961

"Okay, class, since you are in second grade, your song will come right after the first grade. You'll come in from over here..."

Our music class is preparing for the Christmas play. My music teacher doesn't like me for some reason. I don't know why because all my other teachers like me. The first day of music class she called me to her desk and asked, "Where are you from? Who brought you here? You know you're a foreigner, don't you?"

She wanted to know about my family! I started to tell her everything. "My real name is Sousanna. I came from Greece. Mr. Bakas took me from Mama and brought me here. Someday Papa will come to take me ho..."

"Quiet," she interrupted. "You're a very lucky little girl to live in America and be adopted by good parents that love you. Go back and sit down, and don't ever say such things again in my class."

Why was she so mean? And I don't know what "adopted" means. I had to try hard not to cry as I walked back to my seat. Joni gave me a hug when I sat down next to her.

Today the music teacher wants us all to sing so she can arrange us how she wants us to stand in the play. I sing loud so she can hear me. It works because she's coming toward me.

"Nita, come here."

I told her I'm really Sousanna, but she won't say my real name. I don't like the name Nita. It sounds ugly and nobody even says it right. And it's not my name. How come nobody in America wants to say Sousanna?

I leave the group and go to the teacher. Maybe she'll say I can stand next to Joni.

"Nita, you can't be in the musical. You don't have the necessary range."

I've learned to talk American pretty good, but that's another word I don't know. I ask, "Where can I get the right range? Can my mom get it at the store? If I get some, can I be in the play? Please let me sing, and stand by Joni."

"No. You can work the lights. You'll sit by the light switches in the auditorium and turn them on and off when I tell you. I'll write it down, so you can't mess it up."

After school I beg Joni, "Please talk to Mrs. Warenski and ask her to let me sing in the play. She loves you because you can sing so beautiful. If you ask maybe she'll let me."

The next day Joni gives me the bad news. Mrs. Warenski said, "No. There's no place for her in the choir. She'll work the lights."

If that's my part in the play, she can count on me. I'll do my job the best anyone ever did working the lights.

After school I tell Mom what Mrs. Warenski said about me not having range.

"I might have known you wouldn't even be able to sing properly," Mom says. "You'll have to go to the play with Joni; I'm not going to be embarrassed by you working lights instead of being onstage."

Even though she's upset with me for not having range, Mom gets me a new red dress with sparkles on it just for Christmas. I wear it on the night of the musical, with white gloves and white socks with red shoes that match the dress. I feel beautiful. Joni's parents pick me up and take me to the play.

When we get to the auditorium, I go stand near the light switches. They're right by the door. That means I get to greet everybody as they come in. I try to say something nice to everyone as they enter the auditorium.

"Welcome."

"Your dress is very pretty."

"I hope you enjoy the show."

"Merry Christmas."

When Joni's mother and father walk by they both give me a big hug and say they're proud of me for greeting everyone so nicely and working the lights for the play.

"That's a very responsible job," Joni's mother says.

Mrs. Warenski sees me greeting everyone. She frowns at me. But she doesn't say anything, so I keep doing it.

§

1963

"Now let me hear you sing *The Star-Spangled Banner*. Every word has to be correct." Dad is helping me get ready for my test to become an American citizen. I only have to sing one song, but it's a hard one. My music teacher from last year said I didn't have any range, and I guess she was right. No matter how much I practice I can't hit the right notes. Dad laughs out loud at my out-of-tune voice every time I practice *The Star-Spangled Banner*.

"Now say the Pledge of Allegiance," Dad says. "Stand straight and speak loud and clear with your right hand over your heart...Tell me again the name of the president and the capitol of the United States...What are you going to say when he asks why you want to be an American citizen..."

"I'll tell him that America is a very nice place to live with nice houses and plenty of food, and good schools to learn a lot of things, and people can be free." That's true, but I still want to go home to my real family, even if we don't have nice things and a lot of food. But I can't tell that to anyone, especially the judge.

There's so much to remember. What if I forget something? Will Dad have to spank me? Will I be sent back to Greece? Will the judge put me in jail? Nobody tells me. My stomach gets shaky and I can't move when I think about it, so I keep practicing, over and over and over.

Finally Dad says I'm ready. "I have a special bedtime story for you tonight," he says. He pulls out a book that has a picture of an old yiayia sewing a flag on the front. "This is the story of Betsy Ross. She made the first American flag." He reads me the story.

When the story is over, he says, "Tomorrow, you'll get your own American flag. Then you'll be an American. Think of that. You'll be a real American."

Mom comes in and I don't know what to think. She never comes to tell me goodnight anymore, and she never helps me practice for the citizenship test. She says she has to put pin curls in my hair before I go to sleep so my hair will look nice for tomorrow. Dad leaves.

I go stand in front of Mom while she yanks the brush through my short hair, so hard that it hurts. When Mama brushed my hair, she was always gentle, and petted me. Mom never does that. She twists my hair tightly and pins it into pin curls.

"Mom, when did you and Dad become American citizens?"

"Your father and I were born in America, so we've always been Americans. Only people who come from other countries and want to be American citizens must go through this process. After tomorrow you'll no longer be a Greek—you'll officially be an American. I hope you're grateful for what we've done for you."

I don't know what to say so I just tell her, "Thank you." That makes her smile and not pull my hair so hard.

In the morning I wake up early so I can practice my song and the Pledge of Allegiance. Mom comes in my bedroom. "I could hear you singing all the way down the hall. At least you know all the words." I don't think she likes my singing my either.

"Come sit at your vanity so I can fix your hair." She takes out the hair pins and fluffs all the curls until they make a row of curly hair around the sides and back of my head. She looks pleased with the result. I think the curls looks like ear muffs, but I don't dare say anything.

Mom lays out clothes for me to wear to the ceremony on my bed: my favorite white dress with red polka dots that has a double red bow to tie in back; my red petticoat from Sears that still fits; red shoes; white lace socks; white gloves; a white hat with tiny red flowers on it; and a pearl necklace. Mom and Dad and David gave me the necklace to remember this special day.

I ask Mom if I can wear my red sweater. Her answer is direct and simple. "No."

Dad keeps me close to him all day. It makes me feel safe, and I like it because I don't feel that way very much since I left home. Some grownups go first, and I watch what they do so I'll be sure to get it right.

When it's my turn, Dad walks to the front of the courtroom with me, holding my hand as tightly as I hold his. We both stand tall as I answer all the questions and recite the Pledge of Allegiance and sing the national anthem. Then the judge asks me to walk forward, and he hands me a folded American flag.

Dad lifts me high in his arms. All the people in the room clap with Mom and David. Mom takes my picture. Something inside me feels proud. This is what I always wanted to be: The American.

Chapter 34

Marios

May 1967

"Angelia says Papa is getting worse quickly," Marios told Ilias. "I'm going home this weekend to see him and Mama. Do you want to come?"

"No. I have work to do. I don't care to see him, anyway. I don't know why you changed your mind about him, but then he didn't force you to leave home."

Marios recognized the bitterness in his brother's voice; he'd once felt the same, after all. But not anymore. Now he saw his father with the eyes and heart of a man.

As an adult, he could better understand what his father had lived through. As a boy Marios hadn't realized what the war had done to Greece and its people. Years of listening to the stories of older people, who'd lived through the same events as his father, taught him that it wasn't just Papa who'd struggled; it was a whole country.

The war had taken so much from the people, from families and communities, from the land. His father wasn't a coward, but a victim of war and circumstance. In fact, Papa had been one of the most courageous, working with the resistance against the Nazis.

The decisions Papa had made that Marios couldn't understand as a boy—to stay where he knew he had work instead of venturing into the unknown; to let his young sons go off to the city alone; to let his beloved daughter go with a stranger to a foreign land so she'd have a life of plenty instead of a life of hunger and poverty—these were decisions born of true love.

He wished he'd understood that before he'd influenced his little brother to hate Pirgos, and their father. When they first came to Athens, Marios had been full of rage and misunderstanding, and he'd pounded that into Ilias, too. It had set deeper in Ilias. His brother was more hardheaded and determined.

Marios tried to explain the reality to Ilias.

"Listen carefully; I have something important to say," he said, putting his hand on his little brother's shoulder. "I have done a bad thing to you. I was wrong to teach you to hate our home and Papa. I was just a boy, and I was angry. I wanted everyone else to be angry too. Ilias, you must know Papa and Mama are good. They have worked hard and loved us well."

Ilias shrugged off Marios's hand. "I'm working. I don't care about Pirgos or Papa. Go back to work, leave me alone with your sentimental crap. And you don't ever have to tell me our Mama was good. She was the best, and she loved us well—despite our no-good father."

Marios tried again and again, but nothing he said made a difference. He didn't know how to break through the festering resentment Ilias had over being sent away as a boy. Finally he gave up trying and left Ilias with his bitterness in Athens while he went home each month to visit their parents.

In Pirgos Marios spent time simply sitting with his ill father, talking together. It hurt his heart to watch Niko suffer, but their discussions helped Marios understand his father. He knew he would always remember Papa telling him, "You have only known me as a man who failed to provide for his family, but I was not always weak. Once I was a brave soldier, looked up to by everyone for my strength and courage. I love our country and fought many years for her; but we could not keep the bad days from coming and destroying everything we loved."

Marios clasped his father's hand, clutching the amber beads. "My Papa is the most courageous man I know."

He spent time with Mama, too, working in the garden, walking to the market, or having a cup of coffee together in the early evening. She had little to say, but Marios admired her quiet strength and her concern for others. She cared more about helping neighbors than talking about them in the gossip groups. When anyone was in need she was there, helping any way she could, even if it was just to take them roses from the garden. All the neighbors agreed, "Katerina is a good friend to everyone and talks about no one."

Marios

Marios remembered working by her side in the fields as a little boy as she taught him to work hard without complaint, and take pride in his work—even if that work was nothing more than making the best bundles. "Look for broken or yellow leaves and throw them out," she told him. "Always check to make sure all the vegetables are laying in the same direction and tied tight with the twine, so they don't come loose."

Now, caring for Niko, cleaning the house, cooking for the family, and looking after Anastasia's three little girls while she and Nedtarios ran the restaurant, she still worked hard and never complained. There was always a sweet smile on her face, and her beautiful eyes had what Marios thought might have been a gleam of mischief had her life been different.

Marios had come to know and respect Nedtarios, too. He was good to Anastasia and a good father to their three little girls. He was a friend and companion to Niko, doing anything he could to ease his father-in-law's life as much as possible.

Anastasia seemed content and didn't complain. But Marios wished more for her. Her life might be easier if she could get a little education.

"Anastasia, it's important to learn to read and write. Why will you not try?" he asked her.

"Nedtarios says I know everything I need to know to take care of our family and work with him in the restaurant," she answered.

Marios pressed her. "Do you want to be illiterate your whole life?"

"Stop, Marios. I'm a good mother and wife. I take care of Mama and help her with Papa. I may be illiterate, but I am here."

Sobered by her response, and hoping to calm her, Marios wrapped his arm around her shoulders. "Let's go sit in the fresh air together. I'm sorry; please, forgive me. You are a good wife and mother. A good daughter to our parents. I know you're the one with the hard life. You're here taking care of everyone, just as you've always done. You are the one with the courage." He wiped the tears from her cheeks. "Anastasia, you are the cement in all of our lives."

Anastasia gave him a weak smile. They walked outside arm in arm to sit under the pergola covered with tiny white blooms of spicy fragrant jasmine.

Sousanna

After a few moments of silence, Marios said, "Sitting here now I can barely remember the one-room house that stood here, where we were all hungry and sleeping on a dirt floor. Do you remember the cold nights we laid so close to each other trying to keep warm by the fire?"

He paused to close his eyes and breathe in the fragrance of jasmine, then reached to pat Anastasia on the knee. "I know sometimes it's difficult for you with Nedtarios, but I look around and see what he has done for our family. Sister, he is a good man and has built a good house and home for you and our parents."

Anastasia looked away before responding. "Yes, Marios, we have a good home." Then with a lighter tone, as if she wanted to change the mood, she said, "And we have beautiful furniture in our home because I have two brothers that are very talented. You and Ilias have given us the best of your furniture for every room in our house."

That night Marios sat next to Papa's bed. Papa was now too weak to hold his head or body still from the tremors. Even his voice was weak. When he spoke, Marios had to lean in close to hear Papa's words.

"Marios, this has been a hard life for your mother and me. Many days I pray to die so I will no longer burden your mother. She is a good woman, the best woman. I want her to find contentment. Marios, you must find Sousanna to give your mother peace. To give me peace."

Marios pushed the thick, gray hair from Papa's forehead. "I will keep my vow, Papa; I will find her. I, too, want to see my mother resting from all her work and to be content. As Mama always says, God ascends stairs and descends stairs. With His help, I will find my sister, for Mama and for you."

The next morning as Marios was preparing to leave for Athens, Nedtarios pulled him aside.

"Your father is getting worse fast. You must see it yourself."

"Yes. Each time I leave I fear it will be the last time I see him. But what can we do?"

"I talked to a doctor who says we should have an operation done in Niko's head to help with the tremors and convulsions. I've talked with your parents about it. Your father is afraid—he doesn't trust doctors. And your mother can't understand why they must do an operation in his head."

"But you think it would help?"

"Yes, I think so. There's a good hospital in Patras that can do the operation, and you can probably convince them that it'll help, that they should try it. But first we must have enough money. I've been trying to save up, but it's too expensive for me to do on my own. I need your help to pay for the operation. "

"We'll find the money. I'll get Ilias to help, too. He has a lot of money saved up. And I'll convince Mama and Papa to do it, somehow. If there's any chance to help Papa, we have to do it. He's suffered enough, him and Mama both."

When Marios returned to Athens he explained the situation to Ilias. "We need to give Nedtarios the money to pay for the operation," he concluded. "With what he has saved, and what you have saved, plus what I can put in, we'll have enough."

"Why should I give him my money?" Ilias demanded. "He sent me out of his house when I was just a little boy. I owe him nothing."

"He's our Papa—"

"He should have remembered that before throwing me out of his house."

"Then do it for Mama. Do you know how much it hurts her to see Papa like this? And how hard she has to work to care for him?"

"Okay, I'll give you the money. But only for Mama's sake."

Chapter 35

Sousanna

"David, Nita! Come in here. Your mom and I need to talk to you." David comes out of his room the same time I come out of mine. He puts his hand on my arm to stop me.

"It's never good when they want to talk this late." He mimes taking a drink, and he doesn't mean water. "Don't say anything; just listen. It's best that way."

Now I'm really nervous. Mom and Dad can be unreasonable when they've had too much to drink. Will Mom think I've done something wrong again? My stomach turns to jelly as I follow David to the living room.

Mom and Dad are sitting in their favorite chairs. They don't look mad. In fact, they're smiling. Even Mom. And her eyes are sparkling. I can't remember the last time I've seen her so happy and excited.

"We have a surprise for you," she says. She looks at Dad. "Tell them, Jack."

Dad barely has time to open his mouth before Mom dismisses him with a wave of her hand. "Never mind, I'll tell them." She turns to me and David. "We're taking a family trip."

David and I look at each other. Neither of us says anything. It's the middle of the school term, so we can't be taking a trip anytime soon. And by the time summer comes...we know better than to expect any plan to last that long. We just have to be agreeable while Mom and Dad scheme, then forget about it when they do.

"Aren't you excited? Say something. Nita, wipe that look off your face."

I arrange my face into what I hope is a happy expression and glance at David. He always knows how to please Mom.

"It's been a long time since we've had a family trip," he says. "We were in elementary school the last time. Where are we going?"

"I have it all mapped out," Dad answers. "We're going to California. On the way we'll see the Grand Canyon, Carlsbad Caverns, and the Petrified Forest. Maybe some other things, too. You kids should see some natural monuments and learn all you can." He's talking like he used to, when David and I were young and he wanted to help us with our schoolwork.

"When are we going?" I want to be part of the conversation. Against my better judgment, I'm getting excited.

"In three weeks. The whole trip will take two weeks."

"What about school? The writing competition is in three weeks. The whole junior high is..." I blurt without thinking, and stop talking as soon as I realize it. I look down; Mom'll never put up with me talking back like that. I should've kept quiet, like David told me to.

But when she speaks, her voice is kind. "Don't worry; we know the competition is important to you, so we're not leaving until after you compete. We talked to all your teachers, yours and David's, and they've excused you for the trip. They all agree that you'll learn more on an educational trip like this than you will in the classroom."

Dad stands up. "Let's see some excitement, you two. We're off to California. And guess what we're going to do when we get there?"

David and I look at each other, then back at Dad. We both shake our heads. There's no telling what they've come up with.

"We're going to a real, live taping of Truth or Consequences."

"Really?" I bounce up and down, clapping my hands like a little kid. That's my favorite show. Well, that and Bonanza. Little Joe is so cute.

Dad grins and ruffles my hair. Mom gets up and hugs David. Everyone is smiling and jolly. Maybe this trip is just what we need. Someday Papa will come get me and take me home to Greece, where I belong; but until then, this is my family. I want it to be a happy one.

For three weeks we prepare. In the evenings David and I study the map with Dad to mark out the route we'll take, and we read about all the places we'll go in the Encyclopedia Britannica. Mom makes lists of things we need, and on weekends we go shopping for new clothes, and books and games to take in the car.

Sousanna

Finally the day comes. Dad stuffs our luggage in the trunk. David and I each have a small bag of things to do. I have a couple of books, a drawing pad with colored map pencils, and some notebooks to write in. There's a bag of snacks on the seat between us, but we can't have any unless Mom says it's okay.

Leaving Tulsa is exciting, but riding in the car gets boring soon. The road's not smooth enough to draw or write, and reading too much while we're moving makes me queasy. David and I play some car games until Mom says we're too loud and to quiet down.

I spend hours staring out the window, watching the telephone poles pass. I think about Marios and Ilias. Anastasia. Mama and Papa. I miss all of them. I replay in my mind everything I can remember about them. I think about Mama's gray dress and soft arms. Her stroking my hair and kissing my cheeks as she dressed me in the mornings. Papa, tall and strong with blond hair like mine, cuddling me in his lap and telling me stories after his work. Anastasia hugging me and swirling me around and blowing bubbles, and my brothers playing with me. Marios's cigar rings and Ilias sticking his tongue at me. Our house, one little cement room with a dirt floor. It didn't have the things my home in America does—no carpets or sofa or refrigerator or TV. Not much of anything, really, except for the one thing I crave but can't get in America: love.

I remember the morning Mr. Bakas took me away. Papa had given me an egg, and said it would keep me strong until we were all together again. Together again—that's how I know he's going to come get me. When I was little, I didn't know how big America is, or far away it is from Greece; but now I understand why it's taking so long for Papa to find me.

I remember Miss Helena, too. I don't think about her like I do my family, but I want to keep the memory of her telling me to be brave and not let anyone break my spirit. It gives me determination when things are extra hard with Mom.

I guess I'm not the only one letting my thoughts roam back to the past, because out of the blue Dad says, "David, do you remember anything about when you came here?"

"No." David keeps staring out his window. I don't think he wants to reminisce.

"You were a scrawny thing. No teeth, no hair. Three years old and so puny you couldn't even walk. Pitiful."

"But you started improving as soon as we got you," Mom says. Her voice is consoling, like she's afraid David's feelings would be hurt by Dad's comments.

"Yeah, it wasn't long before you were eating us out of house and home," Dad agreed.

"And then you started to sing. We knew from the first time we heard you that you had a gift."

"I always liked to sing."

Mom turned in her seat to look at David. "We were so proud when you were accepted to the Tulsa Boys Choir last year."

"Nita, what do you remember?" Dad asks.

What can I say that won't upset Mom? I remember everything, but she doesn't want to hear it, I'm sure.

"Not much either," I say. That should be safe.

Dad chuckles. "I remember you dancing. We would talk to you, and you were obviously clueless about what we were saying, so you'd just start dancing around. You were so cute."

"I remember how difficult you were," Mom adds flatly. "Most of the time I wondered if we could send you back."

No one says anything else. I look back out at the telephone poles.

§

We're dressed in our best clothes. Mom is wearing a crisp, green, belted dress with blue hat, purse and heels. Dad's in a gray suit, and David's suit is dark blue suit with a red polka-dot bow tie. I'm wearing all pink, from skirt and blouse to jacket, purse and shoes.

There's a whole group of people taking the tour of the studio. We all crowd into the newsroom and watch the news being broadcast. Then we get a tour of the studio, with people showing us how the shows are filmed. Finally it's time to go to the sound stage for the Truth or Consequences taping.

Our seats are in the perfect place, right in the middle. The familiar music starts and lights shine on the stage. In front of the stage, people hold up signs. APPLAUD. Everyone in the room claps as Bob Barker, the host, announces the contestants. "And today's guest star is Michael Landon, our own Little Joe from Bonanza."

I don't need a sign to tell me to applaud now. I'm clapping so hard my hands sting. "Little Joe" on Truth or Consequences. On the very day I get to watch it tape. I can hardly believe it; I get to see him in person. I'm so busy staring at him I don't even pay attention to the show, so it's a surprise when the stage lights go out and it's all over.

Suddenly the lights come back on and Bob Barker walks out again. "Ladies and gentlemen, you are in for a treat. Today we're doing a double taping. In a few minutes you'll be invited to watch another taping of Truth or Consequences."

We clap and cheer with the rest of the audience.

"While we're waiting for the next show to be set, we're going to have a twist contest. The winner will receive a Truth or Consequences board game, and...a dance with Little Joe."

The audience goes wild, but none of them more than me.

"Come on down, everyone. Come on, don't be shy."

A chance to dance with Little Joe? I jump up and excuse myself down the row of people.

"Stop her, Jack. Nita, get back here. Stop her."

I hear Mom, but I don't stop, because I hear another voice, too. *Don't let anyone break your spirit.* I'll be in big trouble later, but it'll be worth it. When will I ever have a chance to dance with Little Joe again? I'm not going to let anyone stop me.

The music comes on and I twist my heart out. I look at the other contestants. A few are really good. They're all adults; I'm the only kid on the stage. I hope that doesn't mean I can't win. I keep twisting until the very last note.

Bob Barker tells the audience to clap for each person as he indicates them; the one who gets the biggest applause wins. He starts pointing to different people. I'm last of all. When he points to me, the applause is thunderous.

Mr. Barker says, "You win, young lady. What's your name?"

He sticks the microphone in front of my face. I start to say "Sou—" but it's not even a squeak. Good thing, because if I said that on TV, Mom would kill me. I take a breath and say, "Nita."

"Well, Nita, you've won a dance with Little Joe Cartwright."

Little Joe—whose real name I now know is Michael Landon—steps out from behind the curtain. He's not as tall as I thought he would be, but he's even cuter than on TV. Chubby Checker starts again and this time I twist with my favorite actor. When that song ends, *Do the Mashed Potato* comes on, and we do the Mashed Potato. It's the most fun I've ever had. The music and dancing ends all too soon.

"You sure can dance," Michael Landon says. He gives me a quick hug and disappears behind the curtain again. Mr. Barker shakes my hand and gives me the board game. I walk off the stage and back up to the stairs to my seat. I walk slowly to savor the moment as long as possible. At least I won't get in trouble until we get back to the hotel. Mom hates to make a scene.

I wish my Greek family was here. They'd be so happy for me. Maybe they'd have gone on stage and danced with me. They're missing so much of my life, and I'm missing so much of theirs.

Mom and Dad don't even look at me when I get back to my seat. Mom's face is set into a deep scowl.

Chapter 36

Marios

Marios paced the halls of the waiting room. His mother and sister, and Nedtarios, sat quietly, but Marios had to release some of the nervous tension in his body. Papa had been in surgery six hours already, and no word yet.

Finally he saw the doctor coming down the hall. Marios read his face immediately; it wouldn't be good news.

"The operation was not as successful as we hoped it would be," the doctor said without preamble. "There is some neurological damage. Be prepared for his condition."

"What do you mean, 'be prepared?'" Marios asked. "This was supposed to heal my father's tremors and make him better."

"We are limited in what we can do," the doctor said, and he walked away.

Mama looked at him, confusion on her face. "Marios, I don't understand. Niko will be better now, won't he? I thought he would be better? What has happened?" Nedtarios and Marios looked at each other. How could they tell her the operation had failed?

"I don't know, Mama; we'll have to wait and see," Marios said. "It will be a while before we can see him. Here, lay here on the sofa and rest until then."

Mama lay on the small leather sofa and closed her eyes. Anastasia sat quietly beside her.

Finally, hours later, they were allowed to see Papa. They tried not to see the patients in the beds on either side of Papa's. The strange smell of the hospital was even stronger here.

Papa was pallid and weak, hooked up to tubes in his nose, his chest, his arms. Marios held his mother, worried she would buckle at seeing her husband in this condition; but she surprised him, again, with her strength. She walked to Papa and put a hand on his.

"Niko, it's me, Katerina. I'm here. You'll be all right. I will take care of you. Rest and get strong so we can go home. Niko, I am here, do you hear me?"

Papa opened his eyes. Marios saw the love that passed between his parents with just a look.

His father's lips moved but no sound came out. Again he tried to speak. It looked like he was trying to say Katerina's name, and the word help.

"I'm here, Niko. Everything will be all right. Rest and get strong."

Papa fell back into a deep sleep. It was obvious he wasn't going to be leaving the hospital anytime soon. No sense in all of them hanging around with no way to help and nothing to do.

"Anastasia, Nedtarios, go home," Marios told them. "It's still early; you can be home before dark. Your children need you. Mama and I will stay here."

They started to protest, but Marios stopped them. "You have a restaurant to run," he reminded Nedtarios, then turned to his sister. "I know you want to help; you always care for everyone. But there's nothing you can do here. Go on home to your children now. You'll be taking care of Papa for a long time to come, once he goes home."

Nedtarios guided Anastasia to the door, while she made Marios promise several times to contact them if Papa got worse, or if he or Mama needed her.

Over the next few days Papa drifted in and out of sleep from the pain medicine. Each time he awoke, his body convulsed. The surgery had stopped the tremors, but the jerking spasms he suffered now were even worse. Marios could hardly stand seeing it. Papa used to be so strong; now he couldn't control his own body.

He and Mama tried to rest in the waiting room. Marios sat on the cold tile floor in front of a chair and leaned his head back onto the seat of the chair. His mother curled on the small sofa. Her small frame fit with little effort. At least she was able to get a little sleep between Papa's periods of wakefulness. It didn't keep her from worrying; Marios could see the creases in her forehead even while she slept.

"Katerina, help me!"

Papa's voice echoed down the hallway. The words were weak and unclear but the urgency was unmistakable. Mama stirred as

Marios jumped up from the floor. He didn't wait for her but ran to his father's room.

"I'm here, Papa. It's me, Marios. I'm here."

"Help me...please...help..." The anguish in Papa's voice, in his face, pierced Marios's heart.

"What do you need, Papa? What can I do?" Marios stroked his father's arm, trying to offer a little comfort.

"Help...can't...move..." Mercifully, he dropped back into sleep.

Marios fell to his knees beside Papa's bed with a sob. Why had he spent all those years fighting with Papa, hating him? He could have been a help to his father, worked with him and learned from him. Why hadn't he seen the strength and courage it took for his father to endure all that life had punished him with? The love that kept him from becoming bitter?

He was still beside the bed when Papa woke again. His father could make tiny movements with his hands and feet, nothing more. Even forming words was a struggle for him. It was a several days before he was able, with Marios's help, to sit up. Marios and Mama had to help him eat. Use the bathroom. Everything. At last the doctor said Papa was well enough to go home.

As well as he's going to get, you mean. The strong, tall, handsome man his father had once been was no more. Now Papa's body was hunched and crippled. He still had convulsions. Was weak. Couldn't do anything for himself. Heaven only knew how Mama and Anastasia would manage to care for him with all the work they had to do. But they'd have to find a way; there was nothing else to do. No one, not even the doctor, could make Papa better.

Nedtarios drove his car to the hospital to pick them up. Marios was so relieved to finally be leaving the hospital he could hardly keep his patience while getting his parents checked out and to the car. He helped Papa into the front seat by Nedtarios, and got in the back with Mama. His mind would be at ease again when they got back to the house, got everything back to normal.

When Nedtarios pulled up in front of the house, a sadness came over Marios. It took him a minute to realize why. Papa was supposed to be well when they came home, not the crippled invalid he became with the surgery. The ghost of his dead hopes, of what Papa should have been, hovered over Marios, unseen and unmentioned but felt down to his bones.

He couldn't dwell on that. As he'd seen his parents do all his life, they would all just have to do the best they could with whatever they were dealt. Right now, he had to get Papa settled so he could go back to Athens. His customers wouldn't wait on him forever.

Marios and Nedtarios helped Papa into the house to rest from the trip home, then Marios stretched out on the sofa for a nap. After all those days in the hospital, sleeping on the floor, he was exhausted.

He tried to relax his mind by thinking about something other than Papa's health. Like this nice house Nedtarios had built. It was a sight better than the old one-room place that had been here when he was boy, with the goat shed behind it.

The goat shed—he'd almost forgotten. It was Papa who taught him how to build, with that old shed.

When they got the goat they had nowhere to keep it out of the weather. Papa told Marios to be on the lookout for discarded boards so they could make a shelter. It took several weeks of gathering boards from around the town, dragging them home one by one until they had enough to begin.

Then one day Papa brought home a bag of nails and a hammer in one hand and a saw in the other. He held them up for Marios to see and bellowed, "Look, Marios. Nails and a hammer from my friend Taki. He knows we have to build a shed for our goat. And Mr. Yanni offered us his new saw to cut the boards. He trusts me because I have always done good work for him. Remember this Marios: make many friends. Help them, and always be good to your neighbors. Then they will be good to you." Another example of Papa's wisdom, that Marios hadn't appreciated as an angry young boy.

As Papa taught him how to build, to meticulously measure and cut each board and hold them in place to be hammered together, he managed to incorporate many good lessons about people and life.

When the shed was finished, Papa wrapped his arm around Marios and pulled him close. "Son, look what we have created," he shouted with exuberance. "A house for a goat. We are great builders." His roaring laughter made Marios laugh too.

It was a good memory. Marios was glad he remembered it. Somehow it made his far-away furniture building seem a little closer, a little more like his family was part of it.

Sousanna

He'd helped build the new outhouse too. Marios chuckled to himself. It was Sousanna that had brought about the new outhouse.

She hated using the "potty house," as she called it. She said it was too dark and rickety. She was often found squatting at the back of the house to relieve herself.

Papa chided her several times. "Do not go by the house. Don't go on the ground, or out in the open where someone might see you. Use the potty house."

Sousanna protested, "But the potty house stinks." She held her nostrils together to make sure he got the point. "And it might fall on me."

"Use it anyway," Papa said. After several warnings, he added, "If you do this again I'll have to punish you."

It wasn't too many days until Marios and his father came out one day and found her squatting behind the house. Papa slapped his hands together and yelled, "Sousanna."

She stood up quickly, pulling up her underpants. The look on her face—Marios wasn't sure if it was guilt or fear or both, but she looked pitiful.

Papa said, "Sousanna, come here. This time I will have to punish you."

She cried and grabbed his hand, pleading for him not to, but he called the whole family out. "Everyone, come into the yard." When they were all gathered he told them, "Sousanna has misbehaved, and she must be punished."

Sousanna was still crying, and now she ran to Marios and held on to him.

Mama cried out, "No, Niko. She's too little."

Ilias didn't say anything but Anastasia also tried to stop him. "Oh, no, Papa, she's our baby." Papa took Sousanna's hand and led her to his broken-down chair. He sat down and laid Sousanna across his knees. With his wife and children still begging him not to, he lifted his hand high in the air and brought it down, swiftly and— very gently tapped her bottom, then swept her up in his arms and said, "Now let that teach you to use the outhouse."

Marios was certain he'd seen Sousanna giggle. And soon after, his father asked him to help build a new outhouse.

When he was a boy it seemed his whole family never did anything but work. And they did work, hard and a lot. But there were good times, too. What else had he forgotten?

The fig tree. He and Papa had planted the fig tree at the side of the house. Papa dug the hole and threw fish bones and other things into it. He explained to Marios how each item would help the tree grow strong and produce figs. Marios held the little sapling upright while Papa put the soil back around it, then he carried a bucket of water from the well and carefully poured it around the tree. The tree was still there, bearing fruit each year.

"Feel better?" Nedtarios interrupted Marios's thoughts.

Marios sat up. "Yes." He hadn't had a nap after all, but still felt refreshed. Maybe he'd just needed to rest his anxious mind with pleasant thoughts.

"Niko is tired of lying in bed. He wants to sit outside, in the fresh air."

"That's a great idea. He's not used to being inside so much. I'll help you take him out."

Marios and Nedtarios helped Papa to his chair in front of the house. Mama followed them out and pressed his amber worry beads into his hand. Papa couldn't toss them back and forth anymore, but he gripped them in his crippled hand.

Marios watched Papa breathe deeply, taking in the fresh air. He did seem to be more at peace out here, where he could feel the sun and the breeze, see the roses in Mama's garden and the fruit trees Nedtarios had planted around their home. Marios had a feeling Papa would spend most of his time here.

The next morning it was time to leave. He'd been gone too long; no telling what Ilias was telling people about his absence. Marios said his goodbyes to his family, Papa last of all.

"Papa, I have to go back to Athens to work. I want you to know, I love you. You've been a good father. I have learned about life from you, and I'm a good and successful man today because of you."

There were tears in Papa's eyes. He strained to speak, his words broken. "Marios. Son. You made...dreams...true. Go...have good life...love you...Marios...I love you."

Chapter 37

Sousanna

"We're moving to Corpus Christi, Texas."

That's all Dad says, out of the blue, as we finish breakfast. No expression, no explanation. He gets up and walks outside. Through the window I see him light a cigarette, take a big inhale, and blow the smoke up into the sky.

I look at Mom. Her expression is even more grim than usual.

"Why?" There's a wail in my voice.

"Because your father has been transferred there." She tosses her napkin onto her plate. "I'm not happy about it, either. I wanted him to get the job in Liberia, where we would have a big house with servants and live like royalty. But they gave that position to someone else; he didn't fight hard enough for it." Her voice sounds the way it does when she says I've been nothing but trouble. Disgusted.

She keeps ranting. "He lets everyone walk all over him. That's the trouble with him. So it's Corpus Christi, Texas. Wherever on God's earth that is." She stands up and strides out of the room, saying over her shoulder, "You two clear the table."

When she's out of earshot I tell David, "I don't want to go. I don't want to leave our school, or my friends. Especially Joni." I have to fight back tears.

"I know; me either. I just made the all-star baseball team."

As soon as I get to school I find Joni in the hall. I grab her arm and pull her close enough to whisper, "We're moving to Corpus Christi, Texas!"

"What! That's so far away. Why?" She throws her arms around me. "I'm going to ask if you can come live with us."

"I wish. You know that won't happen."

"Why not? We both know your mom doesn't even like you." She sighs. "When are you going? Not before school is out?"

"No, the week after." It's my turn to sigh. "Maybe they'll change their minds. At least it's not Liberia. That's where Mom wanted to go."

"That's a whole other country. You'd definitely have to move in with us if that happened." We hug again.

I'm allowed to spend the night with Joni. After supper we sit on the floor in her room, leaning our backs against the twin beds, facing each other.

"I'm scared to leave here," I confess. "I don't want to leave all my friends. My church. You. Mostly you. You're like my sister." The tears won't stay inside anymore. "I feel like I did the day that man took me away from home. I was so scared and confused. Didn't know what would happen to me. Now it's just the same."

"I know. Me, too. I haven't done anything without you since kindergarten. That's how long we've been best friends. I won't know what to do without you." She sniffs. "You'll still be my best friend, no matter where you are. And I'll write to you every day. And in the summer, you can come here and stay. All summer."

We both pull our knees into our chest and wrap our arms around them, resting our chin on our knees, staring at each other. Tears fill our eyes at the same time. We don't say anything, just stare and cry for a long while.

§

The house is packed. School is out for the summer. It's time to move.

I spent one last night with Joni. When I got there, all our friends were there for a surprise going-away party. For a little while, I pushed my fear and sorrow aside and enjoyed the evening. We listened to music, played games, and gossiped.

When the party was over and everybody else had left, I sat cuddled up with Joni on one end of the sofa. Her mother sat close to us.

"Did you have fun?" she asked softly.

"Yes; thank you so much. I was so surprised. I just wish my mom could have come to see all my friends."

"We asked her," Joni said flatly. "She said she was busy."

"Never mind," her mother said. "You know we'll always be here for you, Nita. You're like a part of our family." She chuckled. "I'll never forget the day Joni came home from kindergarten and said she had to help a little girl from another country." She patted Joni's knee. "We talked about how she could be a good friend to you. She took it very seriously. And look at the two of you now. Two peas in a pod, with so many good memories."

"Mrs. Martin, can I tell you something?"

"Of course."

"I'm really scared to move. I don't know what'll happen in Corpus Christi."

She patted my knee just like she had Joni's. "Everything will be okay. You're a strong, smart girl. Just remember: Keep your dreams. Hold on tight to them, and work to make them happen. One day you'll be on your own, making your own decisions, living your own life. When things get tough, remember your future and all the good things you want. And always remember how much we love you, and that we're praying for you."

I moved from Joni's arms to Mrs. Martin's and felt the warmth of a mother. Though not mine, she made me feel warm and safe.

This morning Joni and I say our goodbyes. We hug each other tightly.

"Thank you for being the best friend ever. You're the best thing that happened to me since I left my family in Greece."

A horn honks outside. It's time to go. This time I know the car, the people inside, where I'm going. But the fear and uncertainty and heartache are as strong as the day I got into the green and white car with the strange man and drove away from everyone I loved.

§

The house in Corpus Christi is big, but not as nice as our house in Tulsa was. The land is flat and there's palm trees all around. It's hot, and it's humid, too. The humidity frizzes my hair out to twice its size.

If Joni were here, we'd laugh about that.

But she's not.

§

School starts this morning. A new school, with new kids and new teachers.

I'm going into seventh grade. Junior high. Joni and I have looked forward to being in junior high since first grade. Of course, we thought we'd be going together. Instead, I have to face it alone.

Maybe David can help. I find him in his room.

"I haven't met anyone that goes to our school. Have you?"

"Yeah, I've been riding my bike over to a guy's house. Ricky. He knows a bunch of guys that play baseball. We've gone to fields and played a few times. They're cool."

"Do you think any of them have sisters my age?"

"I'll ask." He seems to suddenly realize I'm nervous about going to a new school. "Hey, it'll be okay. We'll help each other meet friends. Don't worry."

"I feel lost without Joni. Everybody liked her, so they had to like me since I was her best friend."

"Wrong, Sis. Everybody liked you and Joni." He emphasizes the *you*. "Come on; I see the bus."

Binders and lunch in hand, we get on the bus.

"Hey, Brown, back here," some guy calls.

I grab David's arm. "No; sit with me. Please?"

"You'll be fine." He heads to the back of the bus.

I drop into the closest seat, next to the window, clutching my binder for dear life.

"Hi."

I turn from the window. A pretty girl with long, straight, blond hair sits beside me.

"Hi. You've really got pretty hair." *Why did I say that? How stupid.*

"Thanks. I'm Kristi."

Great. Not only is she pretty, with smooth hair, but she's got a cheerful voice, too.

"I'm Nita. We just moved here from Tulsa, Oklahoma. This is a new school and I don't know..." *Quit rambling.*

"You're new? That's hard. Have you met anyone from school?"

"No."

"What grade are you in?"

"Seventh."

"Oh. I'm in eighth, but I have a little sister." Kristi turns and points to the seat a few rows down and across from us. She waves; her sister rolls her eyes.

"Hey, Rebecca, come here. I want you to meet someone."

"No. Leave me alone."

"Come on."

Her sister trudges up to our seat.

"Nita, this is my bratty little sister Rebecca."

"Hi, Nita. Now can I go back to my seat?" Rebecca returns to the same seat and plops down.

It's probably my hair. Who wants to be friends with a chia pet?

At least Kristi is friendly. "I have a brother," I tell her. "David. He's sitting in the back."

"David? You mean David Brown? He's your brother? He's cool. And cute!"

"Yeah, David's my brother. He's going in eighth grade."

"I know. Everybody's talking about him."

"Oh." I turn back to the window.

Chapter 38

Marios

May 1968

"You boys have been ready for your own business for years," Christo said. "I'm glad you stayed with me, but it's time for me to retire. Stathoula and I are going to move to Kafalonia Island. We'll grow old and fat together, laying on the beach in the sun."

"Kafalonia? We must have made your rich," Marios teased.

Christo laughed. "Well, now you can make yourselves rich. I want you boys to have all my tools. Everything you'll need to open your own shop. There's a place in the center of Athens that would be a good place, and I know our customers will continue to give you their business."

"Hmm," Marios drew his eyebrows together questioningly and scratched his head as if trying to solve a puzzle. "I know. Marios's Furniture Building."

"You wish," Ilias said. "You wouldn't be able to build anything if you didn't have me to design it. It should be Furniture by Ilias."

"You make a good team. One to create the style and pattern, the other to build it. Demetriou Custom Furniture Shop will be very successful."

Marios laughed. What would they do without Christo? He always knew just what to say.

And he was right. Demetriou Custom Furniture was successful. The designs Ilias created appealed to a wealthy clientele, and Marios crafted the pieces to perfection.

What Marios liked best, though, was getting new customers. He loved to talk and tease and flirt. Rarely did anyone walk away without a purchase.

He loved to talk and tease and flirt outside the shop, too. Marios played as hard as he worked, socializing, partying, spending time with beautiful women. He was getting a reputation as a ladies' man, which he didn't mind at all.

"Hey, Ilias, come with me tonight. It won't be a big party, just a few people. Even you can handle this one," Marios invited, again. He worried about Ilias. His brother was so serious all the time. Too serious for a teenage boy. All he thought about was how to make more money.

"No." It was the same reply every time.

§

July 1970

"Hey, Ilias, will you loan me a few drachmas?" It was Friday, and Marios was going to hit some clubs after work. He could go to the bank, but it was easier to borrow from his brother.

"Again? You still owe me from the last time."

"I'll pay you back Monday. All the interest, too. Come on, brother. How am I going to buy drinks for the ladies without any money?"

"That's not my problem. You want to live the big life, you pay for it. I'll keep my money, thanks."

Marios sighed. This was a familiar fight. Sometimes Ilias just loaned him the money without comment, but other times he got stingy and cross, refusing to loan him even a few drachmas for just a weekend. Marios never knew which way it would go. He was getting fed up with his brother's moods and greed. He tried one more time.

"There's more to life than money, Ilias. Come have some fun for a change, instead of sitting around here all the time."

Ilias blew up. "You're just like Papa. Careless, with no sense. I've had enough of watching you spend your life like a playboy. Get out. Go find another place to live. You're never here anyway, always with your friends and women."

It was just as well. He and Ilias fought too much. It was time for them to go their separate ways. "Give me a week and I'll be out. But we have to talk about the business. How can we share a business when we can't even have a decent conversation?"

Ilias turned his back to Marios. "You can have the business. All of it. I'm going to leave the furniture business."

"What will you—"

"I've been lending money to people," Ilias said, his voice smug and arrogant. "I make a lot of money from the interest they pay. You can have the furniture business; and you better quit spending everything you make, because I won't be here to give you any more money."

Marios didn't bother to tell his brother that he'd been putting money in the bank for years, saving it up. Back when Christo helped them read the book about money, he told them the benefits of keeping a bank account. Ilias didn't trust banks; he wanted to keep his money where he could see it and count it anytime he wanted. He kept it in a trunk under his bed. But Marios asked Christo to help him open an account, and he'd been depositing money regularly.

He had enough to buy a small home. Ilias could keep this apartment and make money on his loans. Marios would move to his own place, and Demetriou Custom Furniture Shop would be owned and run by only one Demetriou.

Chapter 39

Sousanna

October 1971

"Jane McGee, Drill Team Captain, McGuire High School Panthers." The announcement streams over the football field. The entire crowd cheers, and several people in one section of the stadium call out. "Go, Jane!" "We love you!" "That's my girl!" Jane salutes, does a high kick into a circular split, and waves to the stands.

The announcer introduces me next. "Nita Brown, Drill Team Co-captain, McGuire High School Panthers." The crowd cheers again, but no one calls out my name. I'm not surprised; my parents never come to see me perform. Sometimes I think that if my real Mama and Papa were here, and Marios and Anastasia, and Ilias, they would cheer loudest of all. Thinking of them, I smile my best smile, salute, and do a high kick, falling into a perfect circular split and waving to the crowd.

Even with no one special to watch me, I love to perform with the drill team. I like doing well, learning and achieving and leading. I guess that's why I join so many activities: National Honor Society, Dance Team, Senior Girls Leader.

I've long since given up hope that these things will please Mom. I rarely please her, not since the first year I came to live with her and Dad here in America. I think it's because I wasn't an orphan, like David was when they adopted him. Mom wanted a daughter to love her completely, but I remembered my real mother and never stopped wanting to go back to her and Papa and our loving home in Greece.

So instead of becoming a loved daughter to my new American mother, I was a doll she dressed up, showed off, and put away. She gave me the prettiest clothes and enrolled me in all the socially-expected pursuits. There were piano lessons, dance lessons, sports, the opera, the ballet. She fixed me up and styled my hair and took David and me to church every Sunday. We learned impeccable manners, like how to write meticulous thank you notes and how to behave at our family gatherings. It wasn't unusual to hear Mom being told, "You've raised such well-mannered children." That always made me laugh to myself: I was like a store mannequin, posed in perfect positions but empty inside.

Mom never held me, never hugged me or kissed me or said she loved me. I missed those things, and longed for Mama and Papa, though I didn't say the words out loud after that spanking. Dad and Mom thought they'd erased the Greek in me; they believed Sousanna, the girl born in a one-room house with a dirt floor, no longer existed.

They were wrong; I kept the memory of my family, silent but constant, in my head and my heart. Often at night I cried for them, remembering how it felt when Mama held me in her arms, saying, "I love you, my sweet Sousanna." Waited for Papa to come and take me back to my real home.

I'm still waiting.

Dad wasn't so aloof, at least at first. When David and I were young, he read bedtime stories to us and helped us with our homework. Gradually that dwindled as he kept more and more to himself. Eventually he was like a ghost: always in the background, haunting us, but never really there.

I tried to find comfort with David. When I first came to the Browns, I'd go into his room and sit on his bed to watch him play. He never told me to leave; he didn't pay any attention to me. Every day we became more comfortable with each other. Eventually he let me play with him, and then he'd seek me out and ask me to come play with him.

Best of all was the time with Joni. It was hard to leave her. When I first moved to Corpus, we wrote to each other every week for a long time. Eventually weeks passed without a letter. Then months passed, and years, until the letters no longer came or went. Another part of my life was only a memory.

The move did bring David and me closer. Since he was only one grade above me, we navigated our way together. He was an outstanding athlete and popular. I met people, but never made a good friend. I was just David's little sister, with the really frizzy hair.

It got better after David suggested I join the school paper.

"It'll be great," he said. "You write well. And you'd meet people, make friends."

I found a passion for writing and was given more and more responsibilities to write about school happenings. In the eighth grade I was voted to be editor, and like David said, finally started making some friends. Not like Joni, but friends.

Mom hadn't wanted to move to Corpus any more than I had. She was bitter about it, and her anger turned her coldness into outright hostility. She takes her frustrations out on me, continually berating me any way she can. She's never forgiven me for wanting my own mother instead of her.

She also started drinking—a lot. Then Dad started drinking, too. Joining her was the easiest way for him to deal with her. I remember Mom saying he let people walk all over him, but she's the one who does that. He can't say no to her, or stand up to her. Not even to protect David and me from her outbursts.

My relief comes in the summers, when I get to spend a whole, glorious month with Aunt Lucy and Uncle Ted at their house in Houston. David always has practice and games for his sports, so he doesn't go. I have Aunt Lucy and Uncle Ted all to myself, and I love it. Aunt Lucy's smile is still a mile long, and everything Uncle Ted says ends with a chuckle and a wink.

Mom says they spoil me. They do make my days there special. Somehow they always know exactly what I'll love most. When I was little, there was always a chest full of dress-up clothes waiting in my room. I spent hours dressing up from one outfit to the other.

When I was a little older, Uncle Ted taught me to garden. He showed me how to build a raised trough for strawberries.

"Sweet pea," he said, using his nickname for me, "always grow strawberries in sand. They grow best that way. Look at all these berries! Go tell Aunt Lucy to get a pound cake ready. We're having strawberry shortcake tonight."

Aunt Lucy pampers me with shopping trips, and luncheons and dinner parties that we cook and prepare for together. She shows me how to be a good hostess and friend.

Sousanna

"Nita, Miss Mary, Mrs. Peterson, and Mrs. Jackson are all coming for brunch today," she might say. "I told them you were here for the month and they would like to welcome you. Let's get out the recipe books and look up some recipes we can make for our guests. And what do you think would make a nice centerpiece?"

Uncle Ted plans special outings for us. Once he told Aunt Lucy and me to dress in our prettiest dresses. "I have a surprise for you."

Aunt Lucy and I helped each other pick out our prettiest dresses, and we took special pains to fix our hair just so. I was still a young girl and felt very grown up. When we were ready, we went outside and in front of the house was a limo that stretched across the whole front of the yard. I was as amazed as I had been the first time I saw the green and white car without a top.

A man in a black suit and cap opened the door for us. "Hello, Mr. Brown," he said. "Those are two very beautiful women you have with you." I put my gloved hand over my mouth to hide my giggle at being called a woman. I looked up at Aunt Lucy to see what she thought of it and she smiled her big, beautiful smile.

It's always something fun with Uncle Ted and Aunt Lucy. The best part about visiting them, though, isn't the treats and outings. It's knowing I can be myself. I don't have to keep my guard up, being careful what I do or how I move or what I say or how I say it, lest Mom get mad.

I didn't realize until recently that Aunt Lucy and Uncle Ted are intentionally trying to make up for the lack of attention at home. They look for ways to shower me with love, and also to teach me things Mom isn't. Like what Aunt Lucy shows with her dinner parties and how she treats everyone: how to entertain, and to be gracious and kind, to be respectful to one's husband and enjoy times with children. How to treat friends.

They try to look out for me, too. Uncle Ted always asks, "How are they treating you at home?" He knows it's hard for me, but I don't tell him much. There's nothing he can do about it.

Anyway, when Mom insults or berates me, tells me I'm nothing but trouble and she wishes they'd never taken me, I have a secret way to ease the pain of her nastiness.

I tune her out and focus my mind on my earliest memories. I remember that I am Sousanna, a dearly loved daughter. Even if Papa hasn't found me yet, I know he and Mama still love me.

Sousanna

I think about Mama saying, "My beautiful Sousanna, every day I will think of you in my arms, of kissing your cheeks. Don't forget me. I am always here, and I am your mother." And Papa's words: "This is Sousanna, the best of my children" and telling me to be brave. Even Miss Helena saying, "Don't let anyone break your spirit."

I will be brave, and I won't let Mom or anyone else break me.

Chapter 40

Sousanna

November 1971

I can't wait until graduation. It's uncomfortable and unpredictable at home. Mom and Dad drink way too much, and Mom lashes out at me more and more. If things go well for me, if I achieve something or have a good time, Mom gets meaner. I guess it's because she had such a hard life, and even though she tried to make something of herself, things never worked out the way she wanted. I spend a lot of time hiding in my room to avoid confrontation.

Just a few more months and I'll be on my own. Next fall I'll go to the university, get my degree in Elementary Education. Being a kindergarten teacher has been my dream since the day Mrs. Semeras whispered to me, "I am Greek, too, and I will take good care of you." I made plans with one of my friends to room together. We talk every day, planning our dorm room and the fun we'll have going to football games and parties and meeting great guys.

First I have to get through the rest of the school year. It's our final football game. We're playing our biggest rival, not only in football but also for the dance teams. As one of the captains, I've worked hard to get myself and my team ready.

Our pre-game and half-time routines were perfect. With half time over, I meet up with my best friend Patti in the bleachers. She's sitting with her boyfriend, Rick. I sit on her other side and dig in my purse for money to get a Coke before having to go back onto the field.

"Patti, I'm short a dime to get a Coke. Help?" I say.

"Sorry, I don't have any money with me."

"No worries, I'll just get a drink from the water foun—"

I'm interrupted by someone sitting on the other side of Rick. "I have a dime. Here; go get a Coke. By the way, that was an awesome half-time show you all did. Way better than our team."

I don't know who he is but my heart skips a beat. He has long, blond hair, tanned skin, and is casually dressed in a Pat McGee surfboard t-shirt. A surfer. Just my type. But Mom never lets me go out with guys like that; it doesn't fit the good-girl-from-a-perfect-family image she insists on.

Besides, he's from the rival school. So I give him the cold shoulder. "No thanks," I tell him. "Keep the dime; I don't need it."

He shrugs and smiles, tucking the dime back into his pocket. "Let me know if you change your mind."

We catch each other's eye for just a moment. My stomach flips. I look away. I can't stay there with him looking at me that way so I tell Patti I'll see her in the parking lot.

When she and Rick get here, the surfer guy is with them. Who is he, and why is he hanging around with them? He's cutting up with Rick; they're obviously good friends.

He looks up and sees me watching him. I want to run away but my legs won't move. My eyes are glued to him. He calls my name and walks toward me. Why'd they tell him my name?

I don't know why I'm so nervous. He's relaxed and at ease.

"Rick and Patti and I are going for pizza," he says. "Come join us."

Oh, God, I want to. But Mom would never allow me to go anywhere with a surfer. I can't tell him that, so I say, "I don't know you; I don't even know your name. I don't just go out with someone I've never met. If you want to go out with me, call me seven days ahead of time and give me time to think about it."

Seven days ahead of time? Where did that come from? I feel my face burn and look away, trying to act nonchalant.

He doesn't seem to notice. "No problem, I understand. And my name is Robert. Rick and Patti can vouch for me; I'm a good guy." He gives a casual wave and walks away. My heart falls.

That night all I can think about is Robert. I have to see him again, no matter how mad it makes Mom. I can hardly wait until morning to call Patti and find out all about him.

"Who was that? He's sooo cute."

"And you're so weird. Why didn't you go with us? He's interested in you. You know what you look like after a game, and he still thought you were pretty."

My long hair frizzes out in the Corpus Christi humidity. "He must be weird himself to think I was pretty after a sweaty half-time show."

"Robert's a good guy. Big surfer, great family. I know him from church; we grew up together. You missed out."

"Yeah, I know. But you know how it is here, what my mom is like. I can't wait to get out of this house."

All day I can't get Robert off my mind. I'm day-dreaming about him when Mom calls me to the phone again.

The voice on the other end is playfully sarcastic. "Hey, it's Robert. I'm calling six days ahead of time to see if you want to go out next Friday night."

I can't catch my breath. I'm breathing so hard he can probably hear it. I put my hand over the receiver until I can settle myself down. He's on the line, saying, "Hello? Hello, Nita? Are you there?"

I finally have enough breath to talk. "Robert, hi. Ah, yes. I mean, let me check with my parents. They don't usually let me go out with boys they don't know."

"I understand. They may know my family, Street." He laughs. "We've been around Corpus for a long time and I think we have a pretty clean reputation."

"Okay, call me Wednesday and I'll let you know."

We do go out Friday night—and we keep going out every Friday night for the rest of the school year.

Chapter 41

Marios

Honk—honk!

Marios looked over his shoulder as he hurried down the street. What was all the commotion?

Oof! He caught himself and the person he'd bumped into at the same time. Oranges rolled on the sidewalk and into the grass.

"Sorry, I'm so sorry. Are you okay?" He began picking up the oranges, laughing as he recalled another time he'd run into a woman, Mrs. Stathoula, and how it changed his life.

"You think this is funny?" The woman's voice was insulted as she gestured at the oranges.

She was very pretty. His good luck—if he could make her forget to be mad. He swallowed his laughter and tried to sound penitent.

"No, it's not funny. I'm really sorry; let me help you." He dropped the oranges he'd gathered into the bag and reached for more. "Where are you from? You're not Greek, I can tell by your accent."

"No, I'm not Greek. I'm American," she said in broken Greek. "I'm just visiting."

She didn't sound so mad anymore. He'd take the chance. "Can I buy you a coffee? My way of saying I'm sorry. I'm Marios."

The woman gave Marios a forgiving smile. "Sure, I'd love to have a coffee. I'm Kim."

Six months later, they were still drinking their coffee together. Anytime Marios wasn't working, he took Kim on sightseeing adventures around Athens. Eating, drinking, dancing, shopping—there was always more to see and do. He loved spending time with her, no matter what they were doing. In fact, if he was honest with himself, he loved her.

He was pretty sure she felt the same way about him. But he couldn't do anything about it, not yet, anyway. It was time to have a talk and tell her why.

He planned a day on the beautiful island of Spetses. Everything she'd love. Walking around the picturesque old harbor, looking at the colorful sailboats, having a drink at an outdoor café. A romantic ride in a horse-drawn carriage, admiring the grand mansions along the cobbled streets, telling her about the glorious naval history of the island and how the mansions had been built for the captains and officers. Ending the day with a picnic on the pristine white sand of the beach, listening to the gulls and watching the blue-green waves roll in.

The day was as perfect as he'd planned. After eating and packing up the picnic food, they sat on their beach towels with an open bottle of red wine between them.

"I've never seen a place so beautiful," Kim said. "I love Greece. I love the people, the food, the water, the music...everything." She spread her arms wide as if to embrace all of Greece and fell back onto her towel, almost hitting the wine bottle.

Marios grabbed the bottle just in time and moved it to his other side. He leaned over Kim. "And I think I love you."

Kim laughed. "What? The sun must be getting to you, Marios. Or this beautiful island. You're crazy."

"I'm not crazy. My heart and thoughts are clear."

Kim sat up, serious. "I'm not ready to talk about this right now."

Marios let it drop. He wouldn't push her. When she was ready, she'd let him know.

A few weeks later he took her to the Acropolis. After a day of exploring the ancient ruins, they had dinner in a small restaurant at the base of the hill. Their table beside the window provided an excellent view of the old city, and soft music played in the background.

"Look, Marios." Kim was gazing out the window. "The moon is full, lighting up the Acropolis." She gave him a soft smile. "I've fallen in love with Greece. And with you."

"Then let's talk. I love you, too; but...it's complicated."

"I don't know how it can work. My father wants me to work in his law firm. He'll help me with my career, but only if I go soon."

"I have a problem, too. Even if you would stay here now, I can't—I won't—marry until I find my sister in America. She was taken from us when she was not yet six years old. We've tried to find news about her, or some way to find the man that took her, but we haven't been able to. I vowed to my mama and papa to find her."

"What do you mean, she was taken from you? And why didn't you tell me about her before now?"

"It's not something I like to talk about. It makes me sad, and I don't want to be sad with you. But now you should know this." Marios told Kim how the stranger in white had come and taken his sister, promising that she'd keep in touch and one day return.

"It's been fifteen years, and we haven't heard a word from her, or about her, since the day he took her away." He could hear the desperation in his own voice as his words came faster and faster. "Do you think you can you help me? When you get back to America, can you look for her? Or at least find the man that took her? I know his name: Peter Bakas. And I know the people that she was going to stay with, their name is Brown."

"I might be able to find them. Or at least the man. I'll try, anyway."

§

Marios watched the silver spoon clink from side to side inside the small white cup as Kim stirred her thick, sweet coffee. She placed the spoon on the saucer and took a sip of coffee. "Mmm."

When she set the cup down her expression turned serious. "You know I'm leaving next week to go home to America," she said in her broken Greek. "I need to know what is going to happen to us. Do you want me to come back to Greece to be with you?"

Marios took a sip of his own thick concoction. "Kim, you know I can't make plans for us until I find my sister."

"Don't worry, we'll find her. I'm sure when I get home I'll be able to find Peter Bakas."

"How?" Marios didn't mean to sound so doubtful of her ability, but it couldn't be easy to find one person in a place as big as America. "We don't even know where he lives."

"I'll talk to the partners in my father's law firm, and they'll help me. Lawyers are good at finding people." She reached across the table and placed her hand over his that was fidgeting with his small white cup. "Finding him won't be the hard part; getting him to tell me where Sousanna is will be the challenge. But, that doesn't answer my question. What about us?"

Marios looked into his cup and shook his head. "I don't know, Kim. I have to find my sister before I think about it. I made a vow to my family that I would find her."

§

Marios ripped open the envelope. He hadn't heard from Kim in several weeks. She'd written to let him know she was safely back home and happy with her new job, but nothing since then. He figured she decided to stay there, so he'd moved on with his life.

Dearest Marios,

All is well here. I'm working hard at the law firm, and I like it.

I want to let you know that I have met someone. I won't be coming back to Greece but I will always cherish the memories of our beautiful days together.

What a relief. He didn't have to wonder if she was still thinking about coming back anymore. And he was saved from having to tell her about KiKi, the beautiful woman he'd met a few weeks ago.

Here is the address and phone number for Peter Bakas. I hope you find your sister and will be reunited.

Marios stared at the paper. He could scarcely breathe. It seemed too good to be true. After all these years, would he finally be able to find Sousanna?

He was shaking as he dialed the number from Kim's letter.

A woman answered. He understood the words "hello" and "Peter Bakas."

Didn't they speak Greek? What was he going to do? He didn't know English. Maybe if he talked slowly and deliberately the woman would understand him.

"Greetings, this is Marios Demetriou from Greece. I received—"

"One moment, I think you may want to speak to my father," the woman said in Greek. "Please wait a moment while I will get him."

Marios tapped his foot and drummed his fingers while he waited. It was impossible to keep still. There were voices on the phone but he couldn't tell what they were saying. Then a man's voice came on, speaking perfect Greek.

"Hello, this is Peter Bakas. How may I help you?"

"Hello, my name is Marios Demetriou. I am in Greece. You took my sister from us and we want to find her, to bring her home. I know you know where she is..."

"Slow down. Tell me again who you're looking for. What is your name? How did you find me?"

"I'm looking for Sousanna Demetriou. My name is Marios Demetriou, I'm Sousanna's older brother. I live in Greece. You took my sister from our family. In Pirgos. She was only a little girl. You took her to America and we want her back. Where is she? Tell me how to find her. Please, please tell me."

"I will try to help you, but first I want to know how you found me."

"A woman I know, she's an attorney in America. She found you."

There was a long pause before Peter Bakas answered. "I'm surprised she did, but it's good for you. Give me a minute to look; I kept records where all the children went. I have it here somewhere." He stopped talking and papers rustled.

Was the man really going to tell him where to find Sousanna? Or was he going to play a trick again, say something not true, as he had when he'd taken her?

"Here it is..." The man gave him another phone number and address, for the people named Brown. Marios wrote down the information. His shaking hands made the writing look like an old person's. Then he hung up the phone. There was nothing else to say to the person who took his sister away.

He couldn't call this number himself, though. He'd been lucky Peter Bakas could speak Greek, but the man was from Greece. This Brown family was American; they might not know his language. He better get help.

Fortunately, KiKi could speak English. He dialed her number, and before she could even finish saying hello he broke in.

"Can you come over? Right now? I have Sousanna's phone number. KiKi, I have her number!" *Please let it really be the right number, not a trick.*

Marios would have sworn it was hours before she got there but the clock said it was less than half an hour. He practically dragged her to the phone and thrust the paper with the phone number on it in her face. How could she be so calm? Coolly dialing the number like it was just anybody. He couldn't keep still.

He could hear the ringing of the other phone in the handset KiKi held. He put his head close to the earpiece. It was silly; he wouldn't be able to understand anything, anyway. But he had to hear her voice.

Some kind of electronic voice came on. Kim hung up without saying anything.

"What's wrong? What happened?"

"This number is no longer working," KiKi said.

"What are we going to do?" They'd been so close.

"I'm going to call the operator. Maybe there's a new number."

Marios paced around the room while KiKi dialed again and talked in English.

"Got it," she said triumphantly. "Let's see if this one works."

Marios put his head close, as he had before. One ring...two...three...four...What if nobody answered? Just as he was about to give up hope, a groggy man's voice answered.

"Hello?"

KiKi suddenly hung up the phone.

"What are you doing?" Marios demanded. "Why did you hang up?"

"I don't know; I got nervous. Give me a minute to figure out what I'm going to say." After a few moments she dialed again.

This time the man's voice was angry. Marios wished he knew what he was saying. And what KiKi answered. He caught his name, and Sousanna's, but nothing else.

Then KiKi slowly hung up the phone.

"Well? What did he say?"

"He hung up."

Marios kicked the wall. "Hung up?"

"Marios, calm down," KiKi said. "It's the middle of the night in America. We have to wait a few hours. Let's try again in the morning."

Marios stared at the ceiling all night. Was Sousanna just a phone call away? Would she know how to talk to him, or would she only know English now? Did she even remember him? Or Mama and Papa? She'd been so young when she left. Marios couldn't remember much from when he was five. But no; she would remember them. He was sure of it. Wouldn't she?

KiKi didn't return until ten o'clock the next morning.

"It should be six o'clock in the evening in America," she said when she entered. "Let's call now."

Again Marios stood as close as he could next to KiKi and the receiver, hoping to hear Sousanna's voice.

"Hello?" It was the same man's voice, but this time alert.

KiKi starting talking to the man in English. She and the man talked back and forth. The man was getting more upset, and KiKi's voice was getting more desperate.

Then there was long silence before the man spoke again. His voice sounded calmer. He said Sousanna's name in the middle of a bunch of other words. KiKi grabbed a pencil and wrote some strange symbols down.

Finally she hung up the phone. "What did he say?" Marios asked. "Was Sousanna there? Did—"

"You found her, Marios. You found Sousanna."

Marios picked KiKi up and swung her around. They both began to laugh and cry at the same time. Finally he set her down again.

"What did he say? Was he a nice man? Where is she? How is she? Does sh...."

"Marios, Marios, slow down. I don't know if the man was nice. It was strange; he just gave me her address but he didn't want to know anything about us. I think he's been waiting for this call."

There was something else, something she wasn't telling him. He could see it in her face.

"What else? There's something else; what is it?" he asked.

"They changed her name, Marios. He said her name is Nita now, not Sousanna."

"What? Changed her name? But she was named after our mother's mother; they can't change her name. And, Nita? What kind of name is that? Nita?"

"She's been gone a long time. Fifteen years. She may not even remember her family in Greece."

Marios refused to believe it. "She'll remember us. I know she will. And I'll never call her Nita. Her name is Sousanna. She was given that name to honor our mother's mother, our grandmother. KiKi, let's call her right now."

"I don't have a phone number for her. Just an address at the university she attends."

"University? My little sister, at the university. She always was clever. Okay, I have some paper, let's write her a letter. Now, right now."

Marios kissed KiKi. "Thank you, KiKi. Thank you."

They sat at the small dinner table together. KiKi wrote what Marios dictated. Both of them had to stop often and wipe tears away.

Chapter 42

Sousanna

Tonight's the night. I'm meeting Robert at a coffee shop near campus, and I'm going to tell him about my past. I don't know if he'll think I'm crazy or love me even more. I can't prove anything; all I have are memories.

Sitting here, I'm hesitant. Do I really want to tell him? What if he decides I'm too much trouble, like Mom always said?

He notices my discomfort. "Hey, are you okay? You seem preoccupied; is something wrong?"

I have to tell him. "Robert, I want to share something with you, something about me."

He tilts his head. "Okay..."

I don't plan what to say; I just blurt it out. "I was born in Pirgos, Greece. My name was Sousanna Demetriou. I have two brothers, Marios and Ilias, and a sister, Anastasia. I love my mother and father and I miss them every day. A man came to my house one day and took me away in a green and white—"

"Whoa, slow down, slow down. You're from where? Who took you? I don't understand."

I can't read his expression, except for the confusion. Is there anything else? I can't tell.

"You must think I'm crazy, but I promise this all happened, and you should know this about me. I love you and I want you to know everything about me. You believe me, don't you? Do you know I'm telling the truth?"

Silence. It seems to go on forever. Oh, God, I've blown it. He'll never want to see me again; I'll lose him, too, just like I lose everyone I care about—

Sousanna

His hand reaches toward me. It covers mine, holds it. His look is tender. I think he knows I need reassurance. "Of course I believe you. Whatever it is, I'm standing by you. Tell me; I want to know."

I tell him everything I can remember about my life and family in Greece. Our house with the red dirt floor. My tall father and tiny mother. Marios falling in the well. Playing The American. Ilias sticking out his tongue. The boiled egg my last morning at home. Blowing bubbles in the dishwater with Anastasia. Mama's mended stockings and my faded dress and red sweater and the blue ribbon. The green and white car and the doll. The toilet room with running water in Miss Helena's house, and the other children, and the crib. Throwing up on the plane, and the Sears store. My real name, Sousanna.

Everything.

He's quiet while I talk, but when I finally run out of words, he asks, "Have you ever tried to find your family, to look for them?"

Me? Look for them? I have to confess, "I never even thought of that. I thought they'd come for me. Ever since I was five years old, I've just been waiting for them to find me."

"Maybe it's time we made a plan."

We talk for hours. At last we get in his car to go back to our dorm rooms. Robert pulls me close to him and holds me in his arms.

The next day we look up articles about children taken from Greece in the 1950s. I had no idea there were so many—thousands of them. Lawyers have gone to jail for lying to parents and taking their children.

It'll take forever to research all this; luckily, there's an easier way. We look up the faculty list and find a Greek political science professor at the university. I call his office and make plans to see him next Monday. Maybe he'll have ideas on how I might start searching for my family.

Meanwhile, I have to focus on here and now. This weekend is the big game of the season. Robert and I are going with some friends. I dress in our school color and head out to meet them, stopping on the way to check my dorm mail box.

There's one letter, addressed to Nita Brown. The envelope is made of thin, light blue paper and has 'Airmail' stamped on it. The two stamps in the corner feature pictures of a man I don't recognize. The return address says Athens, Greece.

Sousanna

Athens, Greece!

My hands shake, and I feel my heart racing. I want Robert. I run back to my dorm room and call him. "Robert, meet me at the student union. I have a letter from Greece."

"I'm on my way."

Finally I see him running toward me. As soon as he's within earshot he yells, "Where is it? Show me."

I hold the envelope up.

"You haven't opened it?" His voice is surprised. "Open it. Hurry up, open it."

I wait until he gets to me and we sit down on the closest concrete bench. I can hardly open the envelope, I'm shaking so bad, but I have to do it carefully so the letter inside doesn't get torn.

I unfold the large pieces of coarse paper and begin to read. The letter is dated September 3, 1972. It's traveled two months to find me.

Athens, Sunday, 3 September 1972

My beloved little sister. I wish this letter to find you in full of health and joy. Sousanna, it is very hard for me to compose this letter, because it is a story I wish hadn't happened. None of us can come to himself yet. You have been missed from us hard. I have a puppet at home since many years ago and I have called it Sousanna. When I get home and I see Mama and Papa, I think how you miss from us, how empty is the house. We have always you in our mind. I think of you and I say to myself, why haven't I had my sister to look after and to give us joy?

But fortune played a bad game so that you have been taken by them in the foreign country and so we can't see you and can't know how you are. And that was the blow for us. Many times I quarrel with Papa and I say to him, "why did you send her in the foreign country?"

But he has also worried since you have been leaving. He is ill on the bed, he has a sickness called Parkinson. He is continually with medicines, it is Anastasia and me who look after him. He has also had an operation done in the head. That's the condition of the father. He is almost paralyzed. You must know one thing: you have good parents and good brothers.

Sousanna

Sousanna, our mother is the best in the world. Sousanna, I have loved two persons too much in the world, mother and you. Mama has striven too much to bring us up. If today I am a good man, and I have succeeded to have a good job, it is because I had a good mother and I would like to see her one day to be proud of her children. She must rest now and that is why I have succeeded, for mother. All the worry for us it is you, but I hope that, now, we have learnt your address to have correspondence and to know how you are. And if it is God's will, we shall see you, let it be, once.

Sousanna, we have been looking for you for years to find you, first your address and then to see your letter. A girl, who lives in New York, and who comes in Greece in 1971 and with whom I had an acquaintance, she found your address. I told her the story and we learned your address.

Sousanna you have two brothers and one sister. First the eldest is Anastasia, 27 years, she is married. She has three girls. she is contented and has a good home. Second brother it is me, 24 years. I live in Athens, I am very well but I am not married, because I have sweared to myself one thing: first I must find you then I shall be married. I also have obligations with mother and Papa as I told you before that I help to care for them. When my economic situation is better, I'll come to see you. Third is Ilias, he is 22 years, he has just been married and just made his military service. And the last is you, whom we have not had to rejoice you any.

I left for Athens when I was almost a child, a kid, 11 years old, and I used to live by myself. I left Pirgos, I was alone and the affection of the family was missing from me. Anastasia was married and when I was 19 years I opened a shop with Ilias. I have been becoming the protector of the family since I was 11 years. It was because Papa was ill from that time (when I was 11 years old) and many other bad things found our family. My work is cabinet maker and glory to God we are all right now. I mean our economic situation is better than past years.

This long story I described you with a few words and I would like you to understand the story. We shall expect with agony to learn your news.

I kiss you with much love, you have a lot of greetings from all of us and we send you all of us many many kisses and God with you. Be a good girl as you must be, that I understand very well. Ending my letter I kiss you again, your brother, your family.

P.S. give my greetings to yours and we thank them because they talked with us during the calling with so much politeness.

I read the letter through sobs. The English is broken and hard to understand, but the love of my family is clear. And my name. *Sousanna*. I hadn't realized how much I missed my own name until I read it over and over in the letter. It's like my brother is trying to make up for all the years of not being able to say my name, and now wants to say "Sousanna" as much as I want to hear it, and that makes me cry even more.

I read the letter again, then again. Every few sentences Robert murmurs, "It's just like you told me. Your name, your brothers and sister. How wonderful your parents are, everything."

On Monday, I keep the appointment with the political science professor—not to get ideas about how to find my family anymore, but to ask if he'll write a letter to my family for me in their language.

§

December 1972

I check the mail every day to see if there's an answer to the letter I wrote, with the professor's help, to my family. Every day, when it's not there, I go to my dorm room and read the first letter again. It's getting so worn that I'm going to make a copy before it tears.

My heart stops when I open the box today. There's another blue envelope. I feel tears running down my cheeks as I open it. As I read, the tears of excitement and love become sobs of longing and grief.

My father, my big, strong, kind father, who answered all my questions and carried me on his shoulders close to the sky, has died. The letter says he waited until he heard my news from the letter I sent, and knew I was safe; then, believing I was a good girl with a good heart, he died in peace.

There will be no more waiting for my father to find me and take me home. I'll never be wrapped in his strong arms, or look into his crystal blue eyes and see his love for me, ever again.

Chapter 43

Sousanna

January 1973

A third letter arrives, this one from Anastasia. It's written by a local teacher who taught English in Pirgos, with perfect grammar and spelling. She writes how happy she is to be able to write to me, to hear that I am well. She doesn't say anything at all about herself.

At the end of the letter, Anastasia writes, *Sousanna, our mother wants you to know that she went to find you the day after you were taken away. She and her sister Georgia walked all the way to Patras to bring you home. When they arrived, they were told that you were already gone to Athens, on your way to America. She was too late. Sousanna, part of her heart died when she could not bring you home, and it is only now beginning to come alive again since we have found you.*

Mama was there. Mama was in Patras. She was there the next day, and I was still there, too, at Miss Helena's house. Why didn't Mama find me? Who told her I was gone? Why didn't she keep looking? Why would someone tell I'd already left? I don't understand.

Should I tell Mama I was there? That I stayed in Patras with Mrs. Helena and the other children for a long time before we left to go to America? I imagine different ways of writing it.

Oh, by the way, I was still in Patras...

Whoever told Mama I was gone was wrong...

She was so close...

None of them seem right; each one just feels like another heartbreak. Should I do that to her?

No. I can't. What good would it do to tell her now, anyway? It's over. History.

But not telling feels like keeping a secret. Not being honest. Lying.

I can't do that, either.

All day I pace the floor. Wondering. Questioning. Waiting for Robert to come so I can talk to him about it.

He's barely in the door before I tell him what the letter said and ask him all my questions, as if he'll have all the answers. He may not always know the answers, but he does know exactly what to tell me now.

"You don't have to decide this minute."

My entire body exhales as the stress lifts. This is one of the things I love about Robert—he's so steady, and grounds me.

We discuss all the scenarios, and I decide not to mention it yet. When I know the right words, when the time feels right...

§

December 1973

Our letters now flow back and forth on a regular basis. Every eight weeks I receive a letter from Marios in Athens and one from Anastasia in Pirgos; and they receive mine from Texas. I write my letters in English, having never learned to write in Greek. I'm grateful Marios and Anastasia have translators that can read my letters to them and write their letters to me. We share news of our current lives while trying to fill in the gaps of the life we lost with stories, pictures, and memories.

We tried twice to communicate over the phone with KiKi as interpreter, but that was more frustrating than soothing. I can no longer speak Greek. My native language was taken from me when I arrived in America and I wasn't allowed to speak unless I used English words. Even with KiKi's almost perfect English, bad connections made the strained back-and-forth translating unreasonable, and we resign ourselves to a pen and endless pages of paper to communicate.

Always excited to find a letter from Greece in the mail box, I rip it open before I even get back inside. But a strange anger is building in me. For months I've tried to pretend it doesn't exist, but it's nagged at me until there's no more ignoring it. I can't even concentrate on my studies. I've got to talk to Robert about it.

"I don't know why, but I find myself getting angry when I read my sister and brother's letters," I tell him. "Reading their news, knowing they're together sharing their lives and I can't be a part of it. All these years, even when times were hard, at least they had each other. I was here, alone. So often confused and scared." I hesitate. Can it be true?

"I think I'm angry at my father for agreeing to let me go, and at my mother for letting me get in the car. Not to mention my anger at Margaret and Jack for taking my Greek language and even my name from me. I never felt this before—or at least I never acknowledged that I was feeling it deep inside—and I don't understand why it's stirring so much up inside of me now."

As always, Robert listens quietly and takes time to think before answering. "That anger may have already existed long before your family found you, before the letters, and you just didn't realize it because it was in the background of your life." He lays his book down and leans in. "How can all this not stir something up inside you? Each new revelation awakens you to the reality of what happened." He pauses and studies my face.

"You weren't a baby, Nita; you were a young girl, and you've lived with these memories for years. You've waited, with the innocence of a child, that little girl has waited, for your family to find you." He takes my hands in his, rubs the back of them with his thumbs.

"And they never did. Of course you're angry. I'm angry. But now you can have peace. We'll work through this together. We have our lives, you and me, and we'll make a future with our own family." He stands and pulls me up into his arms.

"Robert, I want you to know without any doubt that I love you. I love our lives together and everything our future holds. I would never leave all this, you, to go back to Greece. My life is here with you. It's important you know that."

Still holding me in his arms, he leans his head back and takes my chin in his hand to lift it so our eyes meet. "I know that." He gently kisses me on the forehead.

Now, when the letters come, I can read them with less anxiety. I often chuckle at the broken English, even though it makes the sentences challenging to understand.

Marios writes lovingly about his beautiful wife, pregnant with their second child. His letters piece together the story of how they found me and the woman that helped him.

Sousanna, I will always owe a woman whose name was Kim my gratitude for the miracle of finding you. She comes to Greece to a visit and we are in love. I tell your story and ask for her help. She is lawyer in New York and said she could help us. We say to talk about marrying if I find you, but first she must understand I have you to find. When she goes back to America she meets a man, maybe she is married to him now, I do not know. But I to met someone, KiKi, and we fall in love. I hope you will not think badly of me, that when KiKi becames pregnant we married. She is a very good wife and we are waiting with great anticipation our next child.

His letters include many stories about our mother and father, how they were good parents and his deep love for them, always giving our mother the credit for *all of her children being successful and good people.*

With each sensitive letter, he allows me to see into his heart. If only through the words on the pages, I'm getting to know him intimately as he shares his thoughts, concerns, beliefs, and the experiences that brought him to the life he has.

Marios is my hero. He did what I had waited for my father to do. Marios found me.

Anastasia's letters are filled with stories about her three girls; but there's a tinge of sadness between the lines. She writes about her longing *"to have my sister with me to talk with and live life together"* and that her life has *"been a hard life Sousanna, it was good you were not here."*

Only once has she spoken of Nedtarios, saying *"he has taken good care of me and our parents and is a good father to our children."* It's from Marios's letters that I learn of the difficult relationship between her and Nedtarios.

There is difficulty with Anastasia in her marriage because of the many years between them. Nedtarios is twenty years older and treats our sister as a child that cannot make her own decisions or have opinions and thoughts. She does not complain, she is like our mother. She is kind and works hard. She takes good care of her family and cared for our father when he was ill. Nedtarios is a good man, but he is difficult. Our sister talks only of you these days. She wants for you to move back to Greece and live by her and share your lives together. I try to explain to her your life is in America now.

I never receive a letter from Ilias. I learn about him from Anastasia's letters.

Sousanna, do not be discouraged about Ilias not writing to you. He cares for you, but lives a life away from us. I have some contact with him though he has remained distant from our family for many years. He and Marios have never resolved their troublesome relationship. Sousanna, you must know they are good brothers, they are just too different to be friends. I pray one day they will behave as brothers. Ilias is married to a kind woman, Stephania, and he is happy. Their only sadness is they are unable to have children, and that makes Ilias bitter. He is no longer loaning his money to people but is now in the shoe business and doing very well.

In my letters I write about school, my dreams of being a teacher, and Robert. I always end by telling them, *"You are always in my heart and I wait for the day we will be together again. My prayers are with you and our mother. Many hugs and kisses. Please kiss our mother for me."*

Anastasia always includes Mama's words for me in her letters, and they're the same every time. *Sousanna, our mother sends her hugs and kisses to you. She prays every day for you and Robert. She is waiting to hold you in her arms and kiss you again. She cries when your letters come. I believe it is because it reminds her of the day you were taken. She was with you, only her, and she can never forget that day.*

Chapter 44

Sousanna

*A*pril 1974

The phone is ringing as I enter my apartment. "Aunt Lucy, hi."

Aunt Lucy and Uncle Ted are the only family I have left in America. Things got so bad with Margaret and Jack—I can't think of them as Mom and Dad anymore—that we're no longer in touch. Margaret got mad that I'm in contact with my birth family, and she's so upset about it that I can't be around her. I think Jack understands, but he goes along with Margaret. It's easier for him that way.

And David—I don't even know where he is. Back when the first letter came from Greece, I called him to share the news. He hardly talked to me, just said what a surprise it was, and then he had to go. I haven't heard from him since. His roommate told me he dropped out of school and joined the Army. The only way he knew was because he had to send some of David's things to Fort Hood. I miss David as dearly as I miss Marios and Ilias, and I pray for him every day.

Anytime I talk to Aunt Lucy, the first thing she does is ask if I've heard from David. When I tell her I haven't, she says, "Don't worry, sweetheart. He'll show up. You know how independent he is. He's so smart, he'll do well no matter where he is. But right now we have another project." Her voice becomes urgent. "When can you take a break from classes and come to Tulsa?"

"I don't know. Why?"

"I found Peter Bakas."

A cold stone falls from my throat to my stomach, and for a moment that's all I'm aware of. Then I hear Aunt Lucy through the receiver, asking, "Nita? Are you there? Nita?"

"Yes, I'm here. I didn't know you were looking for him. How did you find him? Why?"

I see Mr. Bakas knocking the doll—my doll—into the back seat of the green and white car at Miss Helena's house. Holding me on the plane, and handing me to Dad. I see Mama running after the car, reaching for me...

I have to sit down, and realize I've missed whatever answers Aunt Lucy gave. Now she's saying, "...need answers. I love you like my own daughter, you know that, and frankly I want those answers, too...Nita?"

"Yes. Yes, I do want answers. I can come Friday."

§

"Ready?" Aunt Lucy asks. She waits for me to nod before she knocks on the door of the apartment. I make myself breathe, slow and long and deep. It calms my stomach a little bit. I've gone back and forth all week, one minute determined to confront Mr. Bakas, the next deciding I never want to see him again. It was when I remembered a line from Marios's letter that I finally made up my mind.

But fortune played a bad game so that you have been taken by them in the foreign country...

That morning so long ago, I'd thought we were playing a game, with everything so strange. Was it a game to Mr. Bakas? Taking advantage of poor Greek people to show how smart or powerful he was? Did he know how much it would hurt? Hurt me? My parents, my sister and brothers? Did he know and not care? Was he sorry? I owe it to my family to find out, if I can. I'm here for them as much as myself; in fact, if Marios hadn't found me, I don't think I could do this.

The door opens. A hunched-over man with wild, white hair stands looking at us over wire-rimmed glasses that cling precariously to the very tip of his nose. All his clothes are white, down to his shoes.

It's all I can do not to bolt. My throat is suddenly full of cotton. Worse, my stomach is turning somersaults. *Oh, God, please don't let me throw up. Please, God, help me do this.*

Sousanna

The old man reaches out to me and says, softly, "Sousanna. Sousanna."

I've waited years for someone to call me by my real name, but it sounds strange coming from this man. I don't want that connection with him. I want to push him away, but years of Margaret's training make me submit to his embrace.

"Come in, come in. I made coffee."

The spicy smell inside is instantly familiar, but I can't name it. It gives me a feeling of comfort, so it must be from Greece. I look around the simple room but don't see where it's coming from. Everything is in perfect order.

Mr. Bakas holds his hand out to Aunt Lucy. "You must be Lucy. I'm Peter Bakas. I'm grateful you found me."

Aunt Lucy grasps his hand firmly and speaks with authority. "Yes, I'm Lucy Brown, Nita's aunt. Her adopted father and my husband are brothers."

"Nita...that's right; Sousanna is now Nita." From the expression on his face as he looks over at me, I'm certain he's reminiscing some moment from the past. Then his face clears and he invites us to sit and goes to get us coffee.

Aunt Lucy pats my knee. Her raised eyebrows silently ask if I'm okay, and I nod again because I still don't trust my voice with my mouth and throat this dry. It's a good thing Aunt Lucy can take charge until I pull myself together. She takes a small tape recorder from her purse and balances it on her knee.

Mr. Bakas comes back with three cups of coffee on a tray. He hands us each a cup, and takes one for himself. I take a sip and set it down; it's too strong, but at least it moistens my throat.

Aunt Lucy gets right to business. "I have a small tape recorder with me; I'd like to tape our conversation. Is that okay with you?"

"Yes, of course." He turns to me. "Sousanna—I'm sorry; Nita. Tell me about yourself. I've tried to stay in touch with the children I brought from Greece, but the Browns would not allow me to contact you, so I don't know anything about your life here in America."

I clasp my shaking hands tightly together. I don't want to chitchat about life; I came here to get answers. One answer in particular. My teeth are gritting together so hard I can barely open my mouth and my words come out jagged. "Why did you lie to my father?"

He sets his cup of coffee down. "I gave you hope where there was no hope."

"No." My voice is back. My strength, my spirit, my anger. I have everything I need to stand up to him. "No. You lied to my father; you broke his heart. You broke my mother's heart that day you took me from her. You scared me and took me away where I didn't know anyone or anything. And you kept my doll."

Both he and my aunt look surprised and confused. "I kept your doll?" he repeats. "You had a doll? I don't remember a doll."

It seems like a silly thing, considering all that happened, but his keeping the doll was the first time anyone had ever lied to me. Betrayed me. My childish innocence, my security, love—all these were lost with the doll, and the world became a harsh, lonely place in that moment. It still stings.

I can't explain all this, so I just say, "Never mind" and look away, concentrating on the stream visible through the sliding-glass door in the back of the room. I have to get a hold of myself, stop shaking like a nervous puppy.

Aunt Lucy takes over, her voice calm and firm. "Did you intentionally lie to Nita's father? Did you know you would sell her to Jack and Margaret and she'd never go back to Greece to her family?"

"Lucy, those are questions I cannot answer. I believed I was doing good for these children; I still believe this. Nita's had a life here in America that she could never have had in Greece. I can see she is a fine young woman now, healthy and successful. So please, let us not talk about the past." Again he turns to me. "Tell me, Sousa... ah...Nita, about your life. Please tell me."

I acquiesce, no more able to ignore the manners that have been instilled in me since I was a child than a robot is able to disregard its programming. "It's true I had many opportunities with the Browns. I've done well in school, and I'm finishing my degree at the university. I'm engaged to Robert, who I've known since high school." I'm giving in, giving him what he wants: assurance that he'd done the right thing. I've got to stop.

"What are you studying at the university?"

I answer automatically. "I wanted to be an elementary school teacher, but it seems I may end up teaching classical dance..." No. I won't do this. I summon every bit of the old, feisty Sousanna, who bit her playmates and raised her fists to Mr. Bakas and kicked Miss Helena, that I can.

"No. I won't let you get by without knowing you regret what you did to my family, to so many families. Tell me you've suffered for what you did, as I know my mother and father suffered for your lies."

Mr. Bakas takes off his glasses and neatly folds them, lays them on the table next to our un-drunk coffee. "I gave you hope where there was no hope. I know and believe that to be true. Maybe I didn't do it the way I should have; I understood that in the end. I made mistakes, but I also gave children opportunities for a better life. And yes, I have suffered. I still dream of your father. He was one of the most beautiful men I've ever seen. And defiant—like you. The same. I went to your house three times before I could convince him to—"

"You didn't convince him, you lied to him."

He sighs. "I do have regret for that. I can't forget him, or your mother's screams chasing my car. Does that satisfy you?" Tears are forming in his eyes and he squeezes the bridge of his nose. "Sousanna—forgive me for calling you that name but that's who you are to me—I told your father that you'd end up in the street if you stayed in Greece. It was the only way I could convince him to let you go. Your father, so strong and tall, began to cry. Nikolas cried...I will never forget his begging me, 'Bring her home again. Promise you'll bring her back home to me.'"

We all spontaneously stand up at the same time, as if a movie ended. "I'm ready to go," I say to Aunt Lucy. "There's nothing else we can do but cause each other pain." I can't even look at Mr. Bakas as I head to the door, but I tell him, "Thank you; you've finished my story, and for that I'm thankful."

Aunt Lucy follows me to the door but turns back for one last comment. "What you did was wrong. So many have suffered, but I can see you've suffered too. I'm glad of that."

"Wait," Mr. Bakas says. "Sousanna, please, before you go, I want to give you something." He walks to a bookcase and takes down a box as he talks. "I have pictures of the other children that came with you. You'll be happy to know they've all done well. My own grandson Mario—you remember him, don't you?—is studying to be a neurosurgeon. I want you to know."

He rifles through the box for the pictures and holds them out to me. I still don't look at him, just take the photos and leave.

Sousanna

§

December 1974

Standing at the entrance of the church, holding Uncle Ted's arm, I see the church pews filled with friends and family. Everything is perfect. The music begins, and each aisle stands in turn as Uncle Ted and I pass by. My eyes are filled with Robert, waiting for me at the altar. We're creating a new family, borne of love.

Chapter 45

Sousanna

A knock at the door startles me. Robert's engrossed in the football game on TV so I answer it.

"David!" I throw my arms around him, revel in his return embrace. David, on my porch, after all these years—five years, to be exact.

I usher him into the house.

"I'll be damned," Robert says when he sees who it is. He turns off the television and steps forward to shake David's hand and slap him on the shoulder. "Brown, where the hell have you been? Do you have any idea how worried Nita's been?"

"Sit down and tell us everything," I demand. "And it better be good."

"I'll tell you," David said, "but first let me say, 'Congratulations,' since I wasn't here for the wedding."

"So where were you?" I ask.

"Trying to get my life together. I signed up right after you got the letter from Greece. That wasn't the reason, just happened that way. Had a lot of stuff going on in my head, thought maybe the war would give me a break from my life, time to sort things out."

"The war? You went to Viet Nam?" Robert asks.

"Yeah."

Robert shakes his head. "Never heard of anybody thinking war would help them sort things out," he mutters.

"Yeah, it was kind of stupid," David admits. "Especially since it put me in the hospital."

"What?" My heart stops a beat as I look him up and down for signs of damage. "What happened? Are you okay?"

"Yeah, I'm fine. Enemy grenade exploded close enough to knock out my hearing in one ear. But, as you can see, it didn't kill me."

I turn away so they can't see me blinking. David could've been killed, and I might never even have known. He never said goodbye, or told anybody where he was or—

"Hey, I'm okay."

I give him a small smile. "I'm glad. If something had happened to you..." I wipe my eyes.

"Nah, I'm fine. Hey, tell me about you. A married woman. And man," he adds with a glance at Robert. "Did you finish school? What are you doing?"

"Yes, we both graduated. Robert owns his business, and I'm a dance instructor."

"You see Uncle Ted and Aunt Lucy much?"

"Pretty often. We spend a lot of time with Robert's parents; they're great. Aunt Lucy and Uncle Ted come down every few weeks, and we all get together for dinner or something."

"And you're in touch with your other family, in Greece? Things are finally going good for you, family-wise, huh?" David says. There's longing in his eyes, wistfulness in his voice. I don't know what to say. I'm sorry he doesn't have that, but I'm not sorry I do.

"You haven't told us where you've been, what you've been doing, since you got out of the service," Robert says. I'm positive he changed the subject because he knew what I was thinking, what I couldn't say.

"I'm in New York. Got a small apartment there. Working; got a good job," David answers. As he talks the longing and wistfulness fade, replaced with a growing aura of contentment. "Been there a couple of years. Yeah, everything is actually good now."

"That's great," Robert and I say at the same time.

I wish we could keep talking about good things, but I have to make sure he knows about Margaret. He was a lot closer to her than I was; it could be a blow to him.

"Did you know our mother died while you were gone?"

"Yeah, I know. I went to see Uncle Ted and Aunt Lucy before I came here; they told me where you live. And they told me about Mom. I'm sorry I wasn't here; I know it was tough."

"It was. Dad called out of the blue. We hadn't talked in years, but he called us when she was in the hospital. Asked us to come. So we dropped everything and drove to Houston that day."

There's a pause before David asks, "What happened?"

"It didn't go well. When we got there, Dad was sitting out in the waiting room. He was really upset, but seemed glad to see us. Gave us both a big hug. Said Margaret was dying. He started crying, and we tried to comfort him. Then a nurse came in and said he could visit Margaret. I asked if he wanted me to go with him, and he said to wait until he could make sure it was okay with Margaret. When he came back he said she didn't want to see me."

Robert sets a box of tissue in front of me. I didn't even know he got up. Robert takes over while I blow my nose.

"We left a little while after that. Lucy called three days later, told us she'd died. Said her family didn't want us—any of our family, including them—at the funeral. So none of us went."

"I wish we had," I say. "I had a right to say my goodbye. But we didn't want to upset anyone."

David shakes his head remorsefully. "I should have been here," he says.

"She loved you," I tell him. "I'm sure it would've brought her comfort to see you at the end. But you couldn't know what would happen. None of us can blame ourselves. That part of our lives has never been easy. We navigated it the best we could."

Chapter 46

Sousanna

May 1977

"Ladies and gentlemen, we have just been cleared to land in Athens. Please make sure your seat belt is securely fastened."

I shake Robert. He slept through almost the entire flight. Not me; my mind has been going wild. What does Mama look like now? Anastasia? Marios? Will I recognize them? How will we communicate? What will they think of me? Will they like me, or will they think I'm too American?

Robert stirs at my shaking. "Huh, what?" he says groggily.

"We're getting ready to land. Put on your seat belt."

"We're already here? That was quick."

I press my nose into the window to see the land below. There's blue, blue, blue water and mountainous terrain. Even from this height, it's beautiful.

Things below seem small. Fields I know to be acres and acres of land appear the size of a stamp. They're connected in patterns that fit together like an intricate puzzle.

For some reason Margaret comes to mind. Our lives were like a puzzle in which the pieces never fit. I'd tried to force them into place, and I think she did, too, but they weren't meant to meet. She needed to be loved by me; I needed my own mother. Wanting that love wasn't something she could help, any more than I could help my feelings. Margaret didn't treat me as she did because of something personal or because she was mean. Or because I wasn't good enough. It was simply two lives colliding. I can't resent her for that, or blame myself. I accept that she did the best she could with the disappointments and hardships in her life, as did I.

These revelations bring peace. I close my eyes and here, flying high above the world, I just let it go. It's time. I thank God for giving me this insight and peace.

When I open my eyes and look out the window again, it seems the ground is rising to meet us. It gets closer and closer. The closer it gets the harder and faster my heart beats. I take some deep breaths to calm myself.

Robert takes my hand and turns my face toward him. "It's going to be okay. You've waited a long time for this day. So have they."

"I know." I take another deep breath, then ask, "Do I look all right?"

I fretted over my outfit for weeks. Casual or dressy? Heels or flats? Hose or bare legs? I finally settled on a fitted, cream-colored, sleeveless dress with a short, collared jacket. I'm wearing hose because the dress is dressy but camel flats for comfort—I don't know how much walking we'll have to do.

Now I'm positive it's all wrong. "It's too formal, isn't it? Too dressed up?"

"Seriously, you're asking me that now? What if I say yes, what will you do?" Robert laughs at his own teasing. "You look perfect. Besides, they're not going to care what you're wearing—if they even notice."

I guess that's true. And he's right; there's nothing I can do about it anyway. I hold onto his hand as the plane lands with a thud.

It takes forever for everybody in front of us to get their bags and walk off. Finally we get to the door, and I step out of the plane. After nineteen years, I'm back in Greece. I remember the fresh air and inhale deeply.

"Ugh." I sputter. Rubber and jet fuel. Guess I'll have to get away from the airport to smell the fresh Grecian air.

We find our way through the glass-enclosed terminal, gather our bags, and get in line to go through customs. Robert stands calmly, not moving except to step forward with the bags as each person in front of us exits customs. I can't stop fidgeting, shifting from one foot to the other, patting my hair, looking arou—

Anastasia.

My sister is pressing into the glass, looking this way and that. Like a child at a circus, I tug Robert's sleeve, bouncing with excitement. "Robert, there she is. Anastasia. It's her. Look, it's her."

Sousanna

Her eyes catch mine. She jumps up and down, waving her hand high in the air. Her mouth is moving but we can't hear her through the glass that separates us.

I wave back, but...what is this uneasy feeling stirring in my stomach? I've dreamed of this moment for so long, fantasizing its perfection. What if it's not? Why am I coming back to the place that's haunted me for so long?

"Robert, I feel sick. I don't know if I can do this."

"What? You're kidding, right?"

"No, I'm serious. What if we feel like strangers to each other? Or worse, what if we all have our hearts broken again because this doesn't make anything better but digs up too much pain from the past? Maybe we should just keep writing letters, maybe then the past will disappear, or we can pretend it didn't happen."

"Well, it's too late. We're here, and that's your sister over there waiting for you." There's no sympathy at all in his voice.

We pass through customs and barely step into the main hall of the terminal before I'm wrapped in Anastasia's arms. She kisses every inch of my face.

"Sousanna, Sousanna. Se agapo, se agapo. Se agapo mikri koukla mou." I may not know any other Greek words, but these I remember immediately. She's saying, "I love you, I love you. I love you, my little doll." We're laughing and crying at the same time.

She releases me and embraces Robert. "Se agapo, Robert." The way she says "Robert" would be funny if it wasn't so sweet of her to learn to say his name at all. Hugging her back, Robert looks at me over Anastasia's head. Tears are sliding down his face, too. I smile and nod my head to him in assurance.

When my sister steps back from Robert she looks at me. We search each other's eyes. Her eyes are still gentle, her smile still sweet and comforting. This is really happening. I'm in Greece, and this is Anastasia. My sister. I'm looking at my sister. I feel the warmth of love that I used to feel when we snuggled together in the bedroll so long ago.

Chattering in Greek, Anastasia starts gathering all our luggage, putting cases under her arms and grabbing the handles of others, dropping one while trying to pick up another. Robert laughs at her efforts and takes the bags from her arms and hands. He points to himself.

"I will take care of the bags," he says. My sister latches onto one bag and refuses to release it, insistent on helping. I take a bag also, leaving Robert to strap the duffel over himself and pull the two suitcases.

Anastasia talks the whole time we walk through the airport. I have no idea what she's saying, but I hope she doesn't stop, so I can keep hearing the sound of her voice.

Outside the terminal I look across the parking lot, and there he is. All my anxiety, my doubts, the years away—all vanish. Marios, my brother, my hero, is only a few steps away. Handsome, confidently leaning against his Mercedes, arms folded over his chest and a smile on his face. He holds his arms open to me.

Something familiar washes over me: a longing for my father. I close my eyes to remember Papa, wishing it was his arms reaching out to me. Will I never stop waiting for Papa to hold me again?

But Marios is here. I drop my bag and run to him. We cling to each other. Our letters have bound our hearts to each other, and now we can physically feel our love. He kisses the side of my face and holds me back to look at me. I assume his nod means approval. He pulls me in for another embrace, then turns to Robert.

Leaning back, Marios opens his arms wide. "Texan. Cowboy," he jests in broken English, and it's true. Over the years Robert has transitioned from a high school surfer to a tall, lean, boot- and hat-wearing Texas businessman. Marios throws his arms around Robert, who is so much taller than Marios that my brother disappears in his embrace.

We squish our luggage and ourselves into Marios's little coupe. Anastasia is still talking. I always thought she was quiet. Maybe it's nerves and excitement. Robert and I don't understand anything she says, except for twice when I catch Ilias's name. Both times she glances warily at Marios.

Marios drives like a wild man. Robert and I cling to any piece of the vehicle or luggage we can grab as Marios zigzags the car over and around speeding traffic. He even passes another car on the sidewalk! And he's not the only one—everyone on the road is driving the same way.

Robert laughs, even though he's stretched over the luggage and hanging on for dear life. "And you thought I drive reckless. This makes me look like an old lady on the road."

Sousanna

Even while tossing around in the back seat of Marios's little car, I gape at the progressive, contemporary city that whizzes by us. This is not the Greece I left so many years ago. Shopping centers, towering skyscrapers, sidewalk cafés filled with people eating and drinking. This is a modern city, a modern country.

As if to refute my musing, Robert taps my shoulder across the luggage. "Look, Nita. It's the Parthenon. Look; do you see it?" I don't know when I've heard him so excited before.

Finally Marios stops the car. We're in front of a traditional concrete home in the center of Athens. It's painted a brilliant white with shutters open on either side of the windows and a door painted the same light blue as the sky. The yard is filled with fruit trees, roses, herbs, and the biggest fig tree I've ever seen. It's exactly what I've always imagined the perfect Greek home would look like.

We wiggle ourselves around luggage and unfold ourselves from the car. The scents of wood smoke, food cooking, and dill waft by. I close my eyes and breathe it in. When I open them, a beautiful, olive-skinned woman stands at the gate. Her long skirt blows in the breeze, and her feet are bare.

"Welcome, Sousanna and Robert," she says in almost perfect English. Her voice is slow and deep, and her smile shows perfect, white teeth. "I am KiKi, Marios's wife. I write letters to you. We have waited for you for a long time to come and visit us here in Greece. Welcome to our home." She reaches her arms to me, her deep laugh coaxing me into her embrace. She kisses me on both cheeks, then greets Robert with the same kisses. I like her instantly. Her green eyes have a friendly sparkle that makes me think of Joni.

KiKi puts an arm around my shoulders and leans close to speak softly into my ear. "Sousanna, look." She points toward the house. "There, do you see her? Your mother. She is your mother. She is waiting for you. Go to her, Sousanna."

A tiny woman stands just inside the open door with a young boy in her arms. Looking at me, she gently sets the boy down, then stays still.

I can't move. I'm a little girl again, standing in a room filled with the smell of earth from the cool, red dirt underfoot, unmoving, waiting to see what Mama would do so I would know what to do.

My mother is wearing a gray dress with an apron tied at her waist. Her dark hair, pulled back, has streaks of white running through it. Her eyes, even from this distance, shine with gentle kindness. Her lips quiver as she tries to smile.

No longer do I wait for her to move. I'm no longer that little girl, and this is not that time. I want to be in my mother's arms, and hold her in mine. My heart pounds in time to my steps as I walk to her.

She moves to embrace me, her small body falling into my chest as I once fell for comfort into hers. Mama. My mama. I wrap my arms around her and we stand, holding each other without words, for a long time. Then she leans back to look at me, and KiKi comes to translate my mother's words.

"I have prayed for you every day, my sweet child. For God to watch over you and to protect you. I have missed you, but now I can hold you in my arms again. I will never let anyone take you away from me again. Sousanna, my child, my child. I love you, my little Sousanna. I am sorry; forgive us, please forgive us. Thank you, God, that you have brought my daughter home to me."

She strokes my face and repeats my name, "Sousanna."

Holding mother in my arms, I ask KiKi to tell her, "Every day I have missed you. Your love and my father's love kept me going, hoping. Your strength gave me strength. I love you."

Tears flow from my eyes, and from my mother's. We cry for all the years we've lost; for Papa, who I'll never see again; for all the children taken from their families; for everything the wars took from the Greek people; for her regrets and Marios's years searching and my adoptive mother; and for this, this miracle we're part of, being together again. I'm in my mother's arms, and she's in mine.

We hold each other for a long time, not speaking, just feeling our hearts beating together. Anastasia comes and wraps her arms around us, then Marios's arms cover all of us. A long while later we break apart, laughing.

Marios gestures for me to follow him. Robert and Mama tag behind. We walk to the fig tree that covers half of the yard. He pulls a fig from the tree, peels it, and hands it to me. I gulp it down as I had once gobbled the peeled egg my father offered me.

I tell him, "Marios, I've always known my family would find me. Thank you for not giving up. You have filled the hole in my heart. Thank you." He shrugs his shoulders and smiles. I know he can't understand my foreign words, but I hope he understands my heart.

Mama walks to us. She takes my hand and walks me to Robert. She takes his hand also, and walks us toward the house, Marios close behind.

Before stepping inside I turn to Kiki. "Where are Ilias and his wife? I thought they lived in Athens."

"Do not worry, Sousanna; they are waiting for you in Pirgos. They went there to help your sister prepare for your visit. I know Anastasia wrote you once that there were difficult years for your brothers. They quarreled and could not find a way to get along. For many years they did not speak. But they years have softened them, and now they are as brothers again. It is good that they have stopped acting like little boys!" She laughs her rich, deep laugh and leads us into the house, to the dining table.

The table is loaded with a feast KiKi and Anastasia helped Mama prepare. Chicken and fish in rich tomato sauces. Stuffed eggplant and tomatoes brimming with rice and herbs. Fried potatoes drizzled with oregano and oil. Cucumber, olive, tomato, feta salad drenched in olive oil. Crusty bread broken into pieces scattered across the length of the table for us to dip into the salad oil. For dessert we have peeled apples sprinkled with cinnamon and covered with honey, and Marios's figs.

Sitting at the end of the table is an older man. His face is handsome and his thick, white hair is tossed every which way. His huge grin exposes a mouth full of white teeth, but tears stand in his eyes as he slowly pushes back his chair to stand. He's short, not much taller than my mother. He opens his arms wide and quietly speaks.

"Sousanna." He says something to me in Greek and I look to Kiki for translation.

"He says he is your father's brother. Sousanna, this is your Uncle George."

He walks over and gently takes my hand. He speaks many words to me. I can't understand any of them, but I can understand the love in his voice.

Again, Kiki translates his words. "Sousanna, your father, my beautiful baby brother, cannot be here to hold you in his arms or to show you his love. So I will do it for him."

He wraps me into his arms and my mind flashes back to the last time I was in my father's strong arms, my tiny body safe in his embrace.

After a moment, he stands back and grins again. He claps his hands together, lifts his heel and gives it a slap, lightening the mood. He walks to Robert and reaches way up, putting his hands on Robert's shoulders.

"Look at this cowboy from Texas! He is as tall as Niko was. Another man I must look up to see!"

There is laughter around the table, and everyone is jovial through the meal. My stomach is filled with the feast, and my eyes and ears are filled with the sight and sounds of my family chatting and laughing around the table. The best contentment comes from the filling of my heart with the knowledge that my family now has plenty. No longer are they suffering with hunger and hardship. The scars of the wars are finally healing.

Robert and I can't understand most of what's said. Occasionally Kiki translates something, but there's too much conversation for her to keep up with. I don't care. I'm focused on my family's faces, their voices, as each becomes real to me again. I tease Marios's two boys, the oldest of whom is named after my father.

When we're all full and the dishes are cleaned, Kiki tells Robert and me, "Marios will take you, your mother, and Anastasia to Pirgos today. It's a four-hour drive. Anastasia's husband and their girls will be waiting for you there, along with your brother Ilias with his wife Stephania. In a few days, Marios and I will come get you and show you around the Peloponnese. There's so much beauty here; we want you to see your country and how well it has grown since the days of destruction from the war."

"Thank you, Kiki, for everything. You've been so kind to Robert and me, made us feel welcome."

"Of course you are welcome; you are family. You are with your family." She laughs. "But we're concerned with all your luggage. Marios thinks he'll have to tie some on top of the car so everyone will fit inside. Why did you pack so many things, Sousanna?" Her rich, deep laugh fills the room. "We are simple people in Greece. Next time you come, do not bring all this luggage."

The trip to Pirgos is quiet. Anastasia has gotten over her nerves, evidently, as even she's quiet now. I can't communicate with my own mother and siblings. This is the country where I was born and this is my family, but I can't speak their language and I don't know their customs. *Fortune is still playing a bad game with us*, I think wryly, remembering the first letter from Marios.

When we reach Pirgos, I can't believe my eyes. Shops, cars, taxis, cafés, people—life everywhere. Marios slows the car and parks at a corner near the square. He signals all of us to get out of the car. We stand on the corner, wondering, as Marios goes inside a shop. He emerges after a few moments with a woman.

I recognize the mischievous eyes instantly. "Emilia."

"Sousanna," she exclaims at the same time, and we fall, laughing, into each other's arms. How can it feel like we never parted when there are so many years between us?

We look each other over, and in perfect English Emilia says, "I can't believe it. Sousanna, you have come home. Look at us. We are women now. My Sousanna."

We visit a few minutes, and then Emilia says, "Your family is waiting for you. Ilias and his wife are there and they have many kisses and hugs for you. Everyone wants to look at you and your tall husband."

"Oh, Emilia, I'm sorry, this is Robert, my husband."

She puts out her hand to shake Robert's. "Welcome, Robert. We are happy you brought Sousanna back to us."

Marios says something to Emilia and she smiles and nods her head. "Sousanna, do you know where your home is from here?"

"Everything is so different now; how am I supposed to know where I am?" I ask Robert, unsure what to say.

"Just tell them you don't know. Or look around; maybe you will."

I look around and everyone laughs at my perplexity.

But I do know where I am. I know exactly where to go. Where home is. I point. "That way."

Mama says something, and Emilia says, "Robert, you go with Marios and Anastasia in the car. Sousanna, your mother wants to walk you home."

Mama puts her arm around my waist, and I put mine over her shoulders. We look down the red dirt road, the road that once carried me away from her until we disappeared into the years, and walk down it, together. Just Mama and me.

Sousanna

Sousanna arriving in
America

Anastasia on her wedding day, escorted through the streets by her father Nikolas and brother Marios

Marios as a young man

Sousanna

Nikolas
Sousanna's father
Taken not long before his death

Katerina
Sousanna's mother
This photo was taken just days before she lost her battle with cancer. As ill as she was, she could not bear to leave all the work for others, and insisted on helping prepare vegetables, even from her death bed.

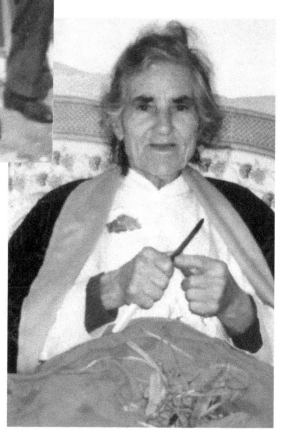

Nikolas and Katerina with their first grandchild,
the first daughter of Anastasia and Nedtarios

The American at last -
Sousanna becomes an
American citizen.

Uncle George teaches
Sousanna Greek dance after
she is finally reunited
with her family.

Sousanna

Katerina (center) and Anastasia (left) teach Sousanna (right) and her son to use souvlaki sticks

Afterword

How Could They Do It?
A Historical Perspective

Some details of the foregoing story have been fictionalized and some names changed, but Sousanna is a real person, and this is her true story.

It is also, sadly, the story of thousands of other children and their families.

People living in first-world countries today often find it difficult to fathom the desperation that would lead parents to turn their preschool child over to a complete stranger. Most wouldn't let a neighbor whose name they didn't know babysit for one night, much less send their child off to a foreign country on the other side of the world with a man they'd never met or even heard of. Knowing a bit about the Greek people and what was happening in their country at that time is helpful to understanding how so many families came to that point.

There is a Greek term, *philotimo*, that sums up the traditional Greek attitude. It means "love honor" and is considered the highest virtue. *Philotimo* is the standard of behavior, dictating how to interact with others. The core concept of *philotimo* is to always do the right thing (determined by compassion and respect for others) so as to bring honor to your family.

This virtue compels Grecians to be loyal and protective of each other. Greek families tend to be very close, and the family and community are considered before self when making decisions. Group unity, cooperation, and harmony are valued over personal success and glory.

Traditionally, everyone acted in ways that benefited the entire community—if they didn't, they were publicly shamed and eventually, if such behavior continued, driven away. This was particularly true prior to the 1950s, and especially in rural areas, where everyone knew everyone else.

When people are raised in a society that values and practices *philotimo*, they get used to trusting one another. It's hard for them to imagine anyone acting dishonorably. They assume that everyone has their interests at heart, that everyone is truthful and acting with integrity.

When a stranger comes to town, he's expected to act with *philotimo* just as the rest of the community does. Thus, he's viewed as a member of the whole, big Greek family, and is treated the same as the rest of the community. He receives the same trust that close friends and family receive.

Of course, that means there's a down side to living by *philotimo*: being taken advantage of by those who don't behave according to the same value.

§

Greece has always been a largely agrarian country. Historically, the economy was based on farming, herding, fishing, commerce, and crafts. Most people were poor peasants who worked on estates belonging to a relatively few wealthy landholders of the Ottoman Empire.

From 1914 into the 1920s, during the First World War and beyond, Greece fought Turkey for control of the land. In 1923, a deal was arranged in which the Turks returned to Turkey and the Greeks in that land returned to Greece.

With the land distributed more evenly (but still far from equally), some peasants began raising cash crops such as currants, olive oil, and tobacco. But The Great War left Greece deeply in debt and with little infrastructure or industry, so economic recovery was not yet within reach.

When the Great Depression hit, Greece was struck particularly hard because their crops were largely luxury items which no longer sold. Unemployment skyrocketed, leading to social unrest. Those lucky enough to own land were able to eke out a living on it, and the practice of *philotimo* helped the rest. Still, hunger became common.

World War II came to Greece on October 28, 1940 when Italy invaded the country. Greece was able to turn them back, but the victory was short lived. A few months later, Germany invaded, and this time Greek forces were quickly overpowered. The government went into exile in Egypt as Greece was divided among three Axis powers: Germany, Italy, and Bulgaria. No goods or persons were allowed to cross the boundary lines.

The first thing the occupiers did was confiscate fuel, food, and goods. Aid worker Laird Archer, who was in Athens when German troops entered, wrote:

> The wholesale looting of Athens has begun. Remaining food and fuel reserves have been taken first...the entire market [has been] sealed under the swastika...flocks of poultry, even the pigeons [have] been machine-gunned and the swastika planted at the four corners of the field. We had been warned to take nothing from the fields on pain of death... The invaders have been taking meat, cattle and sheep...transport has been seized simultaneously with food supplies...Wholesale and retail shops are being systematically cleared out...They took their "purchases" to the parcel post office or to the railway express and promptly shipped them home to the Reich... Raw materials, metal, leather and so on are being confiscated...Finally, hospital and drugstore supplies are being taken...The incredible speed and efficiency of this leaves us dazed, not knowing where to turn for the most ordinary supplies.

To the German and Italian occupiers, Greece was merely a source of food and labor. Anything of value, including foodstuffs, they took for themselves or sent back to their own countries. Food shortage reached a climax in the fall and winter of 1941, and famine was unavoidable.

The Red Cross estimated that in Athens alone, there were 400 deaths from hunger and malnutrition every day, some days reaching as high as 1,000. The sight of emaciated corpses became commonplace. Bodies were piled in the streets and cemeteries. This period of mass starvation, from 1941 through 1944, became known as The Great Famine. Approximately 300,000 people perished during these years as a result of famine and malnutrition.

Afterword

It wasn't long before Resistance groups formed, the main one being the Greek People's Liberation Army. Armed men hid in the hills and carried out sneak attacks against the invaders.

Reprisal was swift and brutal. It became the policy that for every one German killed by the Resistance, one hundred Greeks would be executed in return—including women and children. Villages suspected of supporting guerrillas were wiped out completely.

The aftermath of the Battle of Crete is one example of this. This battle began when German paratroopers dropped into Crete near the village of Kandanos on May 20, 1941. They were confronted by two Allied battalions who were joined by local civilians carrying primitive weapons. The paratroopers experienced strong resistance and suffered the loss of almost two thirds of their troops.

Two days later, a detachment of German soldiers attempted to move through the area. Local civilians from surrounding villages confronted and fought them. They were no match for the Wehrmacht and were quickly scattered.

Nevertheless, the brazen display of resistance infuriated the Germans. Rumors circulated that Cretans were attacking their troops with knives, axes and scythes and torturing and mutilating them. These stories were later proved to be untrue, but when Commander Göring heard them, he authorized swift reprisals against the local population.

The village of Kondomari was targeted first. Four trucks of German paratroopers surrounded the town. All the villagers—men, women, and children—were gathered in the town square. Dozens of men were pulled out, led to a nearby olive grove, and executed by an ad hoc firing squad. The exact number of victims is unclear, as different sources list the number from 23 to 60.

German war propagandist Franz-Peter Weixler captured the massacre on film. Some of his photographs of this event may be found online with an Internet search.

The next day, German forces moved to Kandanos. They killed 180 civilians, slaughtered all livestock, and then torched and razed the entire town. The village was declared a "dead zone" after its destruction, and its remaining population was forbidden to return. Inscriptions in German and Greek were erected on each entry of the village which read, "Here stood Kandanos, destroyed in retribution for the murder of 25 German soldiers, never to be rebuilt again," and "Kandanos was destroyed in retaliation for the bestial ambush murder of a paratrooper platoon and a half-platoon of military engineers by armed men and women."

Several weeks later, German commander Friedrich-Wilhelm Müller, the "Butcher of Crete," planned the destruction of another 20 villages. His directive included the order to promptly execute all males over the age of sixteen as well as everyone who was arrested in the countryside, regardless of gender or age.

Troops divided into groups and surrounded the region. At first, they persuaded the locals that their intentions were peaceful, so that any who had fled the villages would return. But soon, mass executions, along with looting, arson, vandalism, and demolition, took place. Over 500 Greek civilians were killed. Almost 1000 homes were destroyed. The surviving villagers were forbidden to return to their homes, most of which had been burned to the ground, or even bury their dead.

Not far from Nikolas and Katerina's home in Pirgos was the village of Kalavryta. The surrounding hills hid small groups of resistance fighters, who managed to capture and kill some German soldiers. "Operation Kalavryta" was mounted in retaliation. Troops from all around turned toward the village, burning villages and shooting civilians along the way. When they reached Kalavryta, the Germans rounded up all the citizens and separated them. All males over eleven years of age were marched to the edge of town while the women and children were locked in the school building. Then the school was set on fire and the men were machine-gunned down. Of the entire male population of Kalavryta, only thirteen managed to survive. They later stated it was only due to dead bodies falling on top of them and shielding them that they lived. The women, fortunately, managed to break a window after the soldiers left to burn the rest of the town, and most of them escaped with the children. Still, Operation Kalavryta claimed the lives of nearly 700 civilians.

These are just a few examples of what the Greek people endured during World War II. When that war was over, the exiled government returned, only to be challenged by the communist party. Civil war erupted, during which 100,000 Greeks were killed.

After such horrors—the Greco-Turk war, the Great Depression, the Great Famine, World War II, the civil war—it took the villages and the individuals in them many years to recover; some never did. Studies show that after experiencing such trauma, many people experience post-traumatic stress, depression, anxiety, and feelings of helplessness and hopelessness that may last the rest of their lives. They may also have difficulty with memory and concentration, and—germane to Sousanna's story—make impulsive, sometimes irrational, decisions.

These are the circumstances in which Nikolas and Katerina grew up. By the time Sousanna and her siblings were born, the economy was beginning to recover in cities, where international trade could be conducted, but was still in shambles in rural areas. Hunger remained prevalent. Most of those living in the countryside still felt helpless to improve their lot.

The feeling of helplessness was compounded by the lack of education among the people. At the time Sousanna was taken, only an estimated thirty percent of adults could read. Fewer could write. In addition, travel was difficult. Therefore, what the Greeks living in rural areas—like Nikolas—knew of the world was mostly confined to what they had experienced in their own lives.

All of these things played into the decision of Sousanna's parents when they were approached by Peter Bakas. The years of horror still weighed on them. They could barely feed their family, and it didn't appear that things would change anytime soon. All they could see in their children's future was more hard work and hunger.

Then a fellow Greek showed up, offering help. The offer was unimaginable; but then, so was any kind of future in Greece. And Nikolas made a crucial assumption that, tragically, turned out to be false: He assumed the man was acting with *philotimo*.

It is likely many other parents made the same false assumption. In the 1940-50s, an estimated 3000 children were brought to America from Greece and adopted under questionable circumstances. Thousands more were adopted into other countries.

This is not to say that all adoptions from Greece involved deceit. The majority were perfectly legal in every way. Some parents willingly surrendered their children, knowing it was permanent, because they couldn't care for them. In addition, orphanages were running over with both orphans and abandoned children. Many loving parents legally adopted and provided homes for children who had nowhere else to go.

But there were also illegal adoptions, cases of fraud, and outright child stealing. Some babies were taken from unwed mothers who were told the child died; some children simply disappeared. And some, like Sousanna, were taken from parents who were told their children would be returned when circumstances improved.

In all these cases, the adopting parents usually didn't know how the child was taken from Greece and thought the adoption was legal. Sousanna's adoptive parents believed this, and they had no idea that her natural parents expected her back. Indeed, the paperwork was legitimate: It was signed by a judge granting permission for the adoption. The wrongdoing lay in the falsehood given to her natural parents that she would be returned.

It is important to realize that all this was possible largely because of the poverty and chaos left in the wake of World War II. History does not stay in the past—its consequences remain for generations. Sousanna and other children like her are still suffering the after-effects of a war that took place before they were even born.

She's one of the lucky ones—her story has a happy ending.

Teresa Lynn

Sources

In addition to personal accounts, letters, legal documents, government forms, and other documentation, the following sources have been used in compiling this history.

Books

Archer, Laird. *Balkan Tragedy*. Manhattan, KS: MA/AH Pub. 1977.

Beevor, Antony. *Crete: The Battle and the Resistance*. Piscataway, NJ: Penguin Books. 1992.

Fromm, E. *Escape from Freedom*. New York: Holt, Rinehart and Winston. 1941.

Heaton, C.D. *German Anti-partisan Warfare in Europe, 1939-1945*. Atglen, PA: Schiffer Publishing. 2001.

Hionidou, Violetta. *Famine and Death in Occupied Greece: 1941–1944*. Cambridge: Cambridge University Press. 2006.

Kiriakopoulos, G.C. *The Nazi Occupation of Crete: 1941-1945*. Santa Barbara, CA: Praeger Publishers. 1995.

Leigh Fermor, Patrick. *Abducting a General*, John Murray, Ltd. 2014.

Leong Kok Wey, Adam. *Killing the Enemy: Assassination Operations in World War II*. New York: I.B. Tauris. 2015.

MacDonald, Callum. *The Lost Battle: Crete 1941*. New York: The Free Press. 1993.

Mark Mazower. *Inside Hitler's Greece: The Experience of Occupation, 1941–44*. New Haven, CT: Yale University Press. 1995.

Panagiotakis, G. *Documents From The Battle And The Resistance Of Crete; 1941-45*. 3rd Ed. 2007.

Articles

Bonner, Raymond. "Tales of Stolen Babies and Lost Identities; A Greek Scandal Echoes in New York." *The New York Times*. 13 April 1996.

DeLand, Dave. "The Baby in the Box Digs for Her Greek Roots." *St. Cloud Times*. 4 September 2015. Online. https://www.sctimes.com/story/news/local/2015/09/04/baby-box-digs-greek-roots/71710560/ Accessed 11 November 2015.

Dordanas, Stratos. "Reprisals of the German Authorities of Occupation in Macedonia 1941–1944." Aristotle University of Thessaloniki Thesis. Aristotle University of Thessaloniki: 1–848. 2002. doi:10.12681/eadd/20569.

Freh, FM. "Psychological Effects of War and Violence on Children." J Psychol Abnorm Child 2005. S1:e001. doi:10.4172/2329-9525.1000e001.

Hionidou, Violetta. "Send us Either Food or Coffins: The 1941–2 Famine on the Aegean Island of Syros." *Famine Demography: Perspectives from the Past and Present*. Oxford: Oxford University Press. 2002.

History of the United Nations War Crimes Commission and the Development of the Laws of War. United Nations War Crimes Commission. London: HMSO. 1948.

Javakhishvili, D.J. "Victims of war: Psychological problems of displaced people." In: Martinez M., Ed. *Prevention and Control of Aggression and the Impact on its Victims*. Boston, MA: Springer. 2001.

Laiou-Thomadakis, Angeliki. "The Politics of Hunger: Economic Aid to Greece, 1943–1945." *Journal of the Hellenic Diaspora*. Havorford, PA. 1980.

Stefanidis, Yiannis. "Macedonia in the 1940s." *Modern and Contemporary Macedonia*. Athens: Papazissis. 1992.

Voglis, Polymeris. "Surviving Hunger: Life in the Cities and the Countryside during the Occupation". In Gildea, Robert, Olivier Wievorka, and Anette Warring. *Surviving Hitler and Mussolini: Daily Life in Occupied Europe*. Oxford: Berg. 2006.

Websites

http://family.lovetoknow.com/greek-family-values

http://traveltips.usatoday.com/social-culture-greece-17532.html

https://unitedwithisrael.org/the-destruction-of-the-jews-of-greece-during-the-holocaust/

www.occupation-memories.org/en/deutsche-okkupation/ergebnisse-des-terrors/index.html

CPSIA information can be obtained
at www.ICGtesting.com
Printed in the USA
LVHW061525101218
599923LV00008B/82/P

9 780990 497752